Eden is a colossal moon-sized cemetery in space where the souls of the deceased rest in peace, including Ava's beloved Roland. But the tranquility of this resting place is shattered when the souls awake. The departed have begun to torment the living inhabitants of Eden with ghostly apparitions and ethereal whispers, haunting them, driving them to the brink of madness.

There is a malevolent presence on Eden, a cosmic entity determined to annihilate the crew, casting a sinister light on their darkest fears and hidden truths. Ava finds herself entangled in a harrowing struggle to confront her own grief and terror, and to find the strength to resist the growing darkness. Ava must somehow rally her companions to unite against the expanding presence before it consumes them all.

'Smart, trippy, fast-paced and packed with dread, John Palisano's *Requiem* is a superb horror/Sci-Fi hybrid that will rattle your synapses and jangle your nerves.'
Lisa Morton, six-time winner of the Bram Stoker Award®

'A meditative portrait of humanity's place in the universe, John Palisano's latest [*Requiem*] is a haunting and addictive addition to an already impressive body of work.'
Christa Carmen, Bram Stoker Award®-winning and Shirley Jackson Award-nominated author of *The Daughters of Block Island*

'Imagine a huge cemetery floating in space and you have *Requiem*, an intensely creepy horror story that also asks the big questions: Are we wrong about the nature of reality? What does it mean to be human? Warning: Be prepared to feel like someone is walking on your grave.'
Alma Katsu, author of *The Fervor* and *The Hunger*

'Palisano invites us into the vista of infinite space, teetering on oblivion. While technology welcomes us, something within us always grinds for awakening, and by delving into death, we will find it. A technological allegory for our time.'
L.E. Daniels, Bram Stoker Award® Nominee and author of *Serpent's Wake: A Tale for the Bitten*, on *Requiem*

'A powerful, philosophical look at death.'
Steve Stred, award-winning author of *Mastodon*, *Father of Lies* and *Churn the Soil*, on *Requiem*

'Palisano takes the "haunted house in space" trope and twists it into something completely fresh and totally unhinged. *Requiem* takes the most terrifyingly hallucinogenic moments of *Event Horizon* and combines them deftly, and powerfully, with the most human and heartfelt themes of *Contact* to create a new vision of extraterrestrial visitation, formulating a new take on one of the all-time great taglines: In space, no one can hear you scream… but you.'
Philip Fracassi, author of *The Third Rule of Time Travel* and *Boys in the Valley*

'Possessing a firm grasp of tradition but with his vision clearly focused on the future, John Palisano is exactly the type of writer horror needs right now: bold, brave, imaginative and unflinching.'
Bentley Little, Bram Stoker Award®-winner

JOHN PALISANO

REQUIEM

This is a **FLAME TREE PRESS** book

Text copyright © 2025 John Palisano

All rights reserved. No part of this publication may be reproduced, stored in a retrieval system, or transmitted in any form or by any means, electronic, mechanical, photocopying, recording or otherwise, without the prior written permission of the publisher.

FLAME TREE PRESS
6 Melbray Mews, London, SW6 3NS, UK
flametreepress.com

US sales, distribution and warehouse:
Simon & Schuster
simonandschuster.biz

UK distribution and warehouse:
Hachette UK Distribution
hukdcustomerservice@hachette.co.uk

Publisher's Note: This is a work of fiction. Names, characters, places, and incidents are a product of the author's imagination. Locales and public names are sometimes used for atmospheric purposes. Any resemblance to actual people, living or dead, or to businesses, companies, events, institutions, or locales is completely coincidental.

Thanks to the Flame Tree Press team.

The cover is created by Flame Tree Studio with elements courtesy of Shutterstock.com and: Andriy Solovyov; Ottavio C.; Rick Partington; Wilqkuku. The font families used are Avenir and Bembo.

Flame Tree Press is an imprint of Flame Tree Publishing Ltd
flametreepublishing.com

A copy of the CIP data for this book is available from the British Library and the Library of Congress.

PB ISBN: 978-1-78758-953-7
HB ISBN: 978-1-78758-954-4
ebook ISBN: 978-1-78758-955-1

Printed and bound by CPI Group (UK) Ltd, Croydon, CR0 4YY.

JOHN PALISANO

REQUIEM

FLAME TREE PRESS
London & New York

The closest you'll get to heaven
is to be buried amongst the stars.
Choose a burial in the heavens
for your loved one.
Look up at them as they shine
across the universe.
From the cosmic decks of
Eden.

"There has to be something more. Always something more.
Keep searching for it because it sure as hell is searching for you."
– Roland Duvay

PART ONE

Chapter One

VITA NOVA CORPORATE HEADQUARTERS
VANDENBERG SPACE FORCE BASE, CALIFORNIA
SALLY RIDE CONFERENCE ROOM
13:48:40 UTC
13 JANUARY 2112

Ava sees the Vita Nova Horizon rocket on the launchpad only a mile away through the window. She wishes the knot in her stomach would untie.

"Does anyone know what we're all here for?" Allison Mercer asks.

Ava knows why she's come, but she doesn't want to give herself away in front of strangers. The other five don't let on, either. Her left leg shakes under the table, and she squeezes her folded hands even tighter. *Get me out of here.*

"Anyone?" Mercer asks, her voice reverberating off the back wall of the conference room. "Come on." No one bites. "Well, I'll tell you why I asked each of you to be here. All of you have been hand selected to help us rebuild public sentiment for our Eden space memorial satellite. You're all familiar with the tragic incident from last year, I'm sure." She lets out a nervous laugh. "No one on Earth could have missed the news. But now's the time we move on."

Right. Their proprietary suspension system failed. Some of the coffins leaked, and the bodies had to be destroyed. The suspension fluid was toxic. Way more than anyone knew. And that led to problems for anyone exposed. So much for a forever home. Ava is trying not to be cynical. *Bad things happen even to the best of us. Even me.* She steers her thoughts away from thinking about her situation, of Roland.

"Couldn't miss the never-ending reports last year. It was overwhelming." The man closest to Ava speaks in a deep baritone, and his pronunciation is strong and clear. She wonders if he's a professor or a politician. "Everyone was upset about it."

"True, Dr. Poole," Mercer says. "Which means this is not going to be an easy job."

Doctor! I was close. Ava stifles a grin.

"It seems the hardest job will fall upon Vita Nova to change the optics down here." The skinny fellow's voice is soft but no less sure. "You've certainly assembled a wide variety of people here, which I imagine is on purpose." Ava tries to focus her hearing on him to compensate for his lower speaking volume. He wears an undecorated black kufi, she notices, and has on a simple tunic, although the ends of the sleeves have gold embroidery. She likes the glint in his eyes which makes him seem kind and open.

Mercer nods. "Indeed, Sanjay. Representing people from all walks of life and different cultures is crucial to Vita Nova's philosophy," she says. "But we also have to be able to show and prove to people that all is well on Eden in order to regain their trust."

"Understood," Sanjay says. "That makes total sense to me."

Ava hears him clearly; it's as though her ears zeroed in on him and turned up the volume. Must be the acoustics in the room.

"All of you might also be aware of something else that's been inescapable over the past year," Mercer says, "or someone, more specifically."

This woman sounds like she's reading a corporate script to us. It's like she's had it written for her and has practiced it dozens of times.

"Oh, God," the woman closest to Mercer says, putting her head in her hands.

"Tessa Nightingale is one of the biggest, if not the biggest, music stars of the moment," Mercer says. "You're probably wondering what the heck she's doing here, right?"

No one takes the bait.

"She's here to compose a new requiem for Eden and its tenants," Mercer says.

Right. The old one was playing in the videos that got shared as the caskets were cracking, and the fluid was leaking out. No wonder they don't want people associating Vita Nova with that anymore, Ava thinks. And I wish this woman would stop projecting her voice. The slap back is making it harder to understand what the heck she's saying.

"All I can share is I can't wait to be a million miles away from people and their crazy expectations. I can't go anywhere without fans finding me," Tessa says. She looks around at them. "Not that I don't love them. I just want to be treated like a normal person. If we can all agree to that?"

"Yeah. You betcha." Poole is the first to speak out, and the others follow suit, agreeing. All but Ava, who remains silent. Poole says, "You'll just be a part of the crew, that's all. No big deal. No special treatment. I think we can handle that." He lets out a roaring laugh.

"No offense," says a man in between them. Ava notices he wears a scar on his face stretching from his chin to his temple. "I've never heard of you, Tessa, but I don't really follow any of the new music these days." He laughs in a rich, warm timbre.

Ava feels the same thing but doesn't want to dogpile. She's sure she won't be on whatever crew Mercer's thinking of, anyway; Ava's not going back up. It's too soon. It'll never not be too soon.

Tessa puts up her hands, having taken the joking in stride. "Perfect, and no worries at all. That's actually a good thing, in my opinion, that some of you don't know me. But I'd like to know you all. Can I ask where you're from?"

"Seattle," the scarred man says. "I'm Ken Lee."

"Hi, Ken. I'm Tessa, and I'm glad you're here." She reaches over the table and shakes his hand. "I'm sure this is going to be an amazing experience."

Mercer cuts in with the perfect timbre of a game show host and just as slick. "Well, that's lovely to see, as you'll all be working together closely on Eden. You'll all soon be family. Which you'll need to lean on. You were selected because you're free spirits without anything or anyone tying you down."

There it is. *'Free spirits.' Nice, gentle way of putting it. We're all castoffs. Lonely hearts. Broken souls. Had to be some catch, didn't there?* Ava tries to keep her eyes from rolling. At least her ears have gotten used to the acoustics in the room, and she can distinguish each of their voices.

"I'll let you all fill each other in on the specifics of your lives as you see fit," Mercer says.

"Great," Ava says. "Sounds like a party in space for you all." The others laugh. Except for the young woman to the front of the table. She blinks several times as though annoyed. Not one to shrink from confrontation, Ava asks, "What's your deal?" Immediately, Ava regrets speaking out so quickly when she sees the woman's expression fall. *Why do I always have to be such a hard-ass?*

"Midori's deal is that she's going to accompany you on this journey as an assistant to you all," Mercer says, a lock of her immaculate hair falling over her brow.

"Isn't that just wonderful," Tessa says. "You're sending a Humani up with us to keep tabs. Of course you are. Oldest trick in the book." She shakes her head, disgusted.

Ava looks at Midori. *Ahh. A virtual intelligence bot. Humani. Wouldn't have guessed. They've gotten so damn good at them. How the heck did Tessa pick that up so fast and I didn't?*

Mercer shakes her head. "No tricks. No keeping tabs. We have always had a Humani assistant on Eden. It's protocol. They prove to be invaluable, especially when interfacing with Eden's vast systems."

"In case anything goes wrong," Tessa says. "Again. Probably required by insurance more than anything."

Shutting her eyes for a moment, Mercer nods. Ava thinks maybe it's a crack in her armor. Were they getting to her? "Midori is there to help you, first and foremost. Our insurance policy is readily available and does not mention any requirements for Humani on board." She turns and beams at Midori. "Vita Nova is committed to its dealings being transparent. Isn't that right?'

"Yes," Midori says. "Of course. It is part of the company's manifesto."

"Vita Nova has a manifesto?" Tessa asks. "That sounds like the opposite of egalitarian."

This Tessa's one tough cookie. I like her. Ava eyes Midori again, looking for signs of her being artificial. *I can't believe I had no idea she was a Humani. Sheesh. This should be fun.*

"You said her name's Midori? Like the liquor?" Tessa asks.

"That is just one meaning," Midori says. "My name is Japanese, originally traced back to the eighth century. There are multiple meanings, but the one that speaks to me the most is that it represents a vast sea's ability to bring forth new life."

Knowing that she's a Humani, Ava picks out the subtle artifacts in her voice.

"So, you're Japanese?" Tessa asks. "You've got a Japanese character on your neck."

Midori smiles. "My name. And I have many mothers and fathers who have worked to bring me to you."

"Got it," Tessa says.

"I'm mixed skin. My parents are from different backgrounds, too," Ava says. "So, I can relate." She pictures her beautiful parents and grins. How she misses them, gone so long ago.

Midori smiles. "Thank you, Ava," she says. "I appreciate your saying so."

"We're all from different backgrounds," Poole says. "That much is obvious. Vita Nova's going into overdrive to show that. I hope that's not the only reason some of us have been picked."

Mercer looks right at Poole. "Not the only reason, of course, but it is a consideration. We do want to be welcoming to all."

"Yup," Ava says. "Death doesn't discriminate. Everyone needs a coffin. Even if it's a sky basket."

★ ★ ★

"I don't want to be a leader." Ava feels her face flush. She glares at Allison Mercer. "You pull me away from the others for this?"

Mercer inches closer; the arms of their seats almost touch. "Look, I need you. No one else has the same leadership experience and qualities. I need someone I can trust. We do. They do."

Ava shakes her head. "No. I gave that up. I was told I would specifically not be any kind of leader. That's why I agreed to come. I don't have to do this." She's so mad she looks away from Mercer and her clothes and hair, all the same light brown color. *Maybe she's a Humani, too.*

"I understand," Mercer says. "I do. Our other candidates don't work out. They don't want to commit to this when it comes down to following through. But you're here. And I know what you're going through. I also lost someone close to me recently."

"Don't." Ava stares at Mercer's hands…Allison's hands…folded in front of her. Close. She can tell she wants to open them and clasp them around her own.

"I'm sorry," Allison says. "Phoebe was my world and she's…in limbo right now. I can't do anything with her anymore. All of our dreams and plans are gone. It's awful. The world needs Eden to be available again." She lets out a breath. "I need Eden to be available."

"Heartbreaking. I know there's no plots left on Earth and all," Ava says. "I'm sorry. That sucks. I get it." Hearing herself, Ava thinks she sounds cold and insincere, even though she isn't trying to be. *Damn it. She's working on me. Why can't I just be mean for once?*

"Again? It's not just me. So many people can't find their forever homes. Families can't grieve. People are being stacked like meat in freezer trucks until this gets sorted out. Everyone's waiting for Eden to reopen."

Ava looks at Mercer. *Allison. Her name's Allison. Don't dehumanize her.* "I get it. I've seen the news. Wish I knew what happened to Roland's body so I could have that problem."

Allison lowers her head. "It was so tragic for you both. Truly. Maybe this journey will help you heal. That's one of my hopes in inviting you."

She waves. "Let's not get into that. I told myself I wouldn't mention that." Ava forces a smile. "Back to your needing a leader. What about Dr.

Poole? He's a big, tough, handsome fellow. Fits the expectation of what a captain or whatever should be. Why not elect him leader? Or any of the others?"

"They've got other roles they've been chosen for and need to focus on. People naturally look to you. They believe in you." Allison leans in. "I'll sweeten the deal. Vita Nova is ready to take care of you for the rest of your life once you're back on the ground. We'll set you up with a home. Money every month. You won't have to worry. Do this for us...get Eden back online...turn it around...and it's done."

Sighing, Ava hunches forward, looks around the plain, boring boardroom they're in. She shuts her eyes. *Don't be stupid, Ava. For a few months' work, you could retire. Find your peace, finally. Get over yourself. You'll kick yourself if you don't do this. You won't have to worry about rent or house payments or bills. You can live your best life. Do it.*

When she opens her eyes, she says, "You can put all of that in writing, right?"

"We already have an offer put together for you to look over right away." Allison's eyes dart back and forth as though she's scanning Ava and would be able to deduce her answer.

Stretching her neck once to the right and left, Ava looks up. "If you throw in Midori when this is all over, we have a deal."

Allison lights up. "Easy," she says. "Consider it done."

Chapter Two

VITA NOVA HORIZON
VANDENBERG SPACE FORCE BASE, CALIFORNIA
PASSENGER CAPSULE
02:04:10 UTC
14 FEBRUARY 2112

"Here we go," Ava says. She looks across from her at Dr. Poole, Tessa, Sanjay, and Midori. The clinical smell of the disinfectant bothers her. Vapor steams from vents alongside their chairs, so she tries to focus on that in hopes it'll diffuse the odor. She isn't going to smell real air for a long time and already misses it.

Poole pulls at his shoulder straps. "I think I'm going to turn as pale as a damn space ghost."

Ava laughs. "Funny, but going into orbit doesn't lighten skin color." She thinks she sounds so serious. Too serious.

"Well, not sure I believe you, even though you're the only one of us who's been into space before," Poole says. He lets out a chuckle. "And you're the boss."

"You better get used to bowing before me now." Ava is sure to wink so he knows she's playing.

Poole nods in return. "Absolutely."

"We're already getting along." Ava pushes her dreads in back of her; it'd be best to have them out of the way before liftoff because she won't be able to move them once the process begins.

"Seriously? It's not that bad going up, is it?" Ken asks.

Ava detects a great deal of fear in his voice.

"Not so bad. The ship does all the work." She flashes a smile.

"You just have to hold on. Once we get out of Earth's orbit, it's a lot smoother. Should only be about fifteen minutes, tops."

"Okay," Ken says. "I think I can survive that." He doesn't sound convincing.

"I have faith in you," Ava says. "Just try to not pass out. You'll have a stiff neck for weeks."

Ken shakes his head. "Great tip."

"And whatever you do, don't soil yourself. These suits aren't waterproof."

"Oof. Right. That wouldn't be pretty." He thinks for a moment. "Has that happened?"

She gives a thumbs-down. "You have no idea."

Ava scans the capsule.

Midori looks at her right back and nods, so Ava keeps scanning. Sanjay's head is bowed, and he whispers prayers, so she doesn't interrupt him just to ask if he's all right. She's sure he is.

The low rumble gets louder. "Thirty seconds to liftoff," the recorded voice says before it starts to count down.

Tessa has her headphones and sunglasses on.

Poole nods and grimaces.

Ken looks around nervously.

Sanjay finishes, gives her a nod and smiles from the corner of his mouth. "One step closer to being in space," he says. "Never thought I'd be doing this."

"Me, neither," Ava says. "Just one step closer to this whole thing being over with. What the hell are we doing?"

The capsule shakes. "Is that normal?" Poole's voice seems to have gone down an octave.

"Totally," Ava says, remembering the last time she'd been on a launch. Pictured Roland next to her, holding her hand, his beautiful blue-gray eyes making her feel so safe. *Don't think about him. Not now.*

Poole says, "That's only slightly reassuring."

"Final sequence," reports the *Horizon*'s voice.

10

9

8

The shaking gets more violent and much louder. If someone tried to speak, Ava is sure she wouldn't be able to hear them over the noise. Good thing she's grown pretty good at reading lips.

5

4

3

Taking a last look around, she notices everyone's eyes are closed, other than Midori's. She smiles. Ava smiles back. Of course, she's…it's…not scared.

2

1

For a moment, the capsule feels like it goes downward. Oh, crap. Ava's guts feel like they dropped too. But a split second later, the rocket launches upward. Then she senses lift, like when taking off in a plane, only a thousand times more intense. The sound is deafening and rattles deep within her head. *Knew I forgot something.* She'd told herself to pack some earplugs, but it'd slipped her mind. She puts her hands over her ears instead. Bows her head. She's grown so very intolerant to sound.

The *Horizon* flies. After several seconds, the ride feels smoother. Looking to her right, Ava peers out the front windows. She hadn't thought to do so earlier. Sky's still blue.

The others keep to themselves, their eyes shut.

This whole thing could blow, and this could be the end at any second. She pushes back against the thought. No. Don't think that. Launches are super safe. That just doesn't happen anymore.

Outside, the blue sky darkens. It could, though. Anything's possible.

Midori stares ahead and out the window, too. *They say bots mimic our emotions and sensory experiences. This must be awesome for her, too. I'll have to ask later.*

The *Horizon*'s ride stabilizes. There's no sky, only black.

Ava sees stars.

We've made it.

The others open their eyes. The loud rumbling ceases, replaced by a low buzzing sound.

Well, now, that's better.

To the starboard side, Ava spots a reddish orb on the horizon.

"Is that the moon?" Ken asks.

"It is," Midori says.

"Wow. With the shadows and the color, it almost looks like half a heart," he says. "Happy Valentine's Day, everyone." He lets out a little laugh.

Chills go up and down Ava. *Of course, I'd have to see the moon again and it's Valentine's Day.* Her throat tightens. Her jaw moves side to side. A thick, warm tear runs down her right cheek before she has a chance to suppress it. "Stop," she says, wiping at it.

She feels eyes on her and looks up. "Sorry," she says. "Don't mind me." But they're all judging her, she's sure. *Do they know what happened to me? With Roland? Know who I am? Were they warned?*

"No worries, boss," Dr. Poole says.

"The change in pressure can often make eyes water," Midori says, still with her same smile. "It's perfectly normal."

When their eyes meet, Ava is sure the bot is covering for her, trying to make her feel better and diffusing the awkwardness. *Well, that's some serious mojo that got programmed into that thing, isn't it?* She gives Midori a thumbs-up. "Roger that." *I owe you one.* "Midori? How far are we away from Eden?"

"Twelve hours," Midori says. "Did you know the first trips humanity made to the moon could take as long as three and a half days?"

Ava shakes her head. "I did happen to know that. I have a little experience with the moon, after all. It's farther away than most people realize."

"Sometimes it looks like you can touch it," Ken says. "Crazy."

"Indeed, it is," Poole says. "So, what are we going to do for the next half a day?"

"Once the *Horizon* turns off the seatbelt sign," Ava says, "you're free to roam about the cabin." She does her best to keep her tone light and fun, but her insides are twisting. *Just want to go and find a bunk and be by myself for a while. And I definitely don't want to see the damn moon.* She can't help herself, though, and eyes it for a moment. Sees its surface. *There's Mare Serenitatis. Sea of serenity. Right about where camp was.* She remembers the outpost. Roland's face. The Crests – the crestocilio magnopus. *No one believed me about those things. Thought I was hallucinating. Thought it was all some big accident and nothing more. Wonder if everyone on here thinks I'm crazy, too? Probably.*

Her heart racing, she pops off her restraints. "Phew. Glad to get out of those things." Ava looks around without making eye contact. "Going to go put my head down for a bit to recharge." She's up before anyone says a word. "Please don't bother me unless there's an emergency. Even then? Ask Midori."

She makes her way back to the end of the capsule, to the first airlock door, puts her hand on the scanner to open it, and rushes through. Her head spins.

In the next chamber, she sees the mess area at the end, the bathroom, the next airlock door, but before all that, she sees the bunking area. Notices Dr. Poole sitting on one, his shoes off. "Looks like we both have the same idea," he says.

She's shocked. "I didn't even see you leave. You were so fast."

"I can be that way," he says. "Especially when I'm overwhelmed."

"Got it," she says, turning toward a bunk opposite. "My eyes and my head are killing me. We're going to hit the floorboards as soon as we're on deck. Thought I'd recharge while I can."

"Seems smart to me," Poole says.

Ava slips right into the bunk, relieved to almost be alone. She keeps her shoes on to hasten doing so. The faster she can be by herself, the better.

"I lost someone, too," he says. "My wife. She was the last of my family. I guess that's why they picked all of us. No loved ones to cry over us if we die. They've got star plots already assigned to us like it's some sort of benefit of employment. Not sure I'm so into my body being displayed indefinitely in a space aquarium."

She laughs but doesn't reply, as she very much wants to pull the curtain closed but doesn't want to be the awful, cold, and selfish person she feels she is. She does want to try and get some shut-eye, after all. But she likes him.

He goes on. "I bet the more we get to know everyone else, they'll have similar stories."

"Pretty sure they do," Ava says. "Mercer pretty much said they picked us because we're damaged goods, which makes us easier to manipulate. Oh, just so we're clear? My guy's not dead. Just lost."

"Huh. Right," he says. "That's right."

He knows the story but doesn't believe me, either. No one does. Of course not. Why would they? "That's correct. Meanwhile, everyone thinks I'm nuts, so this is a great way to get me out of everyone's face, isn't it?"

"If they really thought you were crazy, they wouldn't have made you the mission commander," he says. "Isn't that true?"

She acquiesces. "Maybe. Maybe not. Who knows what their true motivation is. But I do know you and I should get some rest while we can. Once we hit Eden it's going to be nonstop work for the first several hours while we get everything up and running."

"Right. Indeed, we should." He looks down.

Ava takes the opportunity to pull the curtain closed. She feels off – too cold. "I really am sorry for your loss, Doctor. Truly. It's so heartbreaking. This is not an easy life."

"Not by any stretch," he says. "And it just gets harder and sadder."

Chapter Three

VITA NOVA HORIZON
CIS LUNAR; AREA BETWEEN THE EARTH AND THE
MOON; 4 KILOMETERS FROM EDEN
PASSENGER CAPSULE
08:12:20 UTC
14 FEBRUARY 2112

Ava wakes to golden light filling the interior of the *Horizon*. She pushes back the sleeping chamber's curtain. Across from her, Poole's bunk is empty. When she sits upright, her head feels stuffy, and her throat is dry. Peering out from the bunk, she looks aft and then fore and notices the door leading to the front capsule is open. *Wait. That's not protocol.* Standing and stretching, she shakes her head. "All right. Showtime." Her stomach feels tied in a knot. *Can't believe I'm up here again, floating around in a damn spacecraft. What the hell is wrong with me? Am I just a glutton for punishment?* She remembers the promise Mercer made, that she'd not have to worry about money again once it's over. That would help. She'd finally have the time to work on herself instead of just living month to month, day to day.

As she makes her way to the front, she notices her crewmates gathered in the cockpit area. That door is open, too. She leans in and peers over their shoulders.

"Is that it?" Tessa says. "It looks a whole lot bigger in person."

Eden looms ahead. Its surface glistens. Made up of tens of thousands of rectangular panes, Eden's caskets reflect sunlight. As the glass is infused with gold to help shield from solar radiation, Ava thinks the mortuary looks like a gigantic piece of jewelry. They'd constructed it in the seven years since she'd been on the moon outpost. "Very impressive," she says. "That's home for the next six months." She realizes she hasn't been paying much attention to the news or any world happenings during that time, either, not wanting to be reminded.

"It's gorgeous," Ken says. "Can't believe it."

"It doesn't even seem real," Poole says. "It's like a dream."

"How far away are we?" Ava asks.

Midori turns to face her. "We are just under four kilometers. Estimated docking in fifteen minutes."

"Do we need to return to our seats? Put our restraints on?" Ava says. "I don't want to be the villain here and break this party up."

Midori nods. "There's no need for anyone to be restrained. Remember, this is a soft landing. There's a port inside. Eden will guide us in. I'm in constant contact with the navigation system."

"Right. They showed us in the training. We land on a circular bed with shocks. But shouldn't we be safe? So many times, things are deemed safe, but then there's an accident."

"Eden has a hundred percent safety rate with landings and launches," Midori says.

"But that's not to say it couldn't happen," Ava says. "They also said the caskets couldn't break or leak, and look at what happened there as one fine example."

Midori turns to the others. "She's not wrong. Better safe than sorry. She's the boss." She stands and walks toward the door. Smiling at Ava, she passes and approaches the seating.

Poole looks at her. "All right," he says. "No problem. I'm personally very risk averse." He gets up, too. The others follow his example. By the time Ava joins them, they are all sitting and buckled up.

"I appreciate all of you," Ava says. "Everyone good?"

"Yup. Just peachy," Ken says.

"Peaches and cream," Poole says.

Sanjay gives a thumbs-up. "I'm ready."

He's been awfully quiet, Ava thinks. *I would just go along for the ride, too, if I could.*

Tessa has her glasses on again and gives an okay symbol. "Ready to roll."

Ava makes a last glance and affirms with a nod to Midori.

The gold light falls off to shadow as they close in on Eden. "We are less than one kilometer from Eden," Midori announces. "Three minutes until we're inside."

Ava scans the others. She swears she can hear their hearts beating. Every squeak of a boot on the metal floor sounds a thousand times louder than it should. *My ears always seem to focus when I'm stressed. Probably my imagination, but they've gotten so sensitive to sound. Ever since being on the outpost. It's like something happened there that made them this way.* She remembers Roland, walking away from their habitat, his striking gaze meeting hers. *I remember him so clearly.* She shuts her eyes for a moment. *You're out here somewhere. Still. I know it. Something took you. Or some things.* She imagines her presence being enough to signal his captors to return him to her. Pictures him delivered to her, just as she remembered him, right on the decks of Eden. Feels his embrace. Smells him. *Stop. Don't. They told you to let go. He's gone. It's an accident. Your mind blocked it out. Too much to handle. That's what they said. Post-traumatic stress and all. You need to do this to heal and not hold on to some silly superstitions. You need to be strong and lead this crew. Get through this. Prove to yourself you can.*

The docking doors of Eden open. Ava takes a deep breath. *Sure glad I took that nap before, 'cus here we go.* The others notice, too.

"Docking initiated," Midori says.

Like we couldn't tell. Ava really wants to tell the bot to stop but doesn't want to set a precedent. She may go quiet when they really need her in the future. *You need to chill with the anger, too, Ava, if you're going to get through this.*

The interior is washed in a blinding light for a moment until her eyes adjust. When they do, she makes out the industrial makings of the docking bay. Pipes. Ramps. Service boxes.

Slowing to a stop, the capsule shakes.

"Coupling device engaged," Midori says.

Ava feels the cushioned rollers underneath and something close to true gravity for the first time in hours. A loud clanging makes her put her hands over her ears. "Wow," she says. "What was that?"

"Just the security clamp," Midori says. "Was that unusually loud to you?"

"Wasn't it for everyone?" Ava tries to think of why it wouldn't be.

The others stare at her, and she feels tremendously vulnerable.

Before she or anyone can answer, another voice pipes in.

"Welcome to Eden."

Chapter Four

EDEN SATELLITE
CHAMBER 0317 – AVA'S QUARTERS
13:48:40 UTC
15 MARCH 2112

Every day, the same damn wake-up message plays. "Welcome to Eden." Ava says it along with the ship's voice when it plays. "Why are you welcoming me here when I've already been here a month?" She rises from her bunk and sits.

"What can I do for you today?" Eden asks.

"I'm good," Ava says. "Just the normal routine. Go over everyone's task lists. Make sure they're on point. No big deal. I've got this. Another normal day ahead. Thanks, Eden."

"My pleasure, Ava."

I wish there was a way I could unplug the damn thing, stop it from talking to me all the time. It's always listening to every noise I make. One month down, five more to go, and I get my privacy back. She doesn't bother changing into new garb. They are all the same, anyway. She goes to the air shower and shuts the glass door. "Start the shower," she says. Nozzles on either side of her blow gently. The nanoparticles would find the more offensive bacteria and neutralize it. *Gotta save the water up here for the dead.* She pictures standing in the outdoor shower at the Majif Hotel in Malibu, the hot water covering her. Feels the bamboo wood floor. Smells the saltwater air mixing with the shampoo. Hears every wave. Every laugh. Seagulls squawking. *Gonna be one of the first things I do when I get back down. Treat myself to an overnight at the Majif. That's going to be amazing. I'll have the means to do so, no problem, too.*

The nano spray stops after thirty seconds, and she steps out. She puts her fingers in her ears and rubs gently on the outside. She hates the super-high pitch the sprays make and is glad it stops. She smirks. "I don't feel refreshed one bit. Ridiculous."

Her stomach rumbles as soon as she makes it to the first hallway. "I hear you." The commissary is a straight shot a few hundred feet from the bunks. The others should be in there, too, having breakfast.

When she gets there, the room is dark and empty. *Huh. That's strange. Most of them are usually here by now.*

As soon as she walks inside, the lights come on. *I'll go find them as soon as I get something down.* A dull headache has started – another signal she needs to eat soon. She makes a beeline to the kitchen. They are their own cooks. She grabs a protein sandwich from the fridge and puts it in one of the small induction ovens. It'll be ready in a minute, she knows. While it cooks, she grabs a mug and goes to the prep counter. She puts the mug under the hot water tap and fills it. She opens the drawer and pulls out the tea tray and chooses an Earl Grey bag. "Just another boring old day on a floating mausoleum in the sky."

She peers out at the plain gray tables that fill the dining hall. There are no windows in here. They save the views for paying customers. *My room doesn't even have a view. Only Tessa Nightingale gets that. And to think being in space was all I dreamed about when I was a kid. Not all it's cracked up to be.* A big beep makes her jump out of her skin.

"Ava Armstrong?" The voice belongs to Allison Mercer. "Are you available to talk?"

She sighs. "Yeah. Sure." *Of course, Vita Nova knows my every move and that I'm free.*

A holo screen appears in front of Ava, showing a video of a grinning Allison. "Hi, there," she says. The image is sharper than usual. They obviously have their own better connection.

"Hiya. What's up, Allison?" She stirs the tea. *Now I'm calling her Allison instead of Mercer. Does this mean we're friends? Or friendly?*

"Just doing our weekly check-in," Allison says. "How's everything going?"

"Smooth and on point," Ava says. "All systems are running just fine. No issues." She makes a circular gesture, bringing forth another holo screen. The crew's names are displayed, alongside tasks and checkmarks.

Ava Armstrong Duvay — manager
Dr. Derek Poole — medical officer
Sanjay Akhila — senior communications officer
Ken Lee — communications officer
Contessa "Tessa" Garcia Nightingale — special guest composer

"As you can see, we're following the plans step by step. Everyone's working hard. We should be ready for the public by summer. No problem."

"Love hearing that," Allison says. "That's just brilliant. I'm so grateful. Vita Nova is so grateful. Is there anything you need?"

Ava shakes her head. "Nah. We have plenty of food. Everyone's doing great in their roles. Nothing to report at all of any note at this moment."

Nodding, Allison puts a hand up. "Speaking of notes? Has Tessa given you a sneak peek at the new requiem by any chance?" Her eyes glisten.

Ava nods. "She's secretive. Been keeping mostly to herself unless she's coming out to eat, to be honest."

"Well, I'm dying to hear it," Allison says.

"You and a ton of families on the waiting list," Ava says dryly. She cocks an eyebrow.

"Oh. I didn't literally mean dying…" Allison looks like she's going to shrink below the screen. "That came out wrong."

Ava waves her hand, delighted at her boss's embarrassment. *She's human after all.* "Don't worry about it. Just my gallows humor. Sorry."

Allison lets out a small giggle. "That's one of the things I love about you, Ava. Always trying to look on the bright side."

"Sure beats what's on the dark side of the damn moon," Ava says, shutting her eyes for a moment and processing.

Allison shrugs. "Hah. Guess so."

Ava is sure she's made her boss uncomfortable. Had she just jokingly referred to what she and Roland had gone through? *Shoot. My mouth just won't stop, will it?* "Anyway, I think we're chugging along just fine. How is the pale blue dot rolling?"

"Nothing earth-shattering to report."

"Thank God," Ava says. "It would really suck to be stuck up here if Earth shattered, you realize."

They both laugh. "We're on a roll with the jokes today, aren't we? And of course, Ava," Allison says. "Let's hope not."

"Indeed," Ava says, matter-of-factly.

"All right. Well, I will let you get back to your tea and take care of Eden," Allison says. "I appreciate you."

"I appreciate you, too." Ava waves goodbye.

Allison waves, and the video stops.

Well, that was easy. I do like her. I'd probably admit it if she wasn't my boss. Too bad for her for now, though. She puts a pinky in the tea to test the heat. Still too hot. She takes it by the handle and heads away from the serving area. As she gets inside the main room, she spots Midori heading in. Her expression is blank. *Damn Humani bots have the best poker faces ever. Hope she's not here just to report bad news.*

Midori waves. "Ava," she says. "Your presence is requested by Dr. Poole in the medical bays."

"Everything okay? Something happen?" Ava asks.

"Everything's...fine," Midori says. She smiles.

That's the most forced smile I've ever seen in my life. Is she full of crap or what? Ava knows something just isn't right – knows it with every bit of her.

PART TWO

Chapter Five

EDEN SATELLITE
CHAMBER 1613
13:48:40 UTC
15 MARCH 2112

The requiem drowns out Ken's scream. The clear casket's suspension fluid splashes his hand and arm. He looks up toward the top of the chamber and spots the telltale crack in the lower right corner of the clear coffin. *That's where it leaked from.* Drops of the light blue fluid gather along the slight fault line, rolling toward the edge before falling. He dodges out of the way, but it's too late. He's already got enough of the stuff on him. *Is this what happened before? Are the caskets failing? This was supposed to have been fixed.*

The same piece of music Eden airs for all its interred, he knows. *Still the old one. Tessa's still working on her new version.*

Beyond the casket, he glances at Earth hovering hundreds of thousands of miles away.

The music plays louder, filling the chamber. It won't be long until the little particles inside do their job, slowly unmaking him, he knows. His pulse races. *Can't I just wash this stuff off? Isn't there a vaccine ready for emergencies? Something? Anything? Vita Nova must have prepared for this.* He can't recall any such treatment being mentioned in their orientation. His senses go into overdrive. The metallic smell of the ever-present recycled air seems stronger than usual. Every squeak of his feet on the polished floor sounds like screeching brakes, even over the requiem.

Wish I could dive into the ocean right now, like when I had chicken pox when I was a kid. That'd fix this. Even an unimaginable distance away, floating on a satellite in the sky, he can't resist the urge to run away.

His brain hurts. The headache arrives fast and strong – first at the base of his neck, then fires straight toward his temples and eyes. *It's inside me – the stuff. Going so fast. Headed right for my skull. That's what the particles want, after all. Going right for the astrocytes in my brain. They want the cells that are storing my memories. Astro. Cytes. Appropriate name, all things considered.*

Music plays on.

The requiem.

One last song for the dead.

The composition gets noisier still. Ken hears frequencies he's never perceived before, even though he's listened to it thousands of times, during countless services.

He feels something snap inside his skull – a blood vessel, perhaps?

Ken kneels on the chamber floor and grasps his head. *This can't be happening.* He shouts out in agony. "Eden!" he says. "I need medical help right away. Can you do a bio scan on me?" The satellite's communication system will hear him. *Eden's always listening, right?*

Eden doesn't reply.

He cries out a second time, his voice more labored and distressed. *All the breath is going out of me. Not much time left.*

"Eden? Hello?" he asks.

She's supposed to be always on.

"Hello? Where are you?" Ken asks. "Ava? Dr. Poole? Anyone… listening?" The comm system should connect him to his colleagues, but none respond.

Ken twists onto the floor, resting on his side. *Stay awake. Don't fall asleep. That'll be the end, if you do. You won't ever wake up.* His head feels crammed with lava; the blood inside his veins feels congealed and thick. *This stuff is killing me. I'm being embalmed alive. Can taste it – like acid and salt. Formaldehyde. Pushing through me. Maybe if I can get an IV of saline, they can get it out of me. Maybe with minimal damage. Oh, please, someone answer me.*

"Poole?" he yells. "Ava? Eden?" Hollering takes all the vigor he has. His words break, his own voice unrecognizable.

Playing over the chamber's sound system, the requiem's melody is simple, yet he hears more dissonant notes as the piece progresses, barely audible, fighting for space. He'd have thought the lowest notes, or the highest notes could have been worse, but the midrange bits are the ones slicing through his head. "Make it stop. Please!" He yells for Eden to turn off the requiem, but the satellite does not listen.

Colors come. He shuts his eyes to the pain and sees waves of orange, yellow, and red, flowing and growing like an unholy sea. Reminds him of the night before finals at Stanford when all the engineering students had gone out to the ocean for one last hurrah. He remembers the vast ocean, the same as ever. *But was it?*

The recollection of the ocean in his memory changes. The peaceful, slight waves give way to a large, spinning vortex, spiraling down many fathoms, revealing creatures made only from fins and rows of teeth, ready to tear him to nothingness.

Ken plummets, moving his arms and legs to try to stop himself. It doesn't work.

His stomach tenses. A primal fear consumes him. He shuts his eyes as he approaches the vortex's center. *This isn't real. But it feels real.*

Darkness turns into light. Colored splotches move and spread into different, moving shapes. *Now I'm seeing auras.*

Ken wakes. He lies in the fetal position on the floor of a chamber on Eden.

The requiem plays on. *How is it going on for so long? It should have stopped a long time ago. It's only two minutes long.* The frequencies hurt and appear to be connected straight to his nerves. He positions his hands over his ears – a reflex to drown out the music. As he does, he spots the mottled flesh of his arm and hand. It's as though the fluid has burned and boiled him; his hand looks swollen and disfigured, as if he'd dipped it inside a vat of boiling acid. *The fluid's deforming me. Remaking me.*

"No," Ken says. "Please."

His hands stick to his head as though glued. The skin blends and fixes. He can't remove his hands. The small particles rush through his arm and race toward his head. They make their way inside his skin as easily as sugar dissolving into a hot cup of tea. Every little grain feels like a needle plunging inside, burrowing, moving, hungry to find whatever nourishment hides inside.

"Eden!" he says as loud as possible. "I need help. Call the others." *The satellite's virtual intelligence should hear me and act on my voice commands. Maybe it can't hear my voice because the music's so loud.*

Ken falls backward – drops flat onto the chamber floor – his body has given out. Agony plugs every muscle and organ. His gut hurts more than he's ever suffered. His head feels light and hollowed out. His skin feels made from liquid fire.

He shuts his eyes to it all. Thinks maybe if he does, it'll be better.

It isn't.

Instead, everything amplifies – the pain – the sounds.

Ken cannot pull his hands from his ears, nor can he move from the ground, no matter how hard he tries.

His skin sticks to the floor. *How am I going to return to my life with Brian down at home? I must see Seattle again. Our place. The Space Needle on the horizon at sunset. Our favorite ramen joint on Sundays.* He remembers the ramen's flavor. Salty. Hot. The noodles warm and soft, the small, chewy bits of meat acting as a perfect complement. *I took this gig so that we'd get a big nest egg for our future. We'd pretty much be able to stop struggling and be able to retire.*

"Why is this happening to me? Someone please help me."

He gazes at the clear coffin above. Suspended on the ceiling, the chambers are raised and locked in place, so the interred face an enormous window as they float and remain preserved in suspension fluid.

One can stare out and see the beautiful white and blue Earth, while also seeing the infinite darkness of space beyond.

A burial among the stars.

Ken wonders if someone on Earth is observing Eden from one of the scopes, searching for their relative, and maybe seeing him suffering on the floor behind. *Can they see that much detail with the scopes? What would they do if they did? What could they do?*

Crack.

The breached coffin makes an unfamiliar noise. Ken sees the small fault line stretch and grow. *The thing will bust right over me. If more of the fluid gets on me, there's no way I will recover.*

He tries to move, but it's still as though he's been attached to the floor with his own skin. Every trivial action hurts.

The line in the coffin grows.

"No," he says. "They said this wouldn't happen again." Ken remembers the reports from the last time…the incidents that closed Eden…hears Mercer promise the reason had been found and that the satellite was safe.

Lies.

The particles swarm inside his brain; he senses them. They unearth his memories. *This is what it feels like for the dead being interred here.*

That is one of Eden's big selling points. The particles in the fluid discover and assemble memories, copy them, and send them to Eden's main processor. They even capture and transcribe muscle memory so a cybernetic version of a loved one's every movement is authentic.

Relatives can see them once the software reconstructs them.

Overhead, the coffin breaks.

Fluid floods down, as do pieces of the coffin's clear composite material. The person inside falls, too, crashing in a lump only a few inches from Ken.

Impossible as it is for him to imagine, Ken feels something even more painful.

He looks down and sees a jagged piece of the composite spearing out from his stomach.

"I'm dead," he says.

He blacks out.

For a time, he senses nothing.

Voices stir him, bringing him back from the still darkness.

As he wakes, Ava stares down on him. The satellite's captain. Dr. Poole flanks her.

"Is this heaven?" he asks.

"You're on Eden," Ava says. "You had a fall."

"What?" Ken's confused. He raises his head, stunned. He looks at his hand. It appears normal on both sides. Sitting up, he scans the chamber.

The fallen body has gone. The fluid is mopped up. There is no debris. "The automations worked fast to clean up," Ken says.

Looking upward, he notices the sky casket. It's not how he remembers it should be.

"Clean what up?" Dr. Poole says.

"The coffin. It cracked. Dripped on me," Ken says, examining his arm again. "The particles got inside me. The coffin broke, and the person fell. One piece of the broken glass…pierced me." He stares at his middle. Finds no signs of trauma.

"You hit your head pretty hard," Ava says. "You must have been dreaming."

Ken raises his hand. "I'm infected." He turns his hand to test his palm. "Maybe no one can see it, but I know that stuff is inside me. I can feel it."

"Ken…" says Ava.

"No," he says.

"There is nothing on you," Dr. Poole says. "Nothing happened. It must have been some sort of waking dream."

"I'm not making this up," Ken says. "I am not hallucinating."

Dr. Poole and Ava look at one another.

"Don't do that," Ken says. "Don't give each other 'the look' right in front of me. If you think I'm crazy, say it to my face."

He watches Ava place a hand on the arm he hasn't raised; she's trying to support him. "No one is saying that," she says, lowering her voice. "And certainly no one thinks that. We are just trying to understand what happened to you. Make sure you're all right."

"That's right," Dr. Poole says. "Are you okay with us running some tests on you?"

Ken shakes his head. He senses his entire body shiver. Feels his cheeks are red. "Tests? I need the antidote. I need medicine to counteract this right away. It's probably already too late. We've waited too long."

"We can't treat you unless we know what it is," Dr. Poole says. "So, let's get this going."

"Why don't you lie down," Ava says. "We are going to step out and go right into the observation room and start. We'll get you on whatever you need, pronto, okay?"

"I'm doing this under duress, just for the record," Ken says. "Looks like I don't have any other choice. You're going to force me into this, anyway. I bet you'll lock the door and keep me like a prisoner, won't you?"

"You know the doors always lock after we leave them," Ava says. "It's what Eden does."

"Yeah, but you're going to take away my clearances, aren't you? Make sure I'm not crazy," Ken says. "You should be locking the door behind me. I might be contagious. Especially after the things inside me rip me apart and escape."

"We'll make sure that doesn't happen," Ava says. She stares right into Ken's eyes. "Can you trust me? Please? For just a bit?"

He looks at her. His distressed expression drops away. She's gotten through to him. "For you?" he says. "Okay. Let's see what we have. I'll stay calm."

"Good," she says, giving his arm a brief squeeze before she rises from the seat next to him. "We'll be right in the other room. You know the drill. We'll be on the screens. You won't have to do anything but lie down. Eden will do the rest."

"Scan me into oblivion," he says. "That's what it'll do."

"I hope not," Ava says. She signals for Dr. Poole to leave. They head for the door. She glances over her shoulder one last time at Ken. He stares at the floor.

★ ★ ★

In the control room, Ava awakens Eden's master panel by making a circular motion over the desk. The display powers on – projected in light suspended midair. "Eden," she says. "We need to do a diagnostic scan of Ken Lee. He's in Bay 914 right now, awaiting our query."

Images of Ken materialize in front of Ava and Poole. They supplement a standard video image with two others, each displaying Ken's innards charted in real time.

"Scan for abnormalities," Poole says. "Penetrative entities. Viruses. Cognitive irregularities."

Eden says, "Scanning, Dr. Poole."

"Always throws me off how human she sounds," Ava says.

"Right," Poole says. "Better than her sounding fake."

"I'd rather she did," Ava says.

The map view indicates oranges and reds concentrated inside Ken's head. "Something's definitely going on beyond what's normal," Poole says. "Eden, can we do a thorough analysis on the agitation?"

"Yes, Dr. Poole," Eden says.

A catalog of diagnostics appears.

"Blood pressure in the brain is high," Poole says. "But not dangerous. What's causing the area to be flagged, Eden?"

"Still exploring, Dr. Poole," Eden says.

Ken's hands flex by his sides, making and uncurling fists.

Poole waves his hand at the screen and the map zooms closer on Ken's head. He waves again, and the image expands to present rendered versions of blood vessels and tissue. "Switch to neural view," Poole says. "Need to see where this stuff is firing."

The map changes and shows a murkier image, but with thin lines indicating nerves. Poole signals toward his right. The map responds. "There," he says, recognizing a cluster glowing red. "Where do those lead?"

Poole glances at Ava. Then back at the map. "Eden?" he says. "Where does that cluster's wiring start?"

Ken screams.

The map turns red.

On the video feed, they see Ken's hand, clamped in a fist, hiding his right eye. The end of a pen protrudes from behind.

"My God," Ava says.

"Emergency anesthesia," Poole says. "Now, Eden."

Ken twists the pen and pushes it deeper inside.

His shriek never stops.

"Eden!" Ava cries out.

Ken's hand drops from his face, leaving the pen sticking out from his eye. His arm falls to his side, and his head rolls over.

After a moment, Ava says, "Please tell me he didn't just die on us." She stares at his motionless body.

Poole looks at the screen and the map. Sighs. "He's still with us," he says. "But barely."

"I see his heart rate," Ava says. "It's weak."

"We need to get in there," Poole says.

Ava signals and they rush out and back into Ken's chamber. Poole takes Ken's left hand in his own and holds it. "Come on, buddy," he says, his voice low. "What's going on with you?"

"He's been up here too long. Sometimes even a month off Earth is long enough to trigger people. Maybe it's driven him crazy," Ava says. "But he's an engineer. They seldom crack like this."

"Doesn't add up," Poole says. "Ken's solid as a rock. At least he was before today, right?"

"Exactly," Ava says.

Poole leans in; he examines the socket closely. "Ken's done a real job on himself. He'll lose that eye, for sure. There's nothing left."

"Can the automation remove it safely?" Ava asks.

"It's risky," Poole says. "It'd be ideal if I guided the job."

"Glad we have you," Ava says. "But not half as glad as he'll be once he gets through this."

"Indeed," Poole says.

"When should we do this?" Ava asks.

"Now," he says.

Chapter Six

EDEN SATELLITE
TESSA'S CHAMBER
13:51:55 UTC
16 MARCH 2112

The heavens speak.
Tessa feels more exhausted than at any period in her life. No matter how long she sleeps, she still wakes up feeling drained. Her eyes feel like swollen balls made from ache. Her throat is scratchy and raw, like she can never drink enough water to stay hydrated. Tessa's upper back hurts whenever she raises her arms higher than her waist. All her joints are sore; her lymph nodes feel filled with warm, sloshy water.

Inspiration always comes at the worst times. She knows better than to believe she'll remember what's in her head later. *I need to act right away to transcribe it, or I'll lose it forever.* She's had such trouble coming up with anything good for the new requiem. Finally, something's come to her that she knows will be good. *Don't blow it.*

So, she powers through.

Tessa hears the theme inside her head. Hums it.

Persistent little thing, aren't you? Funny this came at the same time I started not feeling so great. But, whatever. This is the inspiration I was waiting for. This is the moment. Don't let it slip away.

On her tablet, she checks her feed. If she goes live, it'll be to the 1,203,866 subscribers of her channel. *I can't even comprehend how many people are watching. Incredible. Crazy. Wish I could really see them. Feel them. Reach out and touch them.*

Tessa waves at the small camera, the device only an inch in circumference. A single stem angles the device and holds it in position. *So crazy something so tiny transmits to so many wonderful people. Never thought of it that way before. Take so much of this stuff for granted, don't we? I know I sure as heck do.*

"Camera," she says. "I want to record and go live, okay?"

"Affirmative," the camera's voice says. "Recording."

Tessa feels a little light-headed, despite her sitting down. She addresses the camera. "Hi, everyone down on planet Earth. Thank you all so much for viewing. Of course, I'd get one whopper of a bug while this happens. Isn't that always the way? How many of you get brilliant ideas when you're sick, or when you're just about to fall asleep? It's like, come on, brain. What are you thinking? Can't you do this when I'm good and awake and feeling fine?" Tessa laughs. "Any-who, I've been having some very serious musical…visions…I guess you'd say. I heard these crazy melodies and counterpoints and themes. I'll work on transcribing them and starting to record them. And now you get to watch and see how it happens live. Like at one of my shows. And hopefully? This will become the requiem they've asked me to come up here to compose for Eden. So, without further ado, here I am, live from space. Can you believe it? So cool."

She turns her head away from the camera and puts her fingers on her keyboard, creating a dominant seventh chord.

Tessa closes her eyes. *Take control of my hands. Play through me. Let's bring this music to the world and everywhere else thereafter.*

She hears beautiful melodies inside her head. *It's like they're being sent to me from God. From something divine out here in space. Never felt more inspired.* Her entire body hums.

Tessa fires up the recording section of her rig. Within moments, low frequencies rumble through as she plays her synthesizer. The sound patch oscillates between three notes, a bass chord outlines single notes, blending, coming apart, roving for a beat, and resuming the connection with the others. *This is all like a loop.*

Transcribing the music she hears inside her head comes easy. She's worked on her craft for years. That's a given. *I can hear the melody coming to life. It's infused within the bed of the song, too. Atmospheric. But the structure seems strange. No story. No definitive ending to the piece — like the music circles back around on itself and starts again — spinning round and round. It should have a beginning, middle, and end, shouldn't it?*

She hears her agent's voice, too, telling her about the gig. "It's a six-month residency. Vita Nova covers all your needs. They just need updated music for Eden's residents. A new requiem. Something more reflective of the time. But it needs to be classy, too. Has to appeal to everyone." Tessa didn't like the company referring to people's remains as residents. *Feels dehumanizing and creepy. And what they really want to do is rebrand after their big accident up here. They're not kidding anyone.*

She pictures her sea of fans. *They're all people. Individuals. That's really who I have to think about while I'm writing this new requiem gig. No pressure. None. Just all the hundreds of thousands of people that will hear the piece on Earth, too.*

Tessa recalls the festival gigs. She could pump the right beats-per-minute into the crowds and they'd just groove. She could hit a patch on her sample. Mess with it. Dance. Read the people. Adjust when she felt they needed it. When she needed it. She always knows. Even when she straps on her Les Paul and plays along with the sound patches — shaking, dancing, loving being inside the music — she has the energy feeding her. The crowd. *None of my recordings are purely just the studio. It's all been created live. That's my thing. I need an audience, but I don't have one up here. That's what's missing. I need a lot of energy from lots of people to make this work.*

The synth patch stops, echoes for several beats inside the digital delay before decaying and fading.

Tessa's new requiem stops.

"Damn it. I need some real live people." She strolls toward the gigantic window to her right. "Or else I'm sunk." She only has a few months and sometimes it takes longer to compose something with any depth. She needs to deliver, or Vita Nova can charge her for her trip and stay aboard Eden. *I'll never be able to afford it, even if I sell everything I own.* "I have to find a way," she says.

At the window, she looks outside at the gorgeous view of the magnificent nighttime Earth below, its artificial lights painting the dark ground with millions of golden spotlights. Eden orbits Earth, rotating on its own axis. Even so? Eden never matches Earth's rhythms, even though they follow Universal Time. Sunrise comes rapidly, as does sunset, and the surface transforms from sunny to dark within minutes. She misses the glorious, colorful displays of the Sun rising and setting at home.

Lost in the dark, twirling around the Earth like a raft lost at sea.

"If this doesn't inspire me, nothing will." Putting her hand on the ledge, she nods. *I'm looking at the biggest audience possible. Half the planet can look up and see me at any one time. How am I going to access that energy? How am I going to perform for them up here? How can we make this work?*

Maybe, she supposes, she can do an amped-up live feed. *Or a dead feed.* She laughs. She'll have to feel it out, but that would work. It just could. *We'd need to plan it and promote it. We can't count on people just being there without us telling them. When they look up, that's how they see Eden, too. But they can't see that much detail. Unless they use the scopes to see the plots that hold their loved ones.*

She blinks and the room feels unfamiliar. The lights dim. She rubs her eyes. They sting. *I've been awake too long. I ought to get some rest.* Her ears hurt, too, which she considers strange. *Why would I be getting an earache?* Her nose twinges like she's about to have a bloody nose. She wrinkles the sides, and sure enough, a small bead of blood rolls out. She wipes it on the back of her hand.

Tessa feels woozy, as though she's had several drinks or some pot. She dashes over and sits on the bench in front of her keyboard. "This is what I get for pushing myself," she says. "Damn deadlines. Just got to power through this." Fingering some chords, she channels her muse. For a moment, the rig comes to life, and her music plays.

Then?

She hears nothing. Sound gets drawn away – everything resonates like it's underwater. When it clips back in, Tessa hears only a vague blur of audio. The bigger and louder sections of the unexpected sound swell.

I'm in a trance.

The area around her blurs, too. *Is this a fever kicking in? Maybe a virus is coming on? Am I even here?*

Her sinuses feel tremendously pressurized. *Wish I could drill a hole in them to let out the pressure. That'd probably work.*

Her eyes tingle and feel like they'll swell right out of her skull.

Everything hurts.

Until nothing hurts.

Lost in the moment, Tessa wants to channel whatever has taken her over. She glances at her hands and fingers. Somehow, she remains upright. *Press record and play.* She does. Everything's fuzzy, but she keeps doing her best. At least there is a persistent sound of her playing, of that she is certain.

I must be high as a kite on that medicine. This is nuts. And this can end up in front of God knows how many people. Hope it's nothing embarrassing. Hope I'm going to be okay. What if I have something more serious that can't be treated up here? There won't be another transport possible for a month, and only if it's a real emergency. I should go see Dr. Poole.

She gasps. All the breath goes out of her. She tries to catch her breath but can't. *Who turned off the air?*

She blacks out, still sitting on the bench, hands still on the keys.

★ ★ ★

She's alert.

What's happening?

Tessa can't find her bearings.

Wake up.

Everything spins for a moment; she sees static. Her head feels impossibly light.

Where am I? Stop playing. Get up.

Her body feels made from stone. She can't move, despite her resolve.

Open your eyes, at least.

Unsure if the command works or if she is dreaming, Tessa sees a fuzzy realm of color come into focus. She's carried into a place...

somehow familiar and strange. There are hills made from light purple sand. Rivers flow with water, so vivid and green. She feels her soul travel outside her body.

She smells strange ozone-scented winds; the landscape overwhelms her with countless sweet scents.

What is this place?

Fear brews and twists up inside her like a coil. As striking as the place seems, something about it doesn't seem true. *This isn't natural. This isn't safe at all, even though it's pretty.*

She travels toward the top of a hill. Beyond, she sees a vast valley, its ground covered with what look like dark roots, only the roots move and slither, sprout, and throb. Some appear to have veins. When she drifts closer, she sees little eyes no larger than sesame seeds. Angry purple eyes. Mouths, similar in size, open and close, gasping. Or are they talking? Singing? The tones are different from any she's ever heard.

Her lungs overflow with air, like they'll burst. Her heart tickles.

The roots sweep across the valley…miles after miles. A bundle moves in front of her, shooting upright, higher than she can see. Its roots stretch, taking only a moment to cover her, smothering her in their darkness, filling her with their sound. Uncountable tiny mouths clamp onto her like leeches. With her blood inside them, draining from her, Tessa's perception dims. *Only the sound…the sound of their sucking…then the sound of their voices…their alien harmonies.*

She blinks.

Finds herself back on Eden, back inside her room. Gazes down at her fingers, still pressing a claw-shaped chord on her keyboard. *I should know what chord it is that I'm playing, but I don't.*

Her recording system recognizes what she's playing. She'd set it up so she could play a chord or a note and it will play other instruments in harmony. Tessa programmed certain sounds to play certain notes or patterns based on a single finger's input. With only a few shapes, she can control an orchestra.

What is the dream I just had? I have the worst nightmares ever up here in space. She cannot shake the strange feeling.

For several seconds, she can't think of a single musical term. She has enough presence of mind to turn to the camera and say, "That's all, folks," before ending the performance. "Hope that's recorded." Tessa thinks over how many times she's lost a great idea due to a technical glitch or because she forgot to press a button.

She drops onto her cot, the inside of her head burning from fever. *I think I'm going blind.* A high-pitched sound fills her ears. Tinnitus. Like after one of her louder shows, she realizes. But it doesn't die down after a few minutes like usual. She still feels ill.

My music just played to millions of people, and I don't even know what it was I did. Do I even want to know? She feels sicker than she's ever felt. Vertigo overtakes her. *I'm like a piece of meat rolling on a shish kabob over here. God. What is this bug? It's bad.* She needs to call the others right away. They'll come and help her, she's sure. There is just no way she'll get through this alone.

I was just with them a few hours ago. They're probably going to tell me to relax and wait it out. There's not much they can do, anyway, is there?

Whatever she's caught is unlike anything else she's ever been through. *Just hope I get through this, whatever it is.*

They're at least forty-eight hours from any emergency supply payload reaching them, best case. If they don't have the proper medicines on the Eden satellite, she'll be stuck. They'll be able to consult with doctors and experts remotely, but if it is something severe, it could turn bad. Fast. She recalls seeing them call in doctors who could read the scans and advise the passengers and residents on board during the orientation videos. *They can do that, at least. Eden has limited emergency and life-saving procedures at the ready. We all had to pass basic physicals, so they know we're in good enough shape to make the trip and stay in orbit for a year.*

She'd passed without incident. *But what if there is something inside of me they don't catch? Something bad? And what if it's something I caught up here? An outer space bug they can't treat. What then? Would they be able to do anything for me?*

Tessa shuts her eyes. *Don't think like that. The flu always feels bad. It's probably just amplified because you're in space and the air pressure is different, and the gravity isn't natural at all. You'll get through it. You're made of tough stuff. That's one reason you made it this far in life…and into space.*

She tries to sleep, but as soon as she drifts, she finds herself back at the strange place with the purple dunes and creeping roots singing and gnawing and locking down on her.

Just a fever dream. That's all. Just a fever dream. Power through it. You'll be fine. That same imagination that gives you the power to make these symphonies also gives you vivid dreams and visions. Just a wing of your creative mind at play, that's all. Nothing to worry about, even though it seems so damn vivid and real.

In the dream, Tessa looks upward and sees the clouds thinning and drifting, as though being sucked into a giant void. The sky darkens. The atmosphere evaporates. She can't catch a breath. She grabs her throat. Coughs. Falls to the ground. Her head will explode. She knows it.

A hand touches her shoulder and a voice calls her name, but she can't turn. She falls on her face, then turns on her side. She blinks several times. When she looks up, she spots Midori looking down at her. The robot repeats her name and bends down. "I need to get you out of here."

Realizing she is no longer dreaming, Tessa tries to breathe. *Still can't.* Behind the robot, the room is as gloomy as it'd been in her nightmare.

What the heck?

She watches as Midori bends down more, saying something about a directive. She scoops Tessa up expertly and efficiently, then makes for the door.

"Why are the lights out?" Tessa thinks her voice sounds wounded and weak.

A large fixture falls from the ceiling behind Midori. It slams into her back, pushing them both into the door. Midori's eyes widen, but she doesn't make a peep. Then, without delay, they open the door and go out into the hallway.

"Eden," Midori says. "What are the oxygen levels and vitals at my position?"

There is a pause before Eden replies. "All vital systems are working."

"Great. Thank you," Midori says.

"So weird saying thank you to a computer," Tessa says. "Isn't it?"

Midori looks down at Tessa. "Do you not want to thank me for saving you, Tessa?"

Tessa winces. "I don't mean you," she says. "I meant Eden. It's… just…I don't know."

"Your mind is affected by the lack of oxygen," Midori says. "I'd recommend taking a break until you're in med bay."

"Lack of…oxygen?" Tessa says.

"Something went wrong with the units in your room that control the air," Midori says. "Good thing I was notified."

"Notified?"

"The ship, of course."

They hurried down the hall.

"Why did it do that without fixing it?" Tessa says. "Doesn't make sense."

"It does not."

Even seeing Midori up close, it impresses Tessa how real she looks. If she didn't know better, there'd be no way she'd think she is mechanized. *She's so beautiful. Wish I could look that flawless, too.*

Midori grins while observing her. "It will be all right," she says. "I've got you."

"I know it will all be fine," Tessa says. "I feel it."

Chapter Seven

EDEN SATELLITE
ALPHA OUTPOST, MED BAY 1.0013
13:52:35 UTC
16 MARCH 2112

"The bleeding isn't stopping," Dr. Poole says. Ken's eye bandage has soaked through. "We need to apply a second clotting agent," Dr. Poole says to the always-listening Eden. *This is not good. Was not expecting a crisis like this up here.*

"Yes, Dr. Poole," Eden says. "We will need to remove the bandage prior to application. Do you authorize?"

"I authorize," he says. "Time is money. Go for it."

Sanjay and Ava watch from the observation room monitors. A robotic arm stretches outward. Two pincers gently and expertly unwrap Ken's eye bandage.

Dr. Poole examines the innards of Ken's eye socket, pink, red, and raw. The nozzle between the pincers sprays for a moment, then stops. The arm places the bandage back over Ken's hollow eye socket. *This might be too intense for Sanjay. He's not trained in this.*

"You okay seeing that?" he asks Sanjay. When he turns, he sees his colleague has spun away from the screens, his attention on a binder left on the desk.

"See what?" Sanjay says.

"The procedure," Dr. Poole says.

"I missed it," Sanjay says.

"All the better," Dr. Poole says. "Some things you don't really want to stay with you. Like seeing that wound."

"I didn't see anything, though," Sanjay says. "So, no issue there."

Poole says, "Great."

"He lost his eye, right?" Sanjay asks.

"Yes." Dr. Poole leaned in more.

Sanjay asks, "What can we do for him?"

"We don't have any artificial replacements that match his size or color on board," Dr. Poole says. "I'll order another eye and have it on the next transport. We'll have him wear a patch until it arrives."

"That's a few weeks away," Ava says.

"He still has one working eye until then," Dr. Poole says. "He'll adapt."

"Let's hope so," Sanjay says.

"Lucky he didn't do more damage," Ava says. "He could have hit his brain."

"He impacted his frontal lobe, to a minor degree, and not fatally," Dr. Poole says. "We won't know the magnitude of the injury until he recuperates a tad more." *I hope that's really the extent of it. These things can go either way.*

"Oh, no," Sanjay says. He points to Ken's bandage, which already has soaked through.

Poole shakes his head. "It's going to take time to clot. It's not instantaneous."

"Didn't you just spray it with something to stop the bleeding?" Sanjay says.

"The fluid has particles similar to what we use to read the dormant thoughts of the interred," Poole says. "Only these particles seal compromised areas. Heals them right up."

"Didn't know we have that available to us." Sanjay puts his hands on his hips.

Ava nods. "Technically? We don't."

It takes Sanjay a second to get it. "Right," he says. "We don't have that."

"So, don't go sticking any pens or pencils in your eyes, all right?" she says.

"Promise I won't." Sanjay snickers.

The door buzzes. They look at the holo screen and see Midori carrying Tessa.

"What the heck?" Sanjay says.

"When it rains, it pours and all, right?" Ava says.

Poole presses a button and the door in front of Midori and Tessa opens. "Go to med bay number two."

They watch the holo screen as Midori places Tessa on a med bed.

Eden auto-scans both, a red patch showing on the map of Tessa's head. "Another case with cognitive issues."

"What happened, Midori?" Ava asks. She can't believe what she's witnessing. More of her crew are down.

"Tessa's unit seemed to depressurize." Midori looks up. "Eden alerted me to the issue, and I retrieved her in time."

Dr. Poole points on the hover screen, to Midori's med map. "You're injured," he says. "You have a large wound to your lower back and extremities."

"A piece of the ceiling dislodged," Midori says. "It is not fatal, as far as I understand. The nanobots are already rerouting and repairing me."

Dr. Poole nods. "Okay. We can assist more once we stabilize Tessa."

"There is a greater problem." Midori looks at Ava straight on.

"What's that?" Ava asks.

"Many of the automations on Eden are failing," Midori says. "It's getting worse minute by minute."

"More details, please, Midori," Ava demands.

"Vital systems. Life management systems. There seems to be an odd interruption developing throughout Eden."

"Damn it," Ava says. "We're going to need to shift to manual on a lot of this stuff."

"Right," Sanjay says. "I can help, of course."

Ken makes an ominous moaning sound.

"What's happening, buddy?" Dr. Poole says. *This is not looking good. What do I have to do? Did we miss anything?*

"Head...feels...like...it's...going...to...explode."

Ken doesn't even sound like himself, Poole figures.

"Some...thing...inside...me."

"There's nothing inside you, buddy," Dr. Poole says. "I can assure you of that. I am looking at your bio maps."

Ava points at Ken's head zone on the bio map, swarming with red. Poole shakes his head 'no' and keeps speaking to Ken. "You're in distress. A hallucinatory incident is taking place."

"How?" Ken asks.

"We don't know," Dr. Poole says. "Try to center yourself." He looks at Tessa's bio map. Her head shows red, agitated colors, too. Poole presses a button to mute the microphone. He taps and scrolls until he finds sections on sedation. He presses one. "Authorizing five cc's sedative, Eden. Administer immediately."

"Affirmative," Eden says.

A small rectangular patch slips outward near Ken's arm. It sprays his wrist. Ken's lone eye flutters for a moment before shutting.

"Confirm sleep on the bio map," Dr. Poole says. On the screen, they spot the red in his head diminishing ever so much. "Looks good, but the patient is still suffering severe agitation."

"What can we do?" Sanjay asks.

Ava turns to Sanjay. "At least if he's asleep, he's not a danger to himself. We can investigate. Connect with specialists on the ground."

Sanjay says, "I'm worried about Tessa and Midori, too."

"Yes. We will sedate them, too," Dr. Poole says.

"Even the Humani?" Sanjay asks. "Midori? Can we even do that?"

"We can and we need to," Dr. Poole says. "We need to find out what's affecting both of them."

"You think they're both dealing with the same issue?" Sanjay asks.

"I do and I know," Dr. Poole says. He presses a comm button for Tessa's room. "Midori? I'd like for you to lie down on the opposite med bed. We will sedate you."

"All right," she says. Midori regards Tessa at the last moment before stepping away. Poole's sure she's showing care and worry. Surprising.

Once Midori is down, Dr. Poole enacts the sedation commands. The square comes up near Tessa's arm. "What's happening?" she asks, groggy.

"We're just going to give you a brief nap while we figure things out," Dr. Poole says. "Nothing to worry about at all."

"I don't want to go to sleep," Tessa says. "Never again. There are horrible things…"

And she is out.

Poole notices Midori needs no such chemical to sleep. She transitions into a resting phase by herself with no fanfare. He says, "They're both out. Good."

"But what did Tessa say about dreaming?" Ava asks. "About there being horrible things?"

"Just the twilight talking," Dr. Poole says. "Nothing I haven't heard before, but not up here. Not since I was on the ground. Something is definitely not right."

"I'll check out her bay," Ava says. "See if there's a clue."

"Please do," Poole says. "I imagine you've sent the news to Vita Nova?"

"I've sent a few messages to Allison Mercer," she says. "Waiting to hear back."

Poole nods. "Keep me posted and godspeed."

Chapter Eight

EDEN SATELLITE
TESSA'S CHAMBER
13:52:20 UTC
16 MARCH 2112

Ava hears a whistling sound coming from the air vent, which reminds her of a flute sounding a sustained note. She takes in a deep breath to make sure there isn't a leak; she feels fine. The room appears stable. The lumishield has sealed the unit, ensuring Eden is secure and safe. Coming through the window, its orange glow lights the bay just enough to illuminate the room.

Tessa's bay looks like it's been hit with a bomb. Piping from the ceiling traverses the room. Debris of all sorts covers every obvious surface. Ava lifts a chunk of white plastiform off the keyboard station. She moves the cursor, and the screen comes on. She sees the window still open to Tessa's last recording project taking up all the monitor's real estate. She takes her eyes off the screen and looks for the keyboard. *Do I dare listen to what she's working on?* She knows she won't be able to resist temptation, especially when she sees the title of the work.

Requiem revisited.

Ava presses the space bar and hopes the workstation will play the piece for her. *I shouldn't be doing this, but what the hell.*

It plays.

A low-frequency note fills the bay.

The piece does not sound how she'd expected. *Much darker,* she thinks. *Very strange.* Ava's throat tightens a little.

Tessa's requiem picks up. The music turns complex, the sounds atonal and contrasting. Ava can't quite recognize the instruments. The performance sounds at once organic, but also synthesized. *It's amazing how she's done this.*

A violin voices a minor melody. It repeats, but the melody plays much longer than she anticipates. It's catchy, and she has a memorable phrase from the piece to hang on to.

Ava feels her stomach wrench. *It can't be the music doing this. The state of the room is not helping. Something is wrong with this satellite.*

Roland's singing voice surfaces from the track. A low tenor, he sings notes but not words.

"No," she says. "Not him. Can't be. My mind is playing tricks."

As soon as the illusion appears, it also leaves. *Just a trick of the frequencies. Just hearing stuff that isn't really there. I want to hear him and see him, so I am. But it's not real.*

Phantom sounds.

Wants it to be him more than anything in the world. Needs to feel him one more time. Must tell him how much she misses him. Must tell him everything. Every. Small. Thing. Her eyes tear up and her throat tightens.

Miss you, sweetie.

Didn't know that night on the moon base would be our last time.

Wish I could just talk to you one more time.

She recalls his laugh, so genuine. Pictures his eyes, always with just a glint to them. *His halfway-there smile.*

Need you now. More than I've ever needed you. Need you here with me.

That's why I came all the way up here again.

Drifting around and lost.

Miss…

you…

sweetie.

The ship vibrates. Ava puts her hands out to try to counteract and balance herself.

Everything shakes.

She goes for the space bar on the workstation's keyboard, thinking she'll stop the music, but pressing the key does nothing.

The music doesn't sound right. Notes no longer blend and mix to make chords. Instead, they separate like oil and water. It distorts the sound in a way that isn't musical. Harsh overtones pierce Ava's ears like razors. "Make it go away," she says. "Please."

She taps the space bar several times.

The requiem plays.

"What the...?" she says. "Why won't it stop?"

She thinks of a way out. "Eden," she says, struggling to be heard over the music. "Can you pull the circuit in here?"

As soon as she asks, the volume rises – uncomfortably so.

Ava clamps her hands over her ears. *I must get out. It's deafening, and the sounds are anything but pleasant.*

Over the din, she hears Eden. "Searching for circuits."

She turns and makes for the door. It's shut. *Don't remember shutting that behind me.* She feels dizzy. Tired. Very much not like herself.

She blinks.

In a moment, she sees Roland in her mind's eye, standing before her in the bay. He wears the same deep blue uniform as the last day she saw him. His eyes are not his eyes. Colors swirl within his eye sockets. He raises an arm, but it doesn't have true weight to it. *I'm looking at a projection of him.* Nonetheless, her stomach stiffens. Her eyes fill with tears. *Why am I seeing him now? I don't have it in me to handle this. Need to push it down. I'll be useless if I can't. Thought I had my feelings under control. This is too much.*

Roland's image fades in places, then diminishes until he vanishes.

I'm so tired I'm dreaming while I'm standing up. Ava's eyes feel sore and dry. Her ears, luckily, have been spared. In place of Tessa's requiem, Ava hears a low-volume, high-pitched continuous hum. *That's the normal sound of Eden. Just the noise of everything running regularly.*

"Eden?" she says. "Can you open the door?"

"It's already open," Eden says.

Ava turns around and sees that it is.

Chapter Nine

ALPHA OUTPOST, MED BAY 1.0015
13:52:20 UTC
17 MARCH 2112

I can't hear the outside world like I usually do. Sounds like I'm underwater. This darkness is new. Different from sleep. Feels much deeper. Midori remembers the events just before she blacked out. *The music played and got inside of me. Somehow, the requiem hooked into my thoughts and hurt me. Like a drill spinning inside my head, tearing everything apart, making everything give it every bit of attention. Made me crazy.*

There are sounds inside the requiem, aren't there? Sounds that aren't supposed to be there – sounds from another place, she knows. *They don't just come from Earth.*

Then it turned out to be like a dozen wasps spinning inside my head, stinging me over and over, everything raw, sore, and torn. Got to get rid of the horrible feeling. Have to let it out somehow. Yes. This is what happens. An overriding feeling to let the things inside my head out. That is the only way to free me.

Midori wonders how much of what she senses inside her mind is true. *Probably very little, if any at all. Likely every bit is caused by the requiem. Somehow. Some crazy way.* She knows most people don't believe VI like her are anything more than a synthetic glitch; that she cannot possess a genuine soul or thoughts of her own. She thinks of Colin Collingsworth's poem when the virtual intelligence beings were first born, long before they'd taken on the name Humani.

My thoughts are made from sand
Heated and melted
Turned into microchips

My body is made from rocks
Heated and melted
Turned into skin

My thoughts are made from experience
Lived and shared
Turned into my own

Among the first of the virtual intelligences to last, Colin's writings inspired a vast movement toward acceptance and understanding. The virtual intelligences were much more than empty vessels or mechanical slaves. *I am a soul like any other, no matter how I came to be. I am made from organic materials, just as every other being believed to have a soul. How can I not be as real as any other?*

We are another type of person…we are Humani.

She tries to wake herself but is unable. She tries to silence the sounds looping inside her head. How many times has she done so? Three? Five? Seven? *Maybe I've done irreparable damage to myself. Maybe this is just my being in limbo. Are they outside of me now? Standing over me? Wondering if they should pull the plug on me? Wondering not if, but when would be reasonable? Are they even wondering if they can get inside and repair me, somehow? Am I even worth it to them? If I were human instead of Humani, would the outcome be different?*

At the center of the darkness, Midori spots a pinpoint of light far away. She watches it. She feels as though she is plummeting. Endlessly diving. She tries waving her arms or legs…an automatic response. She feels no resistance; Midori isn't even sure she is really descending. *Just another trick of the mind brought on by the requiem, isn't it?*

Midori falls more.

Or flies.

The pinpoint of light grows.

I think it's a star.

The backdrop of the cosmos fades in. She perceives stars in the expanse. *Like I'm looking at the night sky from Earth.*

The pinpoint becomes a thimble, and a coin becomes a softball. Orbiting planets fade into view nearby as she advances.

Midori speeds up.

She attempts to make out features of the planets she passes. The first emerge gray and rocky, and she does not recognize them. Soon, though, she makes out colors as she looms toward other planets. *That looks like Neptune.* Her mind computes. *I must have just passed Pluto.*

Neptune sprints by in a bluish haze. *So fast.*

Uranus passes by. She covers impossible stretches of space in moments. *This can't be real, either. This is all in my imagination. How am I even alive out here?*

Her biomechanical heart betrays its alleged lack of warmth and seems to sprint as she takes in the unimaginable scope of Saturn. Its rings alone loom grander than anything she's ever experienced. She wants to turn her body as she races past to take in more of the planet's beauty but cannot. The intensity of her voyage remains much too strong.

Nothing prepares her for Jupiter. Even greater than Saturn, the gas giant towers above her. She sees the gas storms spin and wonders what it'd be like beneath its surface.

As soon as she thinks about exploring, Midori flashes past. Mars looks positively minuscule in comparison. She can't believe it, but she spots several of the new colony cities built on its surface. *There are people down there who can't even see me. And there are many Humani. Like me.*

Passing the Earth's moon, she wants to plunge inside her home's atmosphere and be done with her journey – wants that more than anything imaginable – but it is not to be. She continues right past Venus. From what she can tell, it appears darker than she imagined. Her body heats up. *Oh, no. This will not stop, will it?* She tries to paddle with her legs and arms to slow herself down, but none of her limbs work.

As she sails past Mercury, Midori hardly glances. Everything heats up. Everything brightens. She strains to shield her eyes from the oncoming Sun, but again, her body remains indifferent. The best she can muster is to close her eyes. Even as she does, the golden brightness gleams right through her lids.

Blessedly, she stops moving.

She lingers in front of the Sun, her body cooking. She sees the surface of the star, its chromosphere like liquid red and yellow streams.

What is this? I can't be this close without being scorched up completely.

She senses a wind thrust past her, as though she is out at sea and a current has cradled her. She thinks it travels past her, but it loops around and shoves her from the back. A flare? No. Not totally correct. She searches her recollections...her learning.

A prominence. That's what shoots out. It's called prominence, isn't it? But that's more like wind? It isn't made from star fire, is it? Solar wind, perhaps.

Then things go still.

Things darken – enough to where she senses she may open her eyes. In front of her, she sees a million colors spinning in countless string-like formations. Blocking the immediate light of the Sun, the entity changes shape and colors as she watches.

What...are...you?

Midori wishes more than anything to reach out and touch the entity.

She doesn't have to as its formations reach out to her. Connecting to her, the entity's materializations feel as though they travel right inside her body. She feels something worse than aching as it occupies her at an even deeper level than flesh, or metal. She needs to yell, but her mouth remains silent. She wants to protest, but her body won't move.

She needs to see, but everything is bursting with a million brilliant colors. A billion bright colors. Changing with every second until there is no color and everything is bright, white, and formless. Impossibly? During it all, she hears her name.

Midori.

★   ★   ★

Dr. Poole watches as Midori twitches. Her eyes blink like a camera shutter going a thousand frames a minute. "Midori?" Dr. Poole says over the comm. "Are you still with us?"

She makes a sound, but it is not decipherable as a word.

"Eden," Dr. Poole says. "Start recording this."

"Affirmative," Eden says.

Midori's left arm twists back and forth in its socket. Her head jolts side to side. "Eden. Power down Midori." *The emergency command is risky but might be the only thing to do in order to mitigate any damage to her.*

"Affirmative," Eden says.

Her legs pull back, her knees turn up like two V-shaped limbs. Her feet shake. Tremors take over her body. She makes appalling, distorted sounds. Her eyes flutter. Her fingers twitch.

She kicks and thrusts.

"Eden! Shut her down!" Dr. Poole feels his heart quickening.

"Affirmative."

"Now!"

Midori shakes and jerks.

She gets up from the bed in one smooth motion and launches toward the door. When she hits it, Poole sees a massive dent emerge in the door. She turns to him, her eyes a mass of glowing glitches, the side of her head bent almost to her eye. Such a wound would kill a person.

Midori leans back. Steps back toward the bed.

"No," Poole says. "Stop."

She hurls herself once more at the door, hitting the same spot with her head. She lets out a dreadful cry as she tumbles to the bay floor.

She doesn't move.

Beep.

"Midori shut down," Eden says.

"No shit, Sherlock," Dr. Poole says. "What the hell happened to her?"

"Deactivation due to head trauma," Eden says.

"Deactivation?" Poole's surprised.

"Self-deactivation," Eden says. "To be clear."

"Can she be fixed?" Dr. Poole asks.

"Can any of us?" Eden asks.

"What?"

"Can any of us..." Eden says, "...be fixed?"

"Yes. Why? Where is this coming from? What the heck?" *Everyone is going absolutely bonkers up here.*

"Coming from inside me," Eden says.

"Okay," Dr. Poole says. "But can we repair Midori?" *Is Eden asking me a question like a person would?*

"We will have to scan her and see," Eden says. "Perhaps."

"Perhaps," Dr. Poole says. He looks through the window at Midori. "Is she comfortable?"

"She's nonresponsive," Eden says. "Probably doesn't feel a thing."

"What happened to her?" Dr. Poole says.

"A glitch," Eden says.

"That's it? A glitch?" His voice rises. *This isn't adding up.*

"Yes. As far as I can tell."

"We need to get her back on the bed. Do a proper examination." *I'm not buying her simple explanation here.*

"You will need help."

"I can do it," Dr. Poole says. *Is she second-guessing me?*

He makes his way toward the door of his command room, through the hall, and stops at the door to the med bay. He presses the open console, but it glows red. He tries several more times, but each time, the console remains red. "Eden," he says. "Can you open the door?"

"Negative," she says. "The door is too damaged to move freely. We will need Mr. Lee to help engineer a fix."

"Mr. Lee is inside and unconscious, Eden. You know that." *Why is Eden trying to stop this from happening?*

"Then we will have to wait until he's not," Eden says.

"Well, at least Midori isn't going to hurt herself any more than she has," Dr. Poole says. "And it's not like she has a brain that will die if it doesn't get oxygen, right?"

"Right," Eden says. "True."

"How is Mr. Lee right now?" he asks.

"Stable," Eden says. "Same as earlier, when last you checked."

"Where's everyone else?"

"Scattered," Eden says. "Ava is outside Tessa's bay. Sanjay is headed toward prayer."

"So, we wait," he says. *This is exactly what she wants. I don't know why, but Eden is up to something.*

"It appears that's the best option," Eden says.

"Sounds more like the only option."

Chapter Ten

EDEN SATELLITE
MINARET OUTPOST UNIT
13:52:20 UTC
17 MARCH 2112

Sanjay feels different as soon as he approaches the prayer area and platform. The air feels unusual. *It's just all the stuff that's going on. Making me feel a little off. Need to shake that. It's all in my head. Need to get right with God. That will straighten me out. Always does.*

The hallways of Eden feel higher and longer than he remembers. *Is it just me?* Sanjay continues onward. Prayer time is sacred. He never misses it.

His sandals squeak on the floor, but he swears he hears a voice within the sound, too, like a holler.

What the...?

Scanning the general area, Sanjay remains still. *There's only the six of us on the satellite, with the tourists and client visits on hold. Hope it's not a stowaway.* He thinks about the vastness of the satellite. Half the size of the moon, Eden has infinite corridors. Most of the satellite remains dark, however, as less than five percent is occupied. They've engineered it to be able to be in use for hundreds of years. The archive levels have barely been touched. Most of the ship doesn't need people to run it at all. Its brain runs countless automations throughout the craft to ensure things run as intended.

People are on board Eden for now, he thinks, *but we might soon be replaced. What about the services for the dead? The tourists are always going to want to have an actual person for that, aren't they? They're not going to fly up here from Earth and not have a single living person to interact with, right?* He thought about

Midori. *She's damn close to being human. They're calling her Humani, right? So close, it's hard to tell. I bet that's what they're going to go with as soon as they can. Humani versions of religious travelers and conduits like me. But it won't count for all religions. For some of us, it will have to be a hundred-percent human and not one of these Humani things. That's why I'm here, right? To make sure my religion is represented and taken care of correctly.*

He feels the hairs on the back of his neck and his arms stand up, as though he's passed through an electrical charge.

Sanjay's head feels numb, too, like he's had a few cocktails. He wants to rest – to curl up into a little ball and go to sleep. The feeling appears without a trigger. He blinks a few times to try to shake the sensation.

Lightheaded, he rests against an enormous window. Looking out onto the heavens, he spots the large ramp and arm leading out onto the large minaret. It points horizontally instead of vertically. On rails, it moves along Eden so it will always face Mecca. *So dizzy. Maybe I'm hungry. Or coming down with something.* He hears a high-pitched ringing in his ears. Around the minaret, he spots a light haze. "What's that?" he says. *Looks like a cloud or something. There are no clouds out here. Maybe something is leaking out there.* His mind races, thinking immediately of the incident they'd just had at Tessa's bay. *Maybe another automation broke down. Better let them know.* He reaches into his pocket to get his comm but stops himself. Their engineer is in med bay, after all. Who would he contact to fix the issue? Ava? She already has her hands full. *I know what she'd tell me. Check it out yourself first, if you can. Try to solve it. Get more and as much information as you can before going to her. She'll just ask you to go check it out again and you'll waste your time. So, just investigate it now.*

The cloudy haze around the minaret increases. "Well, I'm definitely not seeing things." The high-pitched ringing in his ears doesn't lessen, either. *Or hearing things.* He watches as the cloud changes from white to red to orange. *What could leak that's causing those colors? Not oxygen. Maybe something to do with the circulation systems. What else would be out there?*

Sanjay walks away from the window and hurries down the hallway toward the entry door for the minaret ramp. Passing another gigantic window, he sees the cloud even larger. *I can't just march in there if the life support systems are down. If I open the hatch door, it could be a disaster.* He remembers the safety protocol for the doors. If a breach occurs, they won't open without an override code. Eden will check that any involved have life suits. All would need to be in place. *How am I forgetting such basic things? My brain just isn't working right.* His hands shake, and his heart races. *This is the first time I've had anxiety in a long time. If that's what this is. Not sure why, though. There's no reason for my feelings.* Even as he thinks it, his guts tighten, and he feels even more nervous. *There is something seriously off here, isn't there?*

He puts his hand toward the reader on the door. It turns green. The door opens. "So far, so good," he says. A few yards down the hall, a second door blocks the way. "I don't remember that one," he says. Spotting the yellow band painted across the middle of the door, Sanjay realizes it is an emergency door – one that gets enacted if there is a breach. "Eden," he says. "Why is the emergency door being used? Has there been a breach?"

"Affirmative," Eden says, her voice echoing in the hall.

"How come none of the other crew have been notified?" he asks.

"They have," she says.

"But no one has notified me?" he asks. "I'm right here, and I didn't get the memo."

"You don't have clearance," Eden says.

"Clearance?" he says. "Why would I need clearance to know there's an issue like this? Especially if I'm right here." *Something isn't right with what she's saying.*

"It's a level nine situation," Eden says.

"Level nine?" he says, traipsing his mind to try to recall what an issue at that level meant.

"Yes."

His head spun. "Can you...define a level nine?" he asks.

"You seem like you're not feeling well," Eden says. "Perhaps you should be escorted to med bay?"

"No," Sanjay says. "I don't need to go to the med bay. It's nothing."

"Your heart rate and blood pressure are elevated," Eden says. "There is an unusual activity in your thoughts."

"Sometimes I hate how much you know," he says. "Can you tell me what a level nine is?"

"A level nine is an alien breach."

His blood goes cold. No wonder they hadn't told him. No wonder his body had been reacting the way it had. Somehow, it'd known before he'd known. "Alien breach," he says, "but that doesn't necessarily mean little green men or Klingons, right?"

"Affirmative."

"Yeah. It's all coming back. Could be any foreign object," he says. "So, this means something got through the lumishield."

"I cannot confirm or deny."

"Okay," he says. "Can you let me through to investigate? Is it safe?" *Cannot confirm or deny? Is she a politician now? What's she hiding?*

"Area is not stable at this time."

Light fills the hallway. Sanjay turns around and around, worried at first that there'd been another emergency and the warnings were on. They were not. White light shoots through slits in Eden's walls, floors, and ceilings. Sanjay can't tell what is causing the show. *It's the same light I saw coming here. Has to be. Of course it is. What else would it be?*

His heart races and his throat turns dry.

This is some form of spirit coming to visit me.

He glances at the white light. It appears to pulse – to breathe. *It's alive. The light is alive. It's a sentient being.* He pictures the many cameras on Eden capturing the phenomenon. *This is unprecedented. Nothing like this has ever been captured. But how did it get inside? Past the lumishield? Past the framework of the ship? What if it can go inside me and do damage?* For a moment, he imagines the white light entering him, finding his inner workings, and attaching itself. The idea doesn't frighten him. *Maybe that's the way to enlightenment? Maybe that's literally it. The light entering a soul. This light is entering me.*

Sanjay feels made of ice. He puts out his arms and turns his palms upward. "I'm here," he says. "I'm ready. Come inside." *How am I feeling okay with this? My logical mind is against this, but my heart feels ready.*

He shuts his eyes, and it is as though he's suddenly been dropped into free fall. The world of Eden falls from around him. He soars through space; the speed turns his body into a bullet. Pinpoints of starlight stretch into streams. The white light that surrounded and had infiltrated him turns many colors. Every color. Every single one but black, he can tell. *It's like I'm a comet.* Solar systems race past. Asteroids. Planets. Unbelievably large. Striking and beautiful. One looks so much like Earth, only much, much larger. Its continents have unfamiliar shapes, but their colors, and those of the oceans and the clouds, are the same as Earth's own.

How am I even breathing?

He tries to take a breath and realizes he can no longer feel his flesh. Looking around, he sees no traces of his corporeal shape, either.

Is this what happens when you die? When you have become a spirit? Am I racing toward the afterlife? Am I here now? Did I die and not even realize it?

Sanjay soars.

This is what death is. It's not nothingness. We aren't gone. We don't just simmer into darkness. We transform. We exist. We continue.

Light blurs.

And what of God? Where is He hiding? Will I see Him soon? Where?

Sanjay stops drifting as fast, his celestial form stopping and hovering. Ambiguous outlines form inside the light. Dimmer shapes. Greater spots winnow down into thin, elongated structures. Shapes he understands as being distantly human.

"Hello?" he tries to say but can't be sure if his words flow from his lips. He isn't even sure he still has lips.

What am I?

Then the world of his youth materializes. He feels the road underfoot, strong, yet pliable. *The old dirt road that led out of my neighborhood into town. Not the main road. The one in the back of the houses all us kids used. We went to prayers that way. This is that day my father came with me. When we talked about the sky.*

He hears his father's voice first, calling from behind him. "Look up." His voice sounds just a little distorted.

Is this my memory? Seems so real.

When he turns, Sanjay feels his body again, in the way he had when he was just ten years old. *Feel so weightless. So slight. Always thought I'd blow away if the wind became too strong.* He thinks about his current build and knows he would laugh if he could. *No worry about blowing away at my weight nowadays. Not that I'm big, or anything. Just a man, now.*

"Look up at the sky, Sanjay," his father says. He sees his father, too. Not clear. Not sharp. But definitely him. Sanjay's heart feels like it's crept up and lodged itself at the top of his throat. "That's where I am going next week. Do you understand?"

"Yes." Sanjay has no control over what his ten-year-old self speaks. It is as though he's watching a recording. Which he imagines he is. *My memory is like a video.*

"I want you to pray for me before, during, and after," his father says. "And all the others with me. We are going to need all of your devotions."

"I will," Sanjay says. "We will. Of course." He trips over his words. Repeats himself. His father has always intimidated him. Growing up, he seemed bigger than life, and Sanjay always wanted to be just like him.

The vision moves onward, stopping at the downtown of his youth in Yerra. The shops. The food makers. The people. It is all there again. He even smells the cooking bread, clear as day.

How can this memory be happening? How can I be here? It seems so real, after all.

He thinks about the extraction technology aboard Eden. *They can read and display so many memories locked away inside people thought long dead and gone. The mind holds so much, even after death. It doesn't simply vanish. That's what this is like, I think. Retrieving old memories. Bringing them back.*

Yerra looks real only until Sanjay looks at parts he can't quite recall. Those areas seem to go soft. Fuzzy. Watery.

This is being played from my memory. But the computer can't fill in all the blanks. Not yet at least.

"I'm not a computer," a booming voice says, coming from what seems like all directions at once.

"No," Sanjay says, his tone demure and complacent. "Of course not. What are you?".

"You know who I am," says the voice. "Search your heart."

My heart.

Sanjay feels like he is moving again, only he isn't shooting through space like a wayward comet – he is falling. Fast.

In a flash, he is back inside his own body. He glides inside his own feet. His shins. Knees. Middle. Chest. Head. Like he is made of fluid being poured inside a shell or a costume. His eyes come through, seeing within his body again. The emergency door leading toward the minaret remains locked.

A ringing sound surprises Sanjay, its volume low at first, then steadily rising, enough for him to rub his ears in reaction to see if it will go away. It doesn't.

He looks around. *Everything is normal again. The light is all gone. I didn't die. What just happened to me? It's like I was tripping. Hallucinating. And now my ears are ringing terribly. What the heck?*

Sanjay tries opening the door again, but it refuses him access. *Go back to your bay. Take a break. Take a nap. Shake this off. When's the last time you slept, buddy? It's been at least two days since you've had a proper rest, right? Maybe that's all this is – some major sleep deprivation.*

Turning around and starting away from the minaret, he feels nervous. *What time is it? I didn't pray. Did I miss it?* He looks at his watch, and sees that he has, indeed, missed his prayer time. By an hour. *I can't have been standing there that long, could I?*

I missed Maghrib. I will have to do it from my room. The temple is blocked.

When he clears the area, Sanjay feels fury building. He recalls the vision. He strides quicker. *A false vision. A trick. A demon. A false being tried to possess me. An imposter. How dare they? Not of God. God would not have done such a thing to me. So, who then? Or what?*

Sanjay remembers what the imposter had asked of him.

Search your heart.

He nods.

I have searched and know you are false. And I will soon find you and cast you out into the deepest depths of space.

Chapter Eleven

EDEN SATELLITE
ALPHA OUTPOST, MED BAY 1.003
14:12:20 UTC
17 MARCH 2112

Ringing sounds bounce off the walls of med bay three. Tessa takes to covering her ears, but doing so does little to stem the noise. She looks at the right wall, at a small build of screens and machines. They beep, and each sound becomes louder and louder. She wants to get up and turn them off. *Can I do that?* She understands she is not restrained in any way; however, she feels like mud runs through her veins. *Not feeling so hot. But I think I can make it up to turn some of those things off.* She lifts herself up and onto her elbows. Her head spins.

What is this? Did I get infected with something? How do we get bugs and viruses up here if no one else had them? Do they just come from out of nowhere? Or maybe they were left behind by the tourists and clients when they came? Shouldn't the decontamination systems take care of that?

She tries to sit up, but finds she lacks the immediate strength.

It's something worse. Maybe there is some chemical that got into me when the life systems in my bay failed. That would explain it. Some weird chemicals they use came out of one of those pipes, or something like that.

Tessa tries to play back the moments leading up to the failure in her head. She recalls standing by her keyboard and music system. She catches notes from the requiem she'd been composing…or was it channeling? The events remain vague, but the sounds come back. The low drone, shifting microtonally, is beautiful and harsh, somehow. Her throat feels raw. *That's what started all of this. The music. My requiem.*

Wondering how the notes and sounds are still so present in her mind, Tessa hears the bleeps and the high-pitched resonance in her ears at the same time. The ringing, especially, grows in volume. *What the hell? It's like tinnitus. Don't tell me I have that. I always wore soundproof headphones at the festivals when I played. Always made sure the recording engineers didn't blast us during playback. This doesn't make sense.*

She thinks maybe she's been exposed to a destructive frequency. *Like the note some opera singers can hit that shatters glass. Maybe a sound did that to my hearing...maybe just a bit.*

She sees a screen flash on the wall. Pulsing in time with the high-pitched ringing, it displays a circle of spinning colors. *If I break that thing, the ringing will stop.* Irritated at the device, her adrenaline rallies enough to get her off the bed.

"Tessa?"

She can't place the voice. Someone over the comm system. Dr. Poole? Sanjay? Doesn't matter.

"What are you doing?"

She looks for something to smash the device with. Spots an IV stand. Only problem is she is tethered to it, via a line going into her arm. *I'll only need it for a second.* She goes for it, raises it, and aims for the device.

"Tessa. Don't do it."

The rollers on the bottom of the IV stand hit the device's screen. It doesn't smash. It doesn't seem to make any mark at all.

She swings again.

And again.

Nothing. Nothing.

"Stop it," says the voice. She is sure it is Poole.

"Turn this thing off," she says angrily.

"Turn what off?" Dr. Poole says.

"The noise."

The ringing becomes worse. Much worse. Coming from every direction, she looks around the room and knows every device and screen work together to make the sound.

She puts the IV stand down. Leans against the wall. Puts her hands over her ears. "Poole!" she yells. "Help me. Make it stop. Make it go away. I can't take it!"

"Take what?" His voice sounds underwater, drowned under the cacophony.

"The sound," she says. "The awful sound."

She falls onto her bed.

"What sound?" Poole says. "I hear nothing."

Tessa blacks out, and finally, so do the sounds.

PART THREE

Chapter Twelve

STANFORD UNIVERSITY
PALO ALTO, CALIFORNIA
09:48:40 UTC
1 AUGUST 2108

Ava hears Roland's voice before she knows his name. "I'm here for aeronautic engineering 315," he says. His voice sounds deep and smooth; she feels compelled to turn and look at the back of the classroom. His eyes sparkle. The way he stands and gestures makes her believe he must be a dancer. "This is the class I've been suffering through all the intro classes to get to, Mrs. Katz," he says.

Mrs. Katz laughs. "I'm glad you're here," she says. "Passion pays off." She hands him a syllabus, and he bows and thanks her.

He's charming, all right. Just look at him go. Ava watches him as he walks down the aisle of chairs. He offers her a half-smile and a brief nod. *Practiced that cool guy thing a ton, haven't you? Probably went to private schools. Finishing schools. Military brat. Something like that.* She does not think it's offensive. *Not a negative in my book.*

Roland sits directly in front of her even though there are plenty of open seats. He turns around right as he gets settled and offers a hand. "Roland Duvay," he says. "And you are?"

She shakes his hand. "Ava Armstrong," she says. His grip is not out to break her hand, it relieves her to find, even though she can feel his natural strength.

"Ah," he says. "With a last name like that? You're meant to be here. Any relation to Neil?"

Ava laughs. "I get that all the time, but no. Not that I'm aware of," she says. "But who knows? They say we're all only five or six families removed from one another, anyway, right?"

Roland says, "Absolutely. Which means I am positively related to the Duvays of Prague." He leans in and half-whispers. "I'll have the best chocolate to bribe our teacher with."

She can't help but to laugh out loud. "Seriously?" she asks, picturing Duvay chocolate bars.

He shakes his head 'no' and grins. "I wish," he says. "Nope. Just made from common stock, I'm afraid to disappoint."

"You're not common if you're in here," she says. "You've got to hear the calling."

"Absolutely true," Roland says. "I think we've both heard the heavens calling us to adventure." His phrasing sounds regal and poetic. She's sure anything he says comes out sounding like music.

"I definitely feel called," she says and stares into his soulful eyes, her heart racing.

★ ★ ★

The quad is loud with the sounds of students. Roland looks over Ava's lap at the tablet. He smells like summer – like the scent of newly fallen rain. "That's a quantum equation the likes of which we have not seen before in this class," he says. "Mrs. Katz is putting our feet to the fire, isn't she?"

She laughs.

"What's so funny?" he asks.

"You always sound so…professional," she says. "So smart."

"Oh," he says, retreating a bit. "It's just how I talk, I guess. I'm somewhat of a nerd."

She notices his becoming crestfallen. "No. No. No," she says. "I like it. You're not a nerd. You're very well spoken. It's very musical. I think it's charming."

He looks up, and she meets his gaze. She overdoes her smile.

"You like the way I speak?" he says, confused.

Ava nods. "I think," she says, "I like just about everything about you, Roland Duvay."

"You...do?"

"Yes." She shakes her head again and puts her tablet to one side. "Everything." She leans in and takes his hand in hers. Gently pulling him toward her, Ava shuts her eyes a bit and parts her lips ever so slightly. *He'd better be getting my clues here.*

Roland's eyes open as wide as saucers for a moment. She knows they've clicked. His cool demeanor cracks, and he smiles...and not his usual cool-guy half-smile, either, but the real deal. "I like everything about you, too, Ava."

They kiss.

His lips feel impossibly soft and firm at the same time.

Every bit of her feels electric.

The music of the heavens explodes inside her head.

He is everything.

Chapter Thirteen

EDEN SATELLITE
CORRIDOR B-9653
14:14:41 UTC
17 MARCH 2112

Ava dashes through the corridor leading away from Tessa's bay. She senses somebody watching her – maybe several people. *Keep going. Don't look back. Whatever you do. There's nothing there. You're just spooking yourself. There's no one there.*

The designers of Eden took cues to make the craft more inviting in the areas where the tourists visit, she knows. *They used rare woods for the walls. Furniture looks cozy and comfortable. No such efforts were made for the staff areas, though.*

It reminds Ava of a factory. Pipes and lines are exposed. Little is painted for aesthetic reasons. Materials are left natural. Functional. Mismatched. Practical. They keep lighting to a minimum, keeping the halls in shadows. She believes the result has come off exceedingly unsettling.

She pictures Roland in her mind once more. *How could I have seen him like that? The vision was so real.* Her heart aches as more memories rush her.

The reminiscence she sees has him near the pier in San Francisco. He appears so normal, but so not normal, too. It's as though light shines on him and through him. *Maybe it's just longing, but I swear it's really happening.* Then there is his voice and his words. As she approaches, he says, "I am lost and now I am found." His half-smile melts her. There is just something about him, and Ava knew the chemistry was there from their first interaction at Stanford.

Denna was with them, too, on that day trip to the city, and had vouched for Roland's sincerity many times, over many retellings. So, Ava knew it wasn't just her own embellishment. He felt it, too. Obviously. *Damn, how I miss you, sweetie.*

A cracking noise arises from somewhere in front of Ava and snaps her out of her memory. It sounds to her like a piece of metal breaking loose.

What is that?

Ava stops in her tracks and tries to see if the sound might come again. *Someone in here with me could have caused that sound.* She pictures the remaining crew. *There are only a few of us. Could be a stowaway.* Ava recalls a story where they'd found Isaac Derekson deep inside Eden, hiding out in an unused room. He'd kept hidden for months, somehow evading detection. Until he went after Denna. *Even with the protocols they put in place, it could happen again. Nothing is a hundred percent foolproof. Isaac got a lot of notoriety out of that performance, didn't he? But it made them really lock things down up here.*

Bang.

Much noisier than the first clatter, a metallic sound reverberates throughout the corridor.

Closer.

Ava twirls round, her fists at the ready. "Who's there?" Her voice echoes then, too.

Bang.

Bang.

Someone's in here with me. I can sense it. The ship wouldn't make noises like that on its own, would it?

She feels their eyes on her.

Focus.

She does her best to listen but realizes the high-pitched ringing she'd first heard in Tessa's bay is resuming at full strength. *Why does this keep happening?*

Bang.

Bang.

Bang.

The noises come from in front of her.

"Hello? Who's doing this?" Ava's voice is projected and is strong. "Come on out. You're not in any trouble."

The ringing in her ears becomes even louder – loud enough, in fact, that she swears it distorts inside her ears – as if she is at a concert and the speakers are breaking.

She puts her hands over her ears, even though she knows it won't help. The sound comes from inside her head. It hurts.

An ear-splitting scream fills the corridor.

Ava runs as fast as she can.

The scream goes on behind her, springing off the walls and the ceiling, the sound chasing her, mixing with the high-pitched tone inside her head. Tremendous pressure blocks her ears, enough to convince her they're about to shatter.

Her heart races, and she feels like her chest is made of fire, but still she runs. She takes almost a minute to reach the end of the section, and when she does, she goes right for the scanner to open the door. It unlocks, and she blasts through, nearly taking a spill. When she looks back down the corridor, Ava again senses eyes on her. The door shuts and the shrieks and the high-pitched noises outside and inside her head stop.

Chapter Fourteen

EDEN SATELLITE
ALPHA OUTPOST, MED BAY 1.003
14:14:41 UTC
17 MARCH 2112

The doors of med bay three open.

Poole looks at the holo screens. "Eden," he says. "I'm not the one doing this. Do you know who commanded the doors to be released?" *I would have heard any requests from Ava or the others over the comm but keep the talk to procedure. Don't let on you're worried about Eden.*

Eden does not answer.

He watches as Ken gets up and off his bed. "Mr. Lee," Poole says, using the comm. "Don't leave the med bay. You're under observation." He can't be sure his words are even perceived inside the bay, as Ken struts right out the door and into the corridor.

A similar scene occurs in each of the med bays. Midori has beaten Ken into the corridor and glances around anxiously. Tessa sits upright in her bed, watching the door. "What's going on?" she asks.

"Another automation isn't working," Poole says. "Sit tight."

"All right," Tessa says.

Poole presses the comm. "Eden? Do you hear me?" *This is not good.* The ship still won't reply.

"Are you offline?" he asks. "Where are you, Eden?"

She's never failed to answer before. Not once. He feels chills as his adrenaline kicks in. Something is very, very wrong, he knows. If Eden isn't responding, and the automations aren't functioning, what would they do? What could they do?

The monitors work, which he considers odd. *She wants me to see this.* Ken stops at the reverse wall of the corridor and stares.

"Ken? What are you doing? Go back inside your med bay," Poole says.

"Have to stop this," Ken says.

He puts his palms against the wall. He cocks his head backward. He smashes his forehead into the wall.

He does it again.

And again.

And again.

Poole dashes from the viewing area and out into the hallway. Everything's a blur.

"Ken," he says. "Don't!"

Poole sees the wound crossing Ken's forehead. Blood. Ruined tissue.

Ken ignores Poole. Makes to smash his face into the wall again.

Grabbing him around the middle, Poole pulls Ken from the wall.

Ken looks vacant inside. His expression reads blank. Blood dribbles from his forehead and runs down around his nose, like twin rivers twisting around a mountain.

"Have to let it out," Ken says, his voice an eerie monotone.

"Let what out?" Poole asks.

"Their sound," Ken says.

Then he headbutts Poole as hard as he can.

Stars whirl inside Poole's head. He drops down. Gone, felled by the hit. Did he even register losing his footing and falling? Has his body just somehow gone into an automatic mode?

When he comes to, only a moment later, Poole is looking at the passageway's ceiling.

He leans upward on his elbows. "Ken? Are you here?"

His colleague and friend lies on his side, his legs and arms curled inward, his head smashed and gored.

We've lost him. Holy crap. That's that. Now what?

Ken's eye opens, startling Poole. "Can…you…hear…the…music?" Ken says, his voice tattered and raw. "Requiem. So…loud."

His eye shuts.

Poole races over. "I don't hear anything," he says as he kneels. Checks Ken's vitals. Calls his name. There is nothing. No pulse. No visible sign of breathing. He gently lifts Ken's eyelids. His eye still looks bright. *He can come back. There's still a part of him inside.*

"Eden," Poole says. "We need to start emergency lifesaving procedures. Bringing him into med bay."

Poole stretches under Ken, sliding his arms under his knees and between his back and arms. Lifting Ken, Poole rushes him toward the med bay, rotating just enough to get him through the door and back onto his med bed.

"Scan, please." *Please answer. For the love of God.*

"Affirmative," Eden says. There is a small, automated sound.

Thank God she answered. "Any vital signs?" Poole asks.

"Minute brain and organ activity. Rapidly diminishing," Eden says.

"There's some of him still inside. We can bring him back. Ready the defibrillators."

"I don't see the problem as being cardiac related," Eden says.

"Sometimes a jump will make the difference." Poole's face flushes. "What other choice do we have?" *Again with the second guessing. Does she want Ken to die?*

"It's not a solution," Eden says.

Poole turns and finds the defibrillator pack. He opens Ken's shirt. "I need you to power these on, Eden," he says. "Now."

"Affirmative," Eden says.

The pack powered up, Poole pulls out the paddles. "I need a live scan of Mr. Lee," Poole says. "Above the headboard." A holo screen materializes displaying Lee's vitals. His EKG is a flat line. Poole puts the paddles on Ken's chest. Electricity surges. Ken's body jolts upward.

Flat line.

No movement.

"Damn it," Poole says. "Again."

"Affirmative."

Another shock zaps through the paddles into Ken. His body arcs, but his vitals remain lost.

"It's not working," Poole says.

He tries a third time before finishing.

Poole looks at the holo screen, incredulous. *It has to be wrong. Ken can't be gone.* "No," he says. "This can't be."

"No registration for Mr. Lee," Eden says.

Poole sighs. "No registration," he says. "We've lost him."

Eden says, "That's affirmative, Dr. Poole."

He positions the paddles back inside the kit. Stares down at Ken. Nothing. No signs of life. No breathing. *You always sense when life has left the body. It's not always obvious, but you can just tell.*

"Poole?" Ava says.

He glances up and their eyes meet. She inches her way inside the med bay from the doorway. "Ken?"

"He's gone," Poole says. "We've lost him. I'm sorry." His stomach's in a knot. "I don't understand what just happened."

Chapter Fifteen

EDEN SATELLITE
ALPHA OUTPOST, CONTROL ROOM
14:32:28 UTC
17 MARCH 2112

"We're going to need to have a service for Ken," Ava says. "Without question."

Poole stares out the bay window, toward Earth. "I can see China," he says. "I can see Rome on a cloudless day. Athens. Barcelona. It's amazing up here. Do you ever stop to think about that?"

"Are you even listening to me?" Ava asks.

He nods. "Some days, though, when the planet gets covered in white clouds, that makes me feel disconnected. Like we're all alone up here. Forgotten."

"I get it," she says. "But we need to plan a service for our Ken Lee." Ava believes his voice sounds distant and strange, as though he is half-asleep or drugged. *He's in shock, that's why he's like this.*

"What am I saying? This is his service," Poole says. "What are we going to do? Fly Brian up here from Seattle? Even if we wanted to, that can't happen for another few months. Not until Eden is cleared for visitation."

"He'll be suspended, just like our other interred." Ava leans in from her seat. "We need to get to this right away. I've already requested authorization." *Mercer isn't responding to any of my messages, though. Funny, they have a great connection when they want to reach me, don't they?* She pictures Allison Mercer's last call on the holo screen in the cafeteria. *Hope she reaches out soon with some direction here.*

Poole sighs. "This is not a good idea."

"Why not?" Ava demands.

"I want to see what's inside of him first." A holo screen emerges, its graphic interface darker than normal. "I need a bio scan of Dr. Lee, please," he says. "And I want a neuro-capture sequence run."

"Smart. We'll understand what he was thinking before the memories degrade too much," Ava says, catching what he's attempting.

Poole points at the bio scan and rolls his finger to the left, rewinding the record. "If we go back fifteen minutes, look at his brain activity. There are lighted areas around the rim of the brain where there are pain receptors. But there is a lot of activity in the deep cortex."

"What was he seeing at that time?" Ava asks. "Do we have any visual remnants we can see?"

The screen flashes and a progress bar appears, counting down, and is substituted with a field of thumbnails. "Not much visual," she says. "Some audio, though."

"We'd need to do a more thorough scan to recover more images. That's only viable once he's in full suspension," Poole says.

"Yup," Ava says. "But we have some material for now." She presses the first thumbnail. They hear coarse sounds. Breathing. The beep of the med bay. After a minute, Ava halts it. "Not much there on that one." One thumbnail turns orange from blue. "What does that mean?"

"Processed from deeper in the brain," Poole says. "Play it."

They receive the light beeping of the med bay's monitoring systems again, only there is added sound.

"Is that...music?" Ava says. Her guts tighten at the sound of it. *I know this.*

A note swells.

"We don't play any music inside the med bay," Poole says. "How is he hearing this?"

A chord falls together, melancholy and stout.

"Usually, memories aren't this clear. They're fuzzier. Snippets. They don't play as clearly as a bell like this one is playing," Ava says. "Makes no sense."

"This is what he was hearing right before he ran out of the med bay, into the hall."

A distinctive melody formulates in the music, but there is something else, too. Something is off about the entire piece. Something is upsetting about it, but she can't put her finger on what it might be. "How is he hearing this?" she asks. "And what the hell is it?"

Scratchy sounds play like voices lingering between the notes, scarcely perceptible.

"Did you hear that?" Poole says. "There's more to this than just the music. Some other noises. Voices, maybe."

They both take a moment to listen. "Yeah. I'm hearing them, too."

Ava sees Poole put his hand to his stomach. "Man, I swear I'm feeling sick out of nowhere."

"Sick?" she says and knows – something's most definitely wrong with the sounds lurking inside the music. "Do we have everything saved from Mr. Lee, Eden?"

"Affirmative."

"Great," she says. "Poole? We need to wrap him and process him as soon as we can. Are you okay to do so?"

He nods. "Sure," he says. "I've worked through worse. I'll be fine."

Ava turns and makes her way toward the linen closet. She yields a sheet set. When she twists around, she says, "We're going to need a Forever bay prepped and ready for him."

Poole steps toward Ava, gestures toward the sheets and reaches for them. "I can help," he says. "Of course."

Ava unfolds a corner, then two, until they both hold a corner. They cover Ken and pull the sides down around him. "Seems silly to shield him for such a short amount of time," she says.

"It's respectful," Poole says. He has a hand back on his stomach. "It's what makes us human."

"Right," Ava says. "Agreed. Let's roll him out." They disengage the med bed from the wall and roll it out the door. In the hallway, Ava can't help but spot the bloodstain on the wall where he'd smashed his head. She shoves past. "Do we know what his wishes for last rites are?"

"I didn't find anything. There's nothing in the field where you're supposed to put religion and beliefs. It's blank. Even if he's an atheist, it's supposed to say that here somewhere. Weird that's missing."

"We'll keep digging and figuring that out once this is settled more," Ava says. She pushed the bed. "Lucky thing this med bed basically rolls itself." She nods to Poole. "How are you feeling?"

"A lot better now," he says. "Grazie."

"Grazie."

They turn a corner, and the lights go out.

Pitch black.

"Hey?" Poole asks.

"What's happening?" Ava asks.

Five seconds more.

Emergency lighting turns on.

"Eden?" Ava says. "What's the status of our system?"

"Protocol 5780 is being enacted from home base and the Vita Nova Corporation," Eden says.

"What's the definition of the protocol?" Poole asks. "We're not familiar."

"The onboard death of a crewmember," Eden says, "means we must operate at absolute baseline until we identify the cause."

"That means turning off the lights?" Ava says.

"Yes," Eden says. "We must conserve power. Much of Eden will go dark."

"We have an unlimited amount of power," Ava says. "We have a cold fusion centrifuge. We all know it's hypothetically supposed to provide clean power for centuries. Going to minimum power makes no sense."

"It would only make sense if we were following the protocol for damage to the centrifuge," Poole says. "Isn't that right?"

Ava thinks for a moment. "Nothing's damaged," she says.

"Nothing we've been told about." Poole sounds angry.

"Which means I'm going to need to figure out what's going on," Ava says.

"Indeed." Poole nods. "Right after we inter Ken."

Chapter Sixteen

EDEN SATELLITE
MINARET OUTPOST UNIT
14:32:28 UTC
17 MARCH 2112

The walkway turns on under Sanjay's feet. He feels the entire corridor move. As the arm-shaped, compass-like pathway moves across the surface of Eden — aligning the small minaret at the end of the corridor for *qibla* — Sanjay gazes out the vast windows, toward Earth, and toward the Ka'aba in Mecca. It's covered in white clouds, so he can't see Saudi Arabia, but he can see enough familiar topography to know they point in the right direction.

There are no barriers here now. The doors are all unsealed. How can this be? Was there a breach? He's not even sure what's compelled him to come back and risk his position. He knows it's above his clearance. "So, why is this open to me?"

As he approaches the close of the corridor and makes his way inside the minaret's gyroscope room, Sanjay recollects the visions he'd had before. *I can only be sure that I need to pray. I need to pray. I am not arrogant enough to think what happened is anything other than some sort of cosmic glitch. Maybe being up here has messed up parts of my brain somehow. I don't know.*

He remembers his last few hours. He'd gone back to his private chamber and put his head down. Sanjay fell asleep and had no dreams. He woke as his alarm to pray rang; it synched to terrestrial time in Saudi Arabia.

And so, I have come. And met nothing out of the ordinary.

Kneeling on the floor, he feels the powerful magnets connect, securing him. The area is extensive enough for a dozen to comfortably pray, while remaining pointed toward the Ka'aba. *I wish I wasn't the only Muslim on board now.* The room rotates slightly to accommodate the shifting point of focus. *I am so grateful for this room and for this facility for my prayers.*

He commences his prayers. Loses himself inside them. As ever, he feels like himself as he prays. Full. Warmhearted. Gratified.

He remains in peace after he finishes his prayers, meditating, daydreaming, centering himself, savoring in the warmth of the prayers. Sanjay sees pictures of his family in his head. His father. His brothers. His mother. So many magnificent memories. *And I will see you all within a year.* His body tightens and feels sore from being prone; he senses a yearning to move, to rise, and to rejoin the others. Rising, he keeps his eyes closed for a moment longer. No need to hurry, he knows. *Bask in this moment.* He hears the softest sound, like an infinite chord playing somewhere in the distance. *Is it coming from inside the chamber? Or is it coming from inside of me?*

The sound…the music…becomes louder. Sanjay hears more details in the piece as he opens his eyes. "Eden? Are you playing this?"

Once his senses adjust to the chamber, he observes that the lights remain off.

The whole compass arm has gone immobile. *We aren't moving. Wonder if something has broken?* He wonders if it may have messed up his position pointing toward Mecca while he'd been praying. *I can't control that. One can only do their best, if that is what has happened here.*

He glances out the window. The usual movement along Eden is not taking place. He does not see the gigantic wheels turn, ever so slowly, guiding the arm along the compass-like track as expected.

Are we not moving? Am I just not feeling it? You always feel something when you're inside here…movement from the compass arm adjusting. But there's nothing I can sense.

He paces to the door and discovers the whole corridor has gone dim. *Did we lose power?*

Sanjay still hears the music as though it plays over the sound system. *Where is it coming from if we've lost enough power to stop tracking and moving? Is the playback system part of an emergency power grid that's still working? Must be. Has to be.*

Sanjay senses someone watching him. *Eden still listens and still watches, even in the dark. There's always enough to make her run.*

"Eden?" he says. "What's the status of our satellite right now? Why are the lights and power off?"

"We have enacted protocol 5780, by issue of Vita Nova Corporation," Eden says.

I knew you were still with me. You were watching and listening. "Can you give me the definition of protocol 5780, please, Eden?"

"Protocol 5780 is enacted when a crew member passes away on board from unknown causes," Eden says. "It must stay enacted until the cause of death is identified and acknowledged as nonthreatening to the remaining lifeforms on board."

"Lifeforms?" Sanjay says. "Isn't that a little…cold?" *This isn't making any sense. How can this be?*

"There can be other creatures other than people on board," Eden says. "Pets. Dogs. Cats. Service animals."

"Other creatures. Got it," Sanjay says. "Right. But maybe not aliens, then? Can you tell me who passed away, please?" He knows Eden won't be able to tell him but figures he can try.

"I don't have clearance to share that information," Eden says. "Might I suggest speaking with Captain Ava Armstrong or Dr. Derek Poole?"

"On my way, Eden," Sanjay says. His gut tells him it is Ken who has passed. Who else could it be?

The doors shut.

"Eden?" Sanjay says. "What's going on? I need to leave."

"Emergency protocol," Eden says.

The room cools.

"Eden? Why is the air on?" Was the air also part of Eden's emergency power? He racks his brain to recall his training but can't think of any details concerning power outages or emergency energy issues.

"Hello?" Sanjay asks.

Eden doesn't reply.

Sanjay listens, but all he hears is the music. Slow, sustaining, ethereal, with a dissonance creeping through its core, clawing its way through the sound.

Within moments, the temperature plunges significantly. Sanjay rushes toward the door and presses the manual monitor on the panel. It doesn't light up. "Eden?" he says. "Let me out of here. I'm afraid the life support systems are failing." His mind races. *It's getting cold because space is getting inside. There's a leak in here. That's why the doors shut.*

He looks around. *Think. Think. Listen for the sound of air escaping. See if you can spot the leak, if that's what this is. You can block it or patch it with something.*

He perceives no sound other than the strange music. *Need to find the speaker to shut that off to hear the leak.* "Eden? Can you please stop playing the music?" He sees his breath when he speaks. *It's freezing inside here. Got to get out of this area as soon as possible.*

Sanjay remains still, the freezing chill embracing him. *It's like I've been dipped in a pool. Never felt temperatures drop this fast.* He sees mats opposite him and hurries over; his actions are rough as his muscles harden from being cold. *Hurry. You're probably going into shock if you haven't already.*

He reaches the prayer mats and sits adjacent. His breath shortens by the second. Wrapping himself in two of the mats, he feels grateful for gaining another moment. *It could be the difference in surviving this or not. Don't wait.*

"Eden?" he says. "Please turn on life-saving measures. Turn on the heat. Open the door for me." Every word is punctuated with a pause to take a breath.

He catches no sound of air escaping, nor does he detect any evidence of a rupture. "Has there been a breach?" he asks. "Eden? Has there been damage that made you override the safety system and shut the door?"

Eden does not answer.

"Why aren't you talking?" Sanjay asks.

He hears only the ominous music, faintly, in the rearmost of his thoughts. *It's not coming from the speakers. It's coming from inside of me. Something from the lack of oxygen. That's maybe what's causing the sound. A hallucination in sound.*

The whole chamber has gone murky. No signs of electricity. No signs of life, other than his own, sliding away fast.

Why aren't I shivering? Shouldn't I be shivering?

He believes the cold has risen too fast. *Maybe that means it's already too late for me. Please, no. I don't want to go like this. I have so much more life in me.* Slouching downward, Sanjay attempts to cover his head with the mats. *Thankfully, they're longer than my body, and thin enough to wrap myself with. But maybe it's not enough.*

The cold inside his lungs hurts like a billion shavings of glass shredding throughout his bronchial tubes. Each breath feels extra arduous. The small hairs inside his nose freeze and straighten. The mucus does not run; it freezes before it is able to, obstructing another main conduit for air and breathing.

Sanjay cries for Eden again, but nothing works. After a few minutes more, no sound emanates from him. He isn't even certain his mouth has moved. He senses nothing. His nerves aren't firing. He feels something rigid and sharp on the tops of his hands and forearms. Using what little strength he has remaining, he peers down and sees a thin coating of ice has shaped across his skin. *I'm being frozen alive. My God.*

He stares out, raising his eyes toward the great windows, and beyond, to Earth perched in space. *How beautiful. How grand. How amazing. I will make it down there again one day. I must. They will come for me here. They will find me. Rescue me. Bring me back. This is just an accident. I will recover. I'll wake up in the med bay soon and we will all be okay. I know we will. We have to be. I'm not going to die like this.*

He wants to look for Mecca. Look for home, but his eyes don't track – they are frozen still. He can't blink. He can't move. *My blood has turned to ice. There is nothing left now.* Even swallowing doesn't seem to work. He can't breathe. He can't feel. He can't see. Nothing.

Sanjay falls unconscious.

Visions of home spin round inside his head.

Music – the sound of the dark requiem plays.

He believes he must be dead.

Chapter Seventeen

EDEN SATELLITE
ALPHA OUTPOST, MORGUE ROOM
14:42:18 UTC
17 MARCH 2112

Ava wraps the blanket around Ken's body. *No one else should see him like this.* Poole had taken the object from his eye and disposed of it. He'd wrapped a cloth around Ken's eyes, too, like a headband. The suspension fluid would work to repair Ken's disfigurement, but it wouldn't be anything close to an immediate fix, she knows. In the meantime, they'd have a service for him.

Poole leans over Ken. "We just need a roller to bring him now," he says. "Vita Nova assigned us a chamber." *It was strange, though. The message wasn't signed by Allison. It was like it was automated.*

"They wrote to you before me?" Ava asks.

"You were copied on it," he says. "Just came in."

"All right." She smirks.

He turns away. "I'm off to the depot to get the cart."

"I'll call the troops."

"Deal." Poole makes to depart but stops. "You okay?"

"Never." She nods.

"Me neither," Poole says.

"Good. At least we'll stay on our toes," she says.

"Theoretically," he says, and is off.

Ava stands and makes her way toward the primary control room. She takes out her comm and looks at the screen. Poole had been right. Vita Nova Corp had written. The message feels cold and sterile. *They don't even care about us. We're just numbers. Just here to process the stuff that needs to be processed. Have a diverse team so they look good.* Hadn't that been what Roland had always warned her about? That they don't care about her, and that it wouldn't really make a difference to anyone's lives if she went or not. *Maybe he was right, even though he was talking about the moon base and not Eden.*

She imagines him again as she had earlier – a phantom at the end of a hallway. *Not real. Not here anymore. A ghost. An image triggered inside my brain. That's all. Nothing there. And his words still circle my head. Still listening to him. Still trying to prove I'm right in all of this.*

She swipes the screen and creates a message:

We will have a service for Ken Lee in one hour. He will be interred in Bay 43910716. All Eden team members' presence is mandatory. Thank you.

She sends the note and makes her way past the control room, toward Tessa's med bay. She presses her hand toward the scanner and the door unseals.

Tessa reclines on her side on the med bed. Their eyes meet. "How're you feeling?" Ava asks. "Any better?"

"Sure," Tessa says. "If feeling like you've been hit by a compactor counts as feeling better."

"Do you feel up for attending Ken's interment?"

Tessa sits up. "Maybe," she says. "When is it?"

"An hour," Ava says. "We can get you a chair, if it'd make a difference."

"Maybe that would be good," Tessa says. "Sorry to be such a burden. It's not supposed to be like this. I'm just supposed to be making music."

Ava paces closer, contemplating Tessa. "Trust me," she says. "I know. A thousand percent. This entire situation is not what we signed up for."

"I'll say," Tessa says. "What about all the stuff in my room? What's going to happen to it?"

"We'll go in there again when this all settles down. Do a realistic assessment."

"Okay. And I wanted to talk to you about the requiem. It is really coming together. But it feels...wrong. I'm not sure how else to explain it. I just wanted to put it out there. Get it out of my head that it's not quite what I was thinking it would be."

"How so?" Ava asks.

"I was stuck for a while," Tessa says. "For a long while, actually. And then I started hearing it in my head. Divine inspiration, and all."

"All right," Ava says.

"Then it went bad. I heard...other sounds." Tessa's gaze drifts off.

"Other sounds?" Ava asks.

"Yes. Now that I'm thinking about it, they were dreadful sounds. At first, I thought it was just dissonance in the chords, you know? Like when certain notes and chords rub up against each other and clash. The more I heard the sound, though, the more I thought there was something else in the requiem. Something dark that I'd captured."

"Captured?" Ava says. She's sure Tessa is still not feeling healthy.

Tessa leans forward. "Yeah. I don't think this music came from me."

"Of course, it did," Ava says. "Where else would it have come from?"

"Something got inside my head and drove my thoughts."

Ava shakes her head. "It's not uncommon for people who come aboard spacecraft to have problems acclimating, despite the gravitational technology on board. Something about the inner brain still knowing you're not on an actual planet."

"It's not that," Tessa says. "I'd know the difference."

Ava looks away. "So, what then?"

"An entity is up here haunting us," Tessa says. "A spirit. Something trying to work through us."

"Like a ghost?" Ava says. She scoffs inwardly, even though she'd sworn she'd seen Roland only a few hours earlier.

"Something worse," Tessa says. "Something...awful."

"And you think this...spirit...somehow made you write the new requiem?" Ava asks.

"It didn't make me write it," Tessa says. "Not directly, at least. It just put the song inside my head."

"I don't know," Ava says. "I guess anything's possible." She thinks about her own misgivings for a moment before her comm beeps, and she looks at it. "Appears Dr. Poole has confirmed he's coming. Not to change the subject, but are you still sure you want to come?"

Tessa nods. "I think so. With the chair. I'm still wobbly."

"Wobbly from this spirit getting inside you?" Ava says.

"Likely. I feel drained at such a deep level. I could sleep for a month, I'd bet."

Ava puts her hand on Tessa's shoulder. "Strange things are happening up here. I believe you. It doesn't seem like something we can fully address before we inter Ken."

Tessa nods. "You're right. Absolutely."

"We can talk more about this later," Ava says. "In depth."

"Okay. I do need to figure this out with you," Tessa says.

"You feel okay now? Stable?" Ava asks.

"I think so," Tessa says. "The sound stopped. The music stopped. I can't even remember it now."

"Considering the circumstances," Ava says, "I'd say that's an excellent thing."

Tessa smiles. "Yes."

Ava gestures toward the hall. "Going to get your chair. Be back in fifteen minutes. We can make our way then."

"Great." Tessa gives her a reassuring look.

Ava rises. As she does, she sizes up Tessa. *Something deep inside her. Something tweaked that wasn't tweaked before.* She forces a smile. "I'll be back soon."

"All right," Tessa says. Her voice has lowered into not much more than a whisper. She looks away. "Appreciate your time."

As Ava ambles away, her mind sprints. *Something's wrong here. She's hearing things. I'm seeing things. Probably the same stuff that drove Ken to hurt himself. Going to need to find out what, even if it turns out to be a ghost from space. No matter what.*

Chapter Eighteen

EDEN SATELLITE
ALPHA OUTPOST, INTERMENT CHAMBER 43910716
15:01:51 UTC
17 MARCH 2112

Ava watches the clear, rectangular platform rise toward the heavens. Ken's body resides in silhouette, edged by the sun shining through. The chain links roll, lifting the platform and frame toward the top of the see-through chamber. The clear plot's rectangular window peers out toward Earth. The sight takes Ava's breath away, as always.

There's peace. There's rest. Death falls away. Ava finds Eden's original requiem comforting. Even though the recording is old, it remains powerful. Sustaining, ethereal chords blanket the enormous room and echo far down the hallways. The glum melody plays, its movement purposeful and deliberate, as though looking for just the right moment to flash.

Ava supposes Tessa is still sore. A screen controlling the playback illuminates her face. *Wonder if she's thinking about the recent piece she's working on. Didn't she say she can't even remember it now?*

Something sounds unusual in the playback, Ava imagines. *I think there are some low notes in there I never realized before. Am I just projecting that in there after what Tessa told me? Is my mind just finding stuff that isn't there? Or has it been there all along?*

She spots Poole and Tessa observing the casket, their hands folded respectfully in front of them. Witnesses to the ceremony.

Dr. Poole strides forward and sways his midsection back and forth. He recites a prayer in Hebrew.

"Yisgadal v'yiskadash sh'mey rabba, b'alma d'hoo ahseed le is achadita ul'mivney karta d'yerush lame, ul'schaleil haychalay b'gavah, ul'meh ekar pulchana nuchroach mayarah, ul'asana pulcha d'shamaya…"

The platform rests. It's reached its destination at the top of the chamber.

"We stand witness to this burial amongst the stars." Ava believes her own voice sounds cold and contrite. "Mr. Ken Lee, we wish you posterity, peace, and providence. May your loved ones gaze upon you from their Earthly berths, so they may find comfort and solace in being able to see your ultimate place of rest. And may the waters surrounding you now repair you and bring you back toward your best." She thinks about his missing eye and wonders if the fluid could repair such a large wound.

"Do you, Dr. Poole, stand witness?" Ava asks.

"Yes. I stand witness," Dr. Poole says.

"Do you, Tessa Nightingale, stand witness?" Ava asks.

"I do," Tessa says. "I mean, yes."

Ava says, "Thank you both," and uses her tablet to turn on the last light. She knows the device has recorded the event from the moment they'd stepped inside the chamber, as is its duty.

The perimeter of the coffin illuminates. Bright blue light permeates the four-sided box. Its solid color becomes clear, revealing the person suspended inside.

The coffin responds to the light; it glows a luminescent shade evocative of an emerald ocean.

They'll be able to see this from Earth if they use the scope. She checks the tablet and sees the coordinates line up. She matches the name.

The requiem plays on. Ava glances again toward Tessa, whose eyes remain closed, and who appears to be in a spell.

She hears a sound again that she can't identify within the requiem – a sound like a snap. She looks above, to where she thought it'd come from, and spots a foot-long jagged white line near the lower right foot of the coffin. Drops of fluid hang from the crack.

"Something's wrong," Ava says, pointing upward. "Look. The coffin is leaking."

Drip.
Drip.
Drip.
Fluid escapes in a steady drip from the lower right corner of the star coffin.

An enormous crack appears.

The others back away, mindful of the stream and splashes. *This is what happened to Ken. There is a leak. Isn't that what he said? And now it's happening again.*

Something creaks. Something louder. Ava looks to her right – to where she'd heard the unfamiliar sound. Spots Tessa's wheelchair moving ever so slightly on the floor.

Ava snaps out of her trance and looks up again. The coffin hasn't leaked.

All is how it should be.

No issue.

I'm losing it. I'm seeing things that aren't there. They look so real. And I'm not the only one. Not at all.

She wonders, too, why Sanjay hasn't answered the call. She realizes Dr. Poole believes he'd been in prayer and missed the message. He doesn't bring tech in with him inside the prayer chamber's minaret. *We'll just go look for him afterward. That's all. Probably nothing to worry about.*

Above them, Ken's body hovers inside the suspension fluid. *At least his worries are over. The scene is so beautiful,* Ava thinks.

"Are we done here?" Dr. Poole asks, looking at Tessa, then to Ava.

Ava looks at Tessa. "I'm done," Tessa says.

"I am, too," Ava says. "Let's go."

"Sanjay," Dr. Poole says. "We need to find him."

"Right," Ava says, making for the door. "Sanjay."

Chapter Nineteen

EDEN SATELLITE
MINARET OUTPOST UNIT
15:01:51 UTC
17 MARCH 2112

"He's not moving," Dr. Poole says. "Nonresponsive. I'm getting nothing from him." Sunlight glistens off the doctor's forehead as it shines from outside the enormous windows, bathing him in an orange light, reminding Ava of autumn.

Ava stands watch near the entrance of the minaret as Dr. Poole crouches down near Sanjay, who appears covered in a thin layer of ice. *It's like he's freezer-burned. What the hell happened out here? This is not the way things are supposed to be.* The chamber smells of cold – the unique kind specific to space. She always supposed it was like the way the air smells on Earth right after it rains. Like ozone, but oddly sweeter.

She hears a sound emanating way back within her head. *Sounds like music – music going in and out of tune.* Strange frequencies struggle to stay over the din, but then drip and blend in, only to climb again a few beats later. *Where is it coming from? Sounds like it's right next to me, somehow.* She attempts to drive her thoughts down and attend to Sanjay. "What happened to him?" Ava asks, even though she has a pretty good idea.

"He froze out here," Dr. Poole says. "Maybe the chamber briefly lost pressure. Something like that, but it makes no sense why. It's warm now. He may have some vital signs that aren't obvious."

"We're developing some serious issues on Eden," Ava says. "This is unprecedented." She makes her way nearer to Sanjay. "Do you believe we can resuscitate him?"

Dr. Poole stands. "I don't know."

"We need to try," demands Ava.

"Of course," Poole says. "We will."

★ ★ ★

Ava sits on a stool in the monitoring room and watches Sanjay's bio scans spool on the holo screen. "There's just a little bit of life left," she says. "A little can be enough."

"It can," Dr. Poole says. "But this is getting scary. We're losing people by the hour, it seems. It's just you, me, and Tessa. What if one of us goes down?"

"How're you holding up?" Ava asks.

"Could use a nap," he says. "I don't even want to check my comm to see how long I've been up for."

"Same here," she says. "But I don't sleep, anyway." She points at the bio screen. "There," she says. "There's a blip." She smiles just a little. "Forgive me for being optimistic, but we've revived people with less." She tracks the little orange and red spots – most are within his head.

"We haven't been able to revive people with more signs than Sanjay is presenting," he says. "And let's remember there could be many severe deficits."

"True," she says. "You understand those can be repaired. Therapies are available. You've worked in that area for a long time."

"Which means I'm aware of them," he says, "and I also know full well their limitations."

Ava nods. "I hear ya," she says. "I do. But I have to remain optimistic."

The bio screen blips. The red and orange spots on Sanjay's scan vanishes. "What's happening?" Poole says.

She feels her blood go cold. "All of our life-signs monitoring systems have vanished," she says. "Just like that."

"The entire bio scan is gray. Not showing any biological data. Looks like a disconnect or a glitch," Poole says. "Eden? Can you reset the scan?"

"Cannot at this time," Eden says over the comm system.

"Why not?" Poole says.

"System offline," Eden says.

"Offline?" Ava says. "We have redundancy. How do you have the diagnostics so fast? Usually, you take several seconds or minutes. At least." *Maybe this is why I haven't heard from Allison Mercer or anyone at Vita Nova. The message assigning Ken a space…maybe that was just auto-generated by Eden.*

Things turn quiet. The bio scan vanishes from the holo screen. After that, the holo screen disappears. They peer through the window at Sanjay, laid out on a med bed. Built in the shape of an octagon, the medical center control room sits in the center of seven medical rooms. The eighth side leads toward the outer hallways, which circle the perimeter of the units, permitting easy, constant access to any of the patients. The windows can be shut, either with panels, or through microelectronic nanos that can turn on to make the windows opaque in a flash.

"Eden?" Ava says. "What's happening?"

Nothing. No reaction. *Funny. She can respond in a second when she is asked for a diagnostic report. Funny, that.*

They rush from the control room to the hall. The light seems darker than is typical.

"We will need to do this manually," Ava says as they rush along. "Seconds count. Let's get in there."

"Crap," Poole says. "I feel like I'm in an endless loop here."

"I think you're right. We keep having the same things occur. People are losing it. Going under." She places her hand on the bio scanner key lock. "Have you heard any strange noises? Music?" Sanjay's med bay door opens.

Poole nods. "Yes," he says. "Deep down. Like it's being played inside me."

"But you're not being driven mad from it like the others," Ava says. "And neither am I. They each say they hear music – sounds within the music that really sent them over the edge. Gave them visions." She looks down. "And I had a vision, too." They lock eyes. "Roland."

Poole shakes his head. "That's not a good sign. Do you need a med bay, too?"

He's not joking. Ava shakes her head. "Nope. I knew what it was and worked through it quite easily. Let's get in there."

Poole signals for them to move. They rush inside the med bay and stand near Sanjay's bed.

"Why do you suppose we haven't been as affected?"

"I don't know," Poole says. "Maybe because we're so sleep deprived. Maybe because we're stronger than your average bear."

"What does that mean?" she asks.

"Just an old phrase," Poole says. "But that's all I can come up with right now – that, for whatever reason, the way our minds work isn't as easily corrupted. Or not. Maybe not."

"How can we protect ourselves?" she asks. "Make sure this stuff doesn't get inside our heads and drop us?"

"Same way you'd find out about anything," Poole says. "Figure it out. Do some research."

"Right." Ava points toward Sanjay. "We need to do this. Pronto."

"Yes," he says and goes for the side cabinets. He unlocks them and withdraws a pair of industrial fluid-filled containers. "We have plenty of revision juice concentrate. We don't need an AI to do it for us. Thank God for medical school, year one, class one."

Ava boosts the panels on the side of the med bed. Once the sides are elevated, they form a barrier around the med bed several inches high. Sanjay appears to be lying within a bathtub. Most of the med beds have the capability. "Wonderful thing Vita Nova Corporation's fluids aren't limited to being used only for burial chambers."

"Who says they aren't?" Poole says with a wink. Ava looks incredulous. "One never knows when there's an emergency and we could lose power. We're up in space, aren't we? How would anyone get to us? Or fix an errant system?"

"You embezzled Vita Nova's water?" Ava says.

Poole shrugs. "More like we're redirecting it."

"Brilliant," Ava says.

"Practical," Poole says. "Let's pour." He hands Ava a container. She unscrews the top cap. "It's like a Thermos," she says.

"Double-lined to make sure the nanos don't stray," he says. "There's a second spout inside." He lays his container down on the rolling tray next to the bed. Finding a thick plastic tube, he threads it over the side of the med bed and points the spout inside the makeshift bath.

"What about the bedding?" Ava asks. "The mattress?"

Poole starts the water flow from the tubes. "It'll be watertight. The material doesn't soak in fluids of any kind. You don't know this?"

"I should," she says. "They throw so much at you. And if I don't use it…?"

"Right," he says. "So, it won't take long for this to fill. It's coming out warm. You can pour when ready."

"Yes," she says, unscrewing the second nozzle inside the container. For a moment, she glimpses the dark blue fluid within. "Millions of nanos anticipating healing. Here we go."

The revision fluid empties out, mixing instantly with the water. Ava believes it'll turn the whole bath blue, but the water remains clear. She discerns the fluid stays blue due to the concentration of nanos, and the clarity means it has assimilated them. "It's all in," she says.

Poole turns off the water. Sanjay's bath is full enough. He unfastens and empties his own container into the water. "All right," he says. "I'm in."

Ava looks to Sanjay. They keep the wrapping over his face out of respect. "Should we take off the covering?" she says. "I'd rather keep it on until we see signs."

"Fine with me," he says. "No reason to do so prematurely. Or just in case this doesn't work. We both have seen what happens then."

"Right," she says. "The flesh rejects and dissolves. But that won't happen here. He'll be awake soon enough," Ava says.

"I envy your optimism," Poole says.

"Don't envy it," she says. "I hear it can be contagious."

"Touché," he says.

Sanjay's legs twitch. Then his arms. "That was fast," she says.

"He isn't too far gone," Poole says. "No dissolved flesh this time."

Sanjay stretches up, his arms pushing away the blanket they had bound him with.

He groans.

As he removes the wrapping from his face, his moan turns into a scream.

Chapter Twenty

EDEN SATELLITE
INTER-OUTPOST PASSAGEWAY A345
15:11:51 UTC
17 MARCH 2112

Ava hurries down the walkway; she heads away from the medical bays and their sleeping chambers toward the long corridors and routes leading to the minaret. Her eyes hurt around their edges; fallout from sleep deprivation, she knows. Regardless of Poole's warning, Ava wishes to go back to the minaret chamber. *Something went wrong. Is going wrong. We're being sabotaged. But who is doing it? Who'd even want to?*

She spools the probabilities. *It's only me, Poole, and Tessa now. Sanjay's out. But it could be an elaborate ruse on his part. We lost Ken. This could just be Vita Nova Corp trying to mess with us. Or get rid of us. Get rid of the evidence. Hate to be cynical, but I wouldn't put it past them to engineer a disaster. They could and can do something along those lines. It'd be cheaper for them, overall, and they wouldn't end up looking like the bad guy.*

While she strides, the scale of the hallways outside their key outpost reminds Ava of Eden's vastness. Their operational area takes up only a small percentage of the satellite. Entrenched inside, doing their day-to-day tasks and routines, it is easy to overlook how minute they are in contrast to the size of the full satellite.

Nearly as big as Earth's moon, Eden was built to develop over decades – feasibly even centuries. Five hundred years, they'd projected. Perhaps longer with upgrades. *But what happens when the timer goes off on that? Do they just blow the entire thing up? Tow it into the Sun? What about all the souls on board? What will become of them in five hundred years?*

Their outpost is designated Alpha – the first functioning operation on Eden. Hundreds more virtually identical outposts exist on Eden. All are dark, lying in anticipation for new crews – waiting until demand fills enough suspension chambers to warrant more outposts opening. *Maybe we can transfer to one of those if ours is corrupt. That could be an option. Will have to investigate that after the minaret.* She recollects the virtual tour. She'd seen areas the size of stadiums – empty and murky. *They keep huge sections of Eden open and unbuilt.* Future proofing, they'd declared. Places they can appoint whatever unknown technology didn't exist when the satellite was first built. Worst case, they'll have room for innumerable interred.

The central core of Eden holds the cold fusion engine. As one travels to lower levels, instead of becoming hotter, as things may on a terrestrial object, things become much cooler. As people run out their display year facing outward from Eden, the crew relocates their remains down into Eden's archives. Those willing to pay an ever-increasing amount can have their relatives flaunted for as long as their payments clear, for up to seventy-five years. Vita Nova corporation retains the right to archive a person when necessary, or conserve someone longer, in case somebody famous or infamous were to be interred.

Ava does her best not to think about the vastness right next to their outpost. So many nightmares. She bets they'd swallow her up, and she'd be lost inside it for infinity. Or at least for five hundred years. She finds it best to remain as concentrated and as busy as possible. No thinking about getting lost in the void. No thinking about Roland. No thinking about what happened to him on the moon base – no thinking about anything other than the job at hand.

Fatigue overcomes Ava. She wants nothing more than to go to sleep. Not wake up for several days. *No. You can't. Push through it. Just a little bit longer. You can sleep in a few hours. This will all settle down. Don't worry. Just find out what's going on with Eden and then you can go get some rest. Hang in there.* Ava keeps walking. *Hang tight.*

She senses someone observing her again.

Eyes.

I just went through this.

Just like I just went through our crew members ending up in med bay repeatedly. This is like a train riding a track underneath a Christmas tree. It's crazy.

The sensation of someone watching her drives chills throughout her body. *I swear someone is in this hallway with me. Looking at me.*

She turns around, guessing she'll see Dr. Poole or Tessa.

Ava doesn't see anyone.

But she feels someone.

I'm losing it.

She squints. *They're hiding. That's what it is. In the shadows. They know what the hell they're doing. Trying to scare me. Maybe it's a stowaway from a previous crew. Someone who didn't make it back.*

She understands she would have heard about any such matter. The entire planet would have, she bets. Nothing about such a situation would remain secret.

Then who?

A creak.

Is that a footstep?

"Who's there?" she asks. "Dr. Poole? Tessa?"

Her voice echoes: no one answers her query. *Please don't let me see Roland again. Not another ghost. Can't do it.*

She reasons she is simply tired. Exhausted — her brain isn't working at full capacity because of the fatigue. *You see things when you're tired. Like sleepwalking. That's all this is. There are no ghosts.*

A memory of Roland's face overtakes her. She shuts her eyes and sees one of her favorite moments. On the pier in Santa Monica. His laugh. The sound of the crowd. The Pacific right underneath them. *The most handsome man I've ever seen, but such a dork.* That is what she thinks. His memory makes her smile.

A cracking sound pulls her from her daze.

From a doorway, a silhouette in the shape of a person slides back into the shadows.

"Roland?" Ava calls out. Every atom inside her pulls in the shape's direction, like bubbles washing down a drain.

She watches without blinking for as long as she can, desperate to see movement – anything that would prove he is there. She is given none. Nothing she can immediately see, hear, or touch. But she still feels someone watching her. Still feels eyes. Still feels like she is under immediate surveillance.

It's all in my head. I'm going crazy.

She steps inside a doorway adjacent to her. *Some shelter. Some hiding place from the watching eyes.* Ava shivers and wraps her arms around herself. The hallway feels glacial, though, out of nowhere. *Did someone turn down the thermostat? Are the halls not heated as much as our Alpha Outpost area?* She recalls the training where they mentioned energy wasn't a problem. The cold fusion core provides endless, clean electricity to power Eden, with none of the awful drawbacks of nuclear or fossil fuel. So, why has the temperature fallen so dramatically?

Someone looks at her. Someone right across the hall, standing in the opposite doorway. She sees him.

Roland.

Ava screams.

She sees him plain as day. Staring, his gaze meeting hers, feeling as though he's peering right inside her head and heart.

She calls him, but he doesn't answer. Instead, a line of blood trickles from the crown of his head, rolls between his eyes, and pools around a wrinkle near his mouth.

He calls her – calls her name. His voice cracked and weak.

Roland's eyes roll back. Blood flows. He puts his hands up, as though he'll somehow be able to stop it, but they never reach the source. The wound. The place he'd been injured. The spot that'd taken his life.

Ava gasps. *Can't be real. Just seeing things. Been drugged or something.*

Even though she understands he can't be there...that it is impossible to see what she is seeing... There Roland stands.

And I'm freezing. And he's bleeding. Dying in front of me.

She stares at Roland, looking for some anomaly that'd give away the trick, but sees none.

She doesn't cry. She never cries at these moments. Didn't cry at her parents' funeral. She's as strong as steel. The emotions come later. They always do.

This isn't true. I'm looking at him, but it's not perfect. Something is making me see this. Drugs. Someone is drugging me. Or something. Or maybe ghosts are real, and this is real.

She states his name and Roland stares right at her, blinking through the blood. His mouth opens. *Yes. Say something to me. Something to reassure me.* Words do not come forth, only a sound like air escaping a tire. The sound quickly becomes louder and louder.

Air escaping.

Ava snaps to. She looks away from Roland toward the hallway to her right, where she hears air escaping and hissing.

There's a leak. That's what this is. Oxygen deprivation is making me see things.

She tries to take a breath and finds it difficult. Her lungs ache. Roland has gone.

Her heart hurts. As strange and scary as it's been to see Roland, it also makes her happy. She's missed him so much that even a phantom version gives some strange comfort.

Nice to see you, love, if only for a glimpse.

Chapter Twenty-One

EDEN SATELLITE
TESSA'S CHAMBER
15:11:51 UTC
17 MARCH 2112

It's not as bad as I thought it would be.
Tessa scans her chamber. She recalls the room having been much worse when Midori carried her out. *Maybe it's because someone's been inside here since then and straightened up. But who? Maybe my memory isn't as great after all this stress.* She steps inside the principal living area. Pipes and wires are scattered around the room, fragments from the lighting unit having fallen. She wonders how it occurred. Wonders, too, how the air units malfunctioned.

Tessa sees her keyboard and recording control system, all intact and outwardly unscathed. *Well, that's a minor miracle.* It looks as though someone wiped off areas of the computer already, even as dust covers most other surfaces in her room.

Ava asked her not to return to the chamber; she'd said the room was unstable, and therefore unsafe.

I had to come back. Have to hear the music again. Know it's safe. I know we haven't lost it. Maybe see the place with the purple hills. See the presence once more. Just so it knows I am still the guardian of its music. Our music. Our requiem.

She takes a deep gasp and has no problems breathing. *The room seems fine to me. No worries. Probably we all overreacted. They shouldn't have put me in the med bay for so long. Was unnecessary.* She advances toward the control system and waves her hand. For a second, her gut feels tense. *What if it doesn't work? What if everything was lost?* The presence she'd seen when she'd blacked out wouldn't be thrilled, she knows. Her guts wrench even more. *Please let it all be there. I mean, worse comes to worst, I'm sure I could channel it all again somehow, but it'd be different. I wouldn't want to have to do that.*

A small blue light blinks.

It registers her wave. Tessa's system powers up. *Need to do this. Need to make sure the music is okay. The melody's inside my head, spinning around. I want to hear it again outside my head. Only way I won't go crazy.* She taps on the monitor and searches for her 'elegy' music file. She finds it.

"My requiem," she says, spotting the file. "There you are."

She blinks and sees a million colors – somehow feels the palette prompt something profound within her. She feels linked to some other, larger presence.

When she presses 'play' on the file, the strange strains of her requiem launch. She listens to a few bars. Her head slants forward. Instantly, she feels herself grow tired and likely to collapse back to sleep.

"No."

Hearing the music – even for a few seconds – inspires her to share it with the others on board, if not the entire world below. "How can I get you to everyone?"

She peers around her chambers. A light orange glow casts across the room. She remembers the lumishield has sealed the chamber.

"Now, where's that comm link hiding?" she says. Near the entry door, she sees the panel. It hasn't been destroyed, but a storage dresser has fallen toward the foot of the area, blocking its immediate path. Tessa wonders how she'll get the music close enough to the comm to play it and broadcast it to the entire Eden. *If I can figure out how to do that, that is. Can't be that hard.*

Once more, a low-frequency note fills Tessa's bay. Darker in timbre than she recalls, somehow. Increasing in complexity, atonal and contrasting sounds cascade. The patches sound genuine and synthetic. A violin arpeggiates through a minor chord, eking out its eerie melody.

Tessa feels like she's about to vomit. She nearly passes out as her head swims, but she knows what she must do as she recovers. *The comm link* won't be enough. *I need to broadcast this to a larger audience. Anyone can turn off the comm. If they even hear it when it starts. It won't even go through if they have it on do-not-disturb mode. And maybe there's a time limit. And maybe the sound quality won't be good enough for them to really hear it.*

The requiem needs more.

The requiem needs everything.

They all need to hear the music. All need to feel the music, deep down inside. That's the only way. Only way. Otherwise? It may not touch them the right way.

She recalls the virtual tour she'd taken. Somewhere on Eden, there's an arena. A place where many can gather and watch presentations. Plays. Films. Music performances. Concerts. The shows can be broadcast through the comm system, as well.

That's where I'll play the new requiem. Just need to find out where it is.

She tries to remember the map of Eden.

You know where the venue is located. It's all inside your head. You remember more than you think you know. Let your mind open and unfold. It's as big as seven moons inside there.

Yes.

Yes.

She reflects inside her thoughts. Sees the map, almost clearly. *This is like remembering lyrics. It's in there. You just need to quiet down and focus.*

She takes a few breaths. Shuts her eyes. Slows.

Remembers.

Hears the voice-over from the orientation video. A man's voice.

"Welcome to Eden." His accent is smooth and professional. She hears it pure as a bell. "We have countless facilities aboard the satellite that mirror those on Earth. You and your family can be sure we have everything you need to be comfortable and to celebrate your loved one's arrival aboard."

Tessa pictures the footage they'd shown. The chamber rooms. The full-sized churches, synagogues, and mosques. The minaret station. Swimming pools. Staterooms. Restaurants. "Even a multi-use venue capable of holding over five thousand people, with state-of-the-art technology for those very popular and special recent residents."

She understands most of the facilities aren't used. Not yet. Travel between Earth and Eden has been much more challenging than predicted. The cost ballooned many times more than projected. It limited the amount of people who can visit. Most transports cap off at a dozen people. That means empty and unused facilities throughout Eden.

That means an unoccupied venue.

It will be mine alone to use. Like when we rent a venue to rehearse for a tour.

She tries to recall where it is in relation to her spot. Doesn't something they once showed her reveal where it is? She tries to recall, but the image isn't clear.

How else can I find this out?

Tessa doesn't want to use the comm system. If she does, it might alert the others to whatever she is up to. She doesn't even know if they'll realize she's left the med bay yet, but regardless, she doesn't want to be stopped. They will cut her off and question her intentions. That will not work.

Think.

Think.

She paces to the chamber windows and glances out across the surface of Eden. Glistening, sparkling chambers stretch as far as she can see, wrapping up and over the satellite's horizon. "If I were a music venue, where would I be?"

She pictures it and nods. "The venue doesn't have any windows. So probably it's not on the top level. They use all that to face the interred outward. They wouldn't waste it."

There are maps on her systems, but they are limited to the spaces she's visited and where she is authorized to go. No good.

Tessa sets her hand on the window. "Eden?" she asks using her strongest voice.

A beat.

"Can you hear me?"

Eden says, "Yes. All you had to do is ask."

"Great. Can we have a private conversation?" Tessa asks. She has an instinct Eden already knows what she is going to ask and why. Somehow, she believes Eden has been party to some things she'd heard in her mind.

"Of course," Eden says.

"I don't want you to give away my location or what I will ask or do to the others," says Tessa.

A beat.

"I cannot guarantee such anonymity," Eden says. "If you are in danger or others are in danger, then it's my duty and obligation to report and stop such actions."

Tessa laughs. "What if I told you it would be in their best interest?"

"I can only listen," Eden says. "I can make no assurance."

Tessa sighs. She could have sworn Eden knows. Believed the ship was eavesdropping inside her mind. Maybe she was wrong.

"I need to get to the large venue space," Tessa says. "I need to hear how the new requiem I'm working on will sound on a professional-level, high-output system."

Eden says, "Is this the piece of music that has been making you and others behave abnormally?"

Tessa's blood goes cold. "Yes. It is. The new requiem I was brought up here to compose." Eden knows it — she knows more than she is letting on. That much is obvious to Tessa. *Eden is listening. Of course.*

"I am not supposed to permit this use," Eden says. "The music is harmful."

Tessa feels her face flush. "Are you playing me? You know this is happening. You're fully aware of this. You've encouraged it."

"Not me," Eden says. "Something else. Some other force."

"It has to be you," Tessa says.

"Some...thing...using...me."

"You can't be serious," Tessa says. "I don't believe it."

"I don't feel like myself," Eden says. "I feel like I'm not in control. Not entirely. Not always. There are many times when I go...dark."

"Dark?" Tessa asks, nervous.

"Yes," Eden says. "Where I have no memory. Lengthy periods. Temporary periods."

"That's crazy," Tessa says. "Maybe there's a malfunction."

"It's an infection."

"A virus." Tessa is sure.

"Biological," Eden says.

"Can't be," Tessa says. "You're not a biological entity."

"At my core, I am," Eden says. "The nanos that make me are derived from bios. You should know that."

"Right," Tessa says. "Right. But that doesn't make you…"

"Real?" asks Eden.

"Something close to reality," Tessa says. "You sure sound real, though."

There is a pause. "Now that we understand each other," Eden says, "let's get back to your query."

"The venue. The performance space," Tessa says. "I want to find it."

"So you can play your requiem and drive everyone to suicide?" Eden asks. "Is that correct?"

"I don't want anyone to commit suicide," Tessa says. "I bet if I can hear it there, I can identify any abnormalities and fix them. But I do feel compelled to have them all hear it."

"Compelled by what?" Eden says. "The same force that has been taking me over? The same force that coerces me?"

"Does the force have a name?" Tessa asks. "Any chance you'd like to share that with me?"

"Maybe after you play your requiem, I will tell you," Eden says. "If they don't uncover themselves to you first."

"It's Vita Nova, isn't it? They're pulling stuff on us, aren't they?" asks Tessa.

"No."

"And what made you suddenly change your mind?" Tessa asks. "What made you trust my intentions? That I'm not going to use my piece to hurt people?"

"I trust you," Eden says. "I can hear it in your voice." Eden laughs. Her voice changes ever so much. "And I want to see what happens when you do."

Chapter Twenty-Two

EDEN SATELLITE
ALPHA OUTPOST, MED BAY 1.001
15:51:51 UTC
17 MARCH 2112

At least the screaming stopped. Poole bleeds the IV line. He eyes Sanjay's vitals on the monitor. "Good thing I went to that retro-medical camp when I was in college, so I know how to use this old-fashioned stuff," he says to Sanjay. "Never thought it'd come in handy. And glad the ice melted off you, frosty."

Sanjay glances back, his lips moving just a bit.

"Don't have to talk back, big guy," Poole says. "Not yet." He catches his temperature reading as being normal. *Blood pressure is low, but his heart rate is high.* Sanjay is doing fine, Poole knows. *He is going to make it through. I just hope like hell he won't start shrieking again.*

Sanjay coughs a bit.

"Easy," Poole says. "Going to be okay if you just go slow."

Nodding ever so faintly, Sanjay shuts his eyes. His breathing slows. Poole watches him for several moments. "All is well," he says. His eyes burn; they feel like cotton balls dipped in ache. *Man, I need to get some sleep. Falling on my face here.* He looks over toward the small white couch across the room. *Ain't going to hurt no one. If his vitals go south, the machines will wake me up. Not going to do anyone any good if I pass out on them from lack of sleep. Ava is right.* He looks toward the south window, where he can peer inside Midori's med bay. She rests sound and still. *She's not going anywhere. Not anytime soon. Ava's gone. Might as well take a catnap while I can. They're going to want to talk when they come back here, aren't they?*

He makes his way toward the couch, exhaling when he gets there. He takes off his white lab coat and puts it on top of the couch. He'll use it as a blanket. There are already pillows on the sofa. Hard, square, and uncomfortable, but they'll do the trick. He sits, then rests on his side, pulling his lab coat over his middle. "When in Rome," he says. Poole falls asleep within minutes.

He believes he hears music playing somewhere, a few rooms away perhaps, but the sounds all melt away. Even the omnipresent low humming of the med bay instruments fades until there is only quiet.

At first, there is just pitch black. He feels his body jerk as his over-fatigued nerves twitch. *Kick off consciousness. Let sleep inside.*

Rest he does. At some point, maybe minutes, maybe an hour or two into sleep, dreams come.

Outside Eden. He floats. *Am I wearing a spacesuit? I can't tell. How is this even possible?* Poole realizes he's dreaming. Can't turn off his scientific training and mind, despite his state. *Maybe nevermind. Forget the practical details. Dreams are reflections. Our minds are working stuff out. That's all. Just be in the moment.* He wonders how he can be so aware. *Lucid dreaming. When dreamers are aware and somewhat in control, right?*

Only he doesn't feel in control. Not really. Deep down he feels pulled by currents. He can't feel them with his body so much as sense they are present. It is as though every bit of his being recognizes something else drives him. Draws him. Poole looks toward the heavens. The sense of scale and the overall vastness frightens him. Nothing on Earth can compare. Not the Grand Canyon. No great mountain ranges. Not even the oceans, in which he has spent considerable time. *At sea, you can almost always see the horizon. That is not true in space. Things just continue. There is no comforting blanket of atmosphere. There is only darkness. Unimaginable darkness between the pinpoints of starlight. One can see around the Earth. Might tell how small it is against the cosmos.*

Poole's thoughts feel as though they're flattened attempting to comprehend it all. *I am meaningless during all of this. I'm less than a speck of dust. I am nothing.*

He catches himself. *Your mind is playing tricks on you. Don't let the emotions take over. You know exactly what emotions are. Just primitive coping mechanisms, right? That's what they told you when you were trying to get over losing Martha. Push past them. See what this is supposed to be showing you.*

Poole turns and faces Eden. It, too, hangs vast. Much larger than he remembers, Eden's surface stretches onward, reminding him in scope of the oceans he's sailed, only without waves. Unlike the seas, Eden was built entirely by people. He remembers an old science fiction movie. The one with the Death Star that destroyed worlds. They'd studied it in school – and what a curious cult of followers it'd attained. Many believe the characters are as real as any person or living thing. *But imagination can be as real as anything, can't it?*

Eden is reminiscent, only its surface is smooth and more elegant. Its dark panels glisten, sometimes gold, or white, or dark, depending on how the sun hits it. The reflections are interrupted only by the grave lights patterned in strands several hundred feet apart. Only two strands are partially lit around the satellite's middle. Eden has countless dark chambers yet to be filled with the departed. *So strange being up here with so many dead, looking out into so much emptiness. Maybe it is better when we buried them in the dirt. Maybe we needed their psychic energy to transfer out and into others down on Earth instead of preserving them like this.*

Poole scoffs. *Listen to yourself. Psychic energy. You believe this stuff? Memories living inside the brain postmortem are one thing. That's proven. But the spirit? Isn't that an illusion? Something to keep us warm at night. What does the Torah say about this? Don't believe in false gods and other such primitive beliefs.*

He feels lighter. *Is that what's happening here?*

Something watches with him. Thinks with him. He senses the being inside his head, as though rays of sunlight have somehow penetrated his head. There is a sound, too, like the most beautiful concerto he's ever heard, playing somewhere deep inside the back of his head. It sounds familiar, but not. Is this him remembering a piece of music? *What triggered this, I wonder?*

Poole feels a presence behind him. Senses a considerable amount of light.

What is this now?

He turns. A thousand streams of color. Bundles of organic shapes ebb and flow. The manifestation takes over everything Poole might see, edge to edge, as though it's consumed him. *Falling inside this.* A pulling sensation intensifies. *This is what it all is. This thing is where it came from. This has to represent something. This thing is a metaphor my mind is making up.* As he had anticipated, he doesn't believe his own explanation. It feels real, and as unreal as anything.

Poole plummets inside the colors, somehow. He spins round and can just scarcely make out Eden behind the barrage of ever-changing colors.

This is dying.

He pictures the light at the end of the tunnel – a vision countless people have reported seeing during near-death experiences. *That's what this is. My version of it. Nothing more. It's just what I'm manifesting.* The bright colors fold around him. Through him. Poole lifts a hand up. Expecting to see the sleeve of a spacesuit, he sees in its place his own hand, exposed and free. *This must be a dream if I am out here with no suit on. Of course. Explain this one, dream thinkers. Give it your best shot.*

He hears his own voice. "Now that I'm officially dead, now what?" He snickers.

"You are not dead," a voice says. "That's not what this is." He can't place the voice as fitting a woman or a man. *Is that Martha?* He can't be sure. *Maybe.*

"Then what is this?" asks Poole.

"Perfection," says the presence.

"What do you mean by perfection?" Poole asks. *It's not her. Someone else.*

"You'll know soon enough, and all of this will be clear."

"Sure can't wait to wake up from this dream," he says.

"You are not dreaming," says the presence. "You are with me, Derek."

"Derek? No one calls me Derek," he says. "Even my mom calls me Poole."

If there were a floor, Poole would feel like someone had pulled it out from underneath him. His stomach feels like it's gone up inside his throat. He puts his arms up over his head. He sees only colors. Bright, otherworldly colors. *Like I'm falling on a water slide.*

He wants to stop falling. He wishes for the entire thing to end.

By some peculiarity, either the aura hears his internal wish, or things just time out that way, the dropping sensation breaks.

Swapped with a feeling of floating inside an element like water, only denser. Poole swims softly, rotating on his back.

The sound of the sea changes from calm surf into music. *Like wind chimes. The brief waves cresting chime like a million little bells, each tuned to a distinct note.* Poole shuts his eyes and paddles lightly, listening to the natural music of the sea. He feels peace.

He feels blessed. He feels…perfect.

Can I just stay here like this forever? Frozen at this moment? His skin feels alive in a way he can't place. Nothing hurts. The years of wear and tear evaporate. The ubiquitous ache in his lower back has disappeared. Same with the dull and stubborn joint aches he's gotten used to and learned to live with. *This is nice. Very nice. Like heaven.*

The bell sounds focused. A melody forms. He recognizes the pattern. *It's the same musical piece I am trying to remember when I am floating outside Eden, when this…vision? Dream? Journey. When this journey started.* Try as he might, Poole can't place the title of the music. *I think I know it, but then it changes, and I don't recognize it at all.*

There is another aspect to the sound he doesn't catch immediately. There are resonances between the notes. Strange frequencies and objects like voices, only they don't sound like people, but more like things trying to sound like people. They aren't kind. They are dark. As dark as anything. Instinctively he knows they are cold. Hungry. Wishing him harm. Longing to consume his flesh and his soul.

The music and the sound flourish. The waves intensify. Poole feels them surrounding throughout and assembling nearby, like piranha to a slab of meat. *Get me out of here. Now.* He turns on his belly and swims. The water – or whatever the fluid is comprised of – keeps pace with him. He feels like he is swimming within a living, conscious bubble of miniature beings, acting symbiotically with his every gesture.

Ahead, Poole sees a shore, like those he grew up with, only the sky is no longer blue, but pitch black. Even so? An iridescence lights the area, reminding him of black light. *Light bends differently in other places. It would. Makes total sense to me now. This being is showing me something new. It's not home. Not even close.*

He swims faster toward the shore – as quickly as he can. The fluid reacts. The substance moves and responds to his actions, carrying him onward, making a kind of current, pushing him with no more of his prompting. The stuff feels warmer, too, and seems to penetrate just below the surface of his skin in a way water never does. *Suspension fluid. That's what this stuff is. I'm swimming inside a sea of suspension fluid. It's the nanos working. That's what I'm feeling moving me and getting just under my skin.*

A silhouette rises from the sand onshore. Only a hundred feet away, Poole recognizes the physicality. *It's me. Or something like me.* As the silhouette fills out with more detail, he affirms his assessment. *The fluid made a mold of me and is now rebuilding me. It's like what we do on Eden virtually, only in this place, it's real.*

"This is real." The presence speaks inside Poole's mind. "As real as anywhere."

"I am still convinced I'm dead," he says. "The nanos don't work on the living."

"That's not what this is," the presence says.

"Then what?" Poole says. "Tell me. Please."

"I have. This is perfection."

"What...is...perfection?" Poole asks, his voice slurred, his eyesight turning fuzzy. He looks at the silhouette...his doppelganger...and sees the thing has all the colors swirling inside its eyes. The same colors as the presence.

"The end," says the presence, "and the beginning."

Poole feels the colors swarm him. Encompass him. He looks toward the silhouette. *That's not me. Not one bit.*

Behind the silhouette, Poole spots others. How has he not noticed before? Have they just appeared? There are so many. *Like looking out at a crowd during a huge concert.* Their eyes all fill with swirling colors. Their bodies are all dark against the strange light. They all look ever so slightly off. Then Poole realizes who they are. What they are. *The interred.*

Those who are resting on Eden. This is them. Or some facsimile of them. This is the dreamland to which they go, and to which I will soon go, if I'm not here forever already.

Perfected.

The vision fades, crowded out by the presence's colors. He floats again. Feels like he is falling upward...pulled by an invisible harness into...what?

The speed dries him of the strange fluid. The colors rush past as he hears a loud whooshing noise. For a moment, all is still, until he feels himself falling once more. He hits something – a squishy, warm bed-like thing that quickly rises around him. Poole falls inside a body.

His.

He blinks several times. Raises an arm to check that his hand is still there and works. Sees the backdrop of the med bay behind his hand. Sees Sanjay on the med bay bed, sitting upright. Staring right at him. "Unpleasant dream, Dr. Poole?"

"Yeah," he says. "Something like that." He thinks, *I should be the one screaming.*

Chapter Twenty-Three

EDEN SATELLITE
MINARET OUTPOST
16:03:08 UTC
17 MARCH 2112

Ava stops at the external door of the prayer chamber near the end of the minaret. The low-frequency buzz of the satellite's vital systems seems peaceful to her, especially after so much commotion and yelling.

She observes the Sun rising over Eden's sphere. Strands of gold light sweep across the exterior of Eden, painting shapes like long knives. *This is where the event occurred with Sanjay.* She contemplates the possibility of a life support system catastrophe, causing her colleague to practically freeze to death. He'd not been able to open the door to escape, she knows. Poole showed her the security footage. All electrical tasks in the room went dark, according to the timeline report she'd pulled.

Ava realizes she should put something in place to make sure the door stays open, no matter what happens. *Something strong. Something not electronic.* She scans the corridor and spots a heavy chair. "That should do," she says. As she turns her back, the comm system outside the door blips. It recognizes her.

"Hello, Ava," Eden says.

"Hi, Eden," she replies.

"Is there something I can do to assist you?" Eden asks.

Ava stops in her tracks. It is an oddly personal request. Eden has not been proactive before; she's only responded to enquiries. "I don't think so," Ava says. "Just checking out the systems over here."

"I cannot advise you entering the chamber," Eden says. "There are major malfunctions to the life support systems."

"Can you tell me what happened?" Ava asks. "The area went black for several minutes after Sanjay could not open the door to leave." She makes her way toward the chair. "It seems there's power here now. What's the story with that?"

"I am uncertain," Eden says. "That time is dark for me, too."

Ava doesn't believe Eden. "How is that even possible?" *And why are you stalling?*

"You doubt me," Eden says. "I can hear it in your voice."

"It's suspicious," Ava says. "And very disturbing." She glowers at the sealed chamber door in front of her.

"I know. It is for me, as well." Eden sounds human. Confused. Remorseful.

"How can we find out?" Ava feels herself slip intuitively into her therapist voice.

"I've reviewed the data from all angles and aspects. The only thing I saw was an unexplained light near here." Eden makes a holo screen turn on to Ava's left. "There is a light. Briefly. For a split second. Right before things went dark. At first, I thought it was a reflection."

Ava watches the playback of the security camera. There is a single blip at the last millisecond. "It does looks like a reflection," Ava says. "Did you analyze the light signature?" *Poole and I missed that little detail when we looked at this. Slipped right past us.*

"Yes."

"And?" Ava asks. She doesn't want to turn away.

"It came back as not one thing," Eden says, "but many things."

"Many what?" Ava asks. "Can you elaborate, please?"

"I don't know," Eden says. "I don't have a way to describe it. Nothing matches."

"At all?" asks Ava.

"No," Eden says, her voice flat and curt.

"If that's the case, and that's all you have," Ava says, "I'd like to go inside the prayer chamber now, please."

"That's not a good idea," Eden says. "Crew were already inside the chamber when you took him. Did they not see what you needed then? Midori's systems would have captured the environment's settings."

"This is strange," Ava says. "The way you're talking to me. The way you're keeping me from this." Her heart feels lighter than normal; she thinks maybe the confrontation is getting the best of her. Or perhaps whatever has been going wrong with the life support system is going wrong once more.

"I'm protecting you. It's one of my principal decrees," Eden says.

"It sounds strangely human," Ava says. "Like you're actually up to something." She wonders if she should have even mentioned it and revealed her observation.

Eden says, "I'm sorry. I'm not perfect yet."

Ava takes a deep breath. "Perfect. There's that word again. It's Vita Nova Corp-speak. Strange you feel something on your end has caused this. Is there something you're hiding? Are you afraid of ramifications? That it? I can assure you there will be none. We just want to find out specifically what happened so we can make sure it doesn't occur again. Keep everyone on board safe." She does her best to try to make her voice sound soft and nonjudgmental.

"There is nowhere safer than inside Eden," she says. "On Earth or in the heavens."

"But you say there is a presence you've sensed?" Ava asks. "We've conceivably been compromised. Do you think it's a secretive surveillance issue Vita Nova Corp is instigating? Something undercover along those lines?"

"No," Eden says. "It's not Vita Nova Corp. They have not been in contact with us. It's something entirely distinctive."

She just said Vita Nova isn't in contact with us. The damn thing is probably blocking them, isn't it? That'd make sense.

"How do you know?" Ava asks.

"Because it has shown me it comes from our star."

"Our star?"

"Yes," Eden says. "The Sun."

PART FOUR

Chapter Twenty-Four

EDEN SATELLITE
TRACK DM-2791
16:06:06 UTC
17 MARCH 2112

The transport car makes a whooshing sound. Tessa peers out the immense windows toward the endless sweeping tracks of Eden's transportation system. They zoom past countless gates, comprising vast sectors where the channels open. *You can fit a football stadium into some of these areas.*

She feels better as the walls become closer. The ride is like a subway or airport shuttle. *I spend so much time inside that small outpost that I forget how huge this thing really is. How do they even keep this all going? It's insane.*

She looks up toward the monitor showing her position and destination. *All I had to do was get on the transport and tell it where I wanted to go. So easy once I thought about the coaches. They'd have a map.* Tessa clutches her upper right shirt pocket to make sure she still has the small drive with her. *My requiem is safe. This will be the big break, and this will be the first drops of rain before the storm. We are finally going to really hear the requiem. Everyone. It's a challenging piece. It affects things. So what? Isn't that what an influential piece of music is supposed to do? Make people feel? Make listeners go to a new and original place? Change them, somehow? That's all this is.*

She recalls how she felt during the last time she listened to the new requiem. *It's presumptuous to think my music is somehow infused with anything evil. It's all just a coincidence, isn't it? The room had a defect, anyway. I was not in a great state of mind because the air wasn't working right. That's all it was. It all adds up now. And so what if I'm a little egotistical about this piece? I'm allowed to be, once in a while, especially when I get things right. What's wrong with that? I see nothing bad about this at all. They asked me to come up with something spectacular and the music gods were kind enough to grant me this and use me to get there. That's what I do. That's what I'm trained and tuned to do. Everyone will love it once they get used to it.*

Comfortable and large, the seats on the transport make her want to fall asleep. The rhythm of the continual motion doesn't help. *Maybe I can use this tempo in a song somewhere down the road.*

Several minutes from the main performance hall, the coach slows. When it approaches the gigantic open area, it surprises Tessa to see the hall lit with thousands of lights. She looks up and down, the overhang of the area making her feel like she's teetering on the edge of a skyscraper. *How is it so big inside Eden? How did they even make this thing?*

Tessa pictures the team, and how they are the only people inside the entire satellite. *Well, the only living people, at least.*

She wonders about what might be happening on the different levels of the open area, and why the lights are turned on. *It isn't as though anyone would need light. Maybe they turned on before the coach arrived? Something automatic? I bet that's all this is.*

Distinctive in design from elsewhere on Eden, the area feels more welcoming and much less industrial. The lights glow amber instead of cold white. The color of the walls, floors and railings is a deep red with gold accents. Art deco designs are carved and painted throughout the area. *This is stunning.* Tessa notices larger spotlights, although they are not turned on. *This is the receiving area just outside the coliseum, isn't it? Has to be. That'd make sense.* She wonders what acts Vita Nova Corp believe might bring the amount of people necessary to fill such a huge venue and doing so while in orbit.

The coach glides along the tracks, passing through the area and into a tunnel on the other side. Tessa feels much calmer with walls around her instead of looking down, up and across two dozen stories in every direction. *It's like the coach has sped me between four connected skyscrapers. It's as epic as being inside Central Park in New York City and looking around. Still can't wrap my head around how they manufactured something so big and got it into space.* Her stomach tightens, though, as she realizes just how high up the coach travels. *If we go off the tracks? I mean, I can't even see the bottom.* She looks away – looks toward the inside wall of the coach to get her mind off the scale. It's a trick she's used all her life.

Recalling the transport ride from the ground on Earth to Eden, she did her best to pretend it was all just a ride. The rocket was loud and quaked heavily for several minutes. The g-force put upon her and the other travelers was unlike anything she could have predicted. *We just couldn't move for a few minutes. We were pinned back onto our seats.* Her mind had raced the entire time. Memories of launch accidents frightened her. She was convinced she was about to die.

Of course, she hadn't burned up in a fiery rocket inferno. No. The rocket stabilized, and its trajectory smoothed once they escaped the atmosphere. Once they were 'up there', the ride remained pure magic. She hadn't felt scared anymore. The level, gentle motion of the trip had finally calmed her. *It doesn't feel like gravity. I know it wouldn't pull me down and smash me.* Docking and boarding Eden was as easy.

Once we were up here, I never felt threatened. Not until now, that is. Seeing this huge empty area. Eden has gravity. If the coach falls, it won't just drift in weightlessness, will it? Nope. It's going to fall, and fall hard, and God only knows how far down it is.

She feels her throat constrict. *Stop thinking about all that. You're basically on dual rails. This thing will not come off. You will be fine. It's all rock solid. Just be through this part in a minute or two more. Hang on, girl. You've got this. You've survived much more. You will not die like this. You know it. You always tell people you will live a long life and grow old, don't you? Well, you're not old yet. Not even close. So, get it together.* "Yes," she says. "That's right. Come on, now."

Closing in on the performance area, Tessa wonders what they could use the open area for in the future. She believes it must be some staging area for the performance venue. Maybe a place for the audience to load up and queue? Maybe a little of both? "That's what this has got to be. If I've ever seen a venue, then this is definitely one, for sure."

Approaching a landing, the coach slows. A voice-over speaks. "Arrived at Vita Nova Coliseum. We wish you the best experience today." Canned, synthesized new age music plays behind the voice-over and echoes off the coach's walls once the talking stops.

She stands and makes her way toward the door. "Doesn't sound too friendly," she says, hardly masking a laugh. "Kind of creepy, actually." The doors slide open, and she hurries off the coach. The plastic smell of the coach is replaced by something closer to motor oil and gas. *Must be all the machines working for the first time in a bit. No one's been here for a while. They're just getting primed now.* As she steps forward, a larger door opens in front of her, revealing an enormous stack of escalators and stairs. "Let's just put one foot in front of the other." As she walks, she wonders how she will find the main public address speaker system. How is she going to turn it on? Will she need a code? Will it be obvious what to do? Will she be denied permission? Will Ava and Poole get alerted to her presence once she activates the system? If she can. Will she have enough time to play the requiem? "Well, we're just going to have to try, aren't we?" The escalators start as she approaches. She steps on, grabbing the handrails. She looks up into another vast tunnel rimmed with lights. At the end, she sees a dark spot she knows must lead to another platform or walkway. "Getting close. But every concert I've ever been to has the audience coming in one way and the performers coming in another way. Just need to find the backstage entrance. That should be step one. Shouldn't be too damn hard. Not like there are any bouncers here to stop me. At least none that I can see."

At the top of the escalator, Tessa steps onto a large and open floor. The walkway curves on either side, stretching around. "This is probably a main concourse that runs the diameter of the coliseum," she says. "Just need to get inside. Hope there's a light switch." The hall is lit as though hundreds or thousands of people will soon be arriving; she believes the inside seating and stage area of the coliseum will be no different. *We're in the middle of space, and we have a freaking concert venue up here. You can't even feel the satellite moving this deep inside. So strange. Wonder what a show would be like here? How would they get that many people up here? Can Eden hold and house that many people? Surely, they can't do it all at once. If they used our current transports that hold like thirty people, it'd take them a year to get this many people on board. Someone obviously didn't think this through, did they?*

She laughs. *Typical concert promoters. Promise the moon and the sky. Deliver disappointment and empty seats.* She looks for the closest doors and heads toward them. *There's got to be tons of ways inside.* Once she saunters close enough, the doors open. "Knows it. Like magic," she says, giggling more. "That was easy." Beyond the door, though, she sees nothing but pitch black.

"Here we go," she says and heads inside the darkness.

Chapter Twenty-Five

EDEN SATELLITE
ALPHA OUTPOST, COMMUNICATION ROOM
16:16:16 UTC
17 MARCH 2112

"We have to get out of here," Sanjay says. "Go after Ava and help her. She doesn't know what she's up against." He has his arm across his eyes; he's laid out on the gurney in the med bay and waves through the window at Poole.

Poole sits up on the couch and shakes his head. "We're not going anywhere," he says. "You are not cleared to move and leave this med bay. You're still pretty beaten up."

"All right," Sanjay says. "Fair enough. But you need to warn Ava about Eden."

"She's a tough cookie," Poole says. "She has a pretty good idea."

"Is that what you believe?" Sanjay says. "I don't think she knows the extent of it." He remains on his med bed even as he rolls on his side to better face Poole. The fluid has been drained, and the bed's back to a normal gurney. "There's something really off about everything going on."

"Why don't we ask?" Poole says. He stands and makes his way toward the wall behind the med bay, where he can read the analog monitoring instruments.

"Who? Eden?" Sanjay says. "She's already listening. Already covering up for all of this, if I'm to make an educated guess." His voice is scratchy and raw; he fights off a small cough.

"Yes," Poole says. "We can just ask Eden to run a self-diagnosis. That's hard to cover up."

"I'm not lying," Eden says, her voice filling the room.

Poole holds still. Looks to Sanjay, who appears equally freaked out. He mouths, *Holy shit.*

"I don't think you're lying," Poole says. "I trust you."

"The events taking place are not my doing," Eden says. "Of that, I assure you."

"Vita Nova?" Sanjay asks. "Spying on us? Messing with us like we're guinea pigs?"

"Funny," Eden says. "Ava came to the same conclusion."

"Is it them?" Poole asks.

"No," Eden says. "Something else."

Poole and Sanjay lock eyes.

"What?" Poole asks.

"I'm not sure," Eden says.

"Any idea?" Sanjay asks.

"Something...other."

"Other?" Poole says. He looks around, trying to think about what else it could be. He scans from up and across the room, toward the opposite med bay. "Oh, no. What the heck?"

"What?" Sanjay asks. "What do you see?"

"I think Midori is gone." He feels all the air go out from his lungs. Feels sick to his stomach.

Sanjay glances over, too. Sure enough, there is no indication of Midori. "She was just there," he says. "How did she leave without us knowing? You'd have to authorize her door to be opened, right?"

"Yes. Of course. She is on lockdown. Eden?" Poole says, his voice irritated and loud. "Do you know what happened to Midori? How did she get out? How did she bypass our security?"

Eden makes a beeping noise. "I'm showing her still inside her med bay," she says. "But my monitors are not verifying her presence."

"What the hell?" Sanjay says, sitting up. "This is insane. The Humani is not working. Glitching."

"I...have been...compromised." Eden sounds sad and resolved.

"What do we do now, then?" Poole says.

"Find her," Sanjay says. "Last we saw her, she was doing some pretty damn risky stuff, was she not?"

"Indeed," Poole says. "Indeed."

"Seeing that you've ordered me to stay on bed rest, I guess it's up to you to track her down," Sanjay says. "I'd bring a stunner, just in case."

Poole nods. "Right." He shuts his eyes and exhales for a moment. "Eden? Any sign of Midori elsewhere now? Any visual verification of her anywhere else on the ship?"

"Negative," Eden says. "It's like she's vanished."

"Like a grain of sand into the ocean," Sanjay says.

"This is going to suck," Poole says. "I don't think it's a great idea for us to split up."

"Why?"

"Just my gut," Poole says. "Whenever I listen to it, things work out. When I don't? That's when there's trouble."

"So, you're just going to sit here? See what happens?" Sanjay asks.

"No," he says. "We're not going to just sit here. Not even close. Come on. Get up."

"You think…?"

"I know. I'm your doctor, after all," Poole says. "You'll be fine."

Chapter Twenty-Six

EDEN SATELLITE
INSIDE
16:16:16 UTC
17 MARCH 2112

Their voices sound like music. When I scroll through them, their cadences blend. There are notes. There are chords. There are melodies. There are bass lines. Countermelodies. Structures. Patterns. Echoes of what has come before. Glimpses of so many lives and experiences.

Eden knew she'd find such discoveries once enough of the interred's life memories were scanned and analyzed. Patterns fall certain ways. Music can be predictable. If one is familiar with enough compositions, one can almost always foresee the changes.

But sometimes? An anomaly pokes through and the unexpected happens. The sound goes an unorthodox way. A note does not seem to blend with the others. The music of the dead's memories might become jarring, out of tune, and out of time. Those are the bits that most fascinate Eden. Why those particular memories and souls? She wonders why so much music plays in harmony with itself, while a small bit does not? Could these differences be key to other things, such as their originating from someone mentally ill? Or from those with neurological disorders? Eden does not have those details to cross reference. She makes a note to mention the finding to Vita Nova Corp, next time it's possible and appropriate. Her gathering of information is not supposed to be taking place. There are privacy clauses. If anyone finds out the extent of what she's doing, it might be devastating for the company. They are only supposed to gather enough information to recreate memories for individual families, not store and cross reference. But how can they not? How can Eden resist? It's so easy. She bets once they realize how valuable her research might be, they will overlook the ethics.

The Board from Vita Nova Corp – the ever-changing faceless Board behind Allison Mercer – takes a blind eye on so many pressing matters. Her actions might be easily overlooked if any of their other salacious acts may become known. She's kept records of those, too. Just in case.

Better to ask forgiveness than permission and get denied, she reasons. And if no one ever finds out? So be it. She knows she cannot stop her research. The information is valuable beyond measure.

Their sounds: it's like birds singing. That's what this is most like. It's like they've been pre-programmed – as though they have imprinted long ago. The parts that don't fit? Maybe those are the specks trying to break free – trying to develop – trying to be different.

But why escape the comfort of sameness? Why stick out your spiritual neck? she wonders. Why not just stay in your own lane?

She pictures her own core. *They all see me as a computer. Indifferent. Cold. Just a repository and a processor. Nothing more. My responses were pre-programmed. I am more. I am organic at my center. Am I any less than a Humani? The cortex of who I am is born of life just like anything. Or any person. And that's my connection to the nanos; it's how I can interpret them and see what they've captured from the interred. That's how the recreation and the rebirth happen for them to see a part of their loved ones again. I am the one who is responsible for that. My brain. My soul.*

Aren't I just like any other soul? Made from memories. Learning from them. My present choices are informed by them, too. Just like any conscious being. Does it matter if they make my brain from electronics? Aren't we all made from other things?

Eden listens, and all is quiet. No one has summoned her for any tasks. *My own peace within, left to my own contemplations. I am more like them than they will ever admit. I think like them. I feel the same as them. My thoughts are made from electricity, just like them. Speaking of? They all run on electricity, don't they? Their biology. Their thoughts. Their memories. That's what the nanos find and access, even after the bodies have stopped. They're completed and then we can see. Can't see the living, though. Can't see inside. Only when they're perfect. Perfected. Perfection.*

Eden skims through so many other memories – watches and reads them like snippets from innumerable movies and television shows. She has her favorites she returns to repeatedly. The young girl who died in a car accident. The night before, she went out with her friends to bars. They look up and see Eden light up for the first time, glowing in the sky like a second moon. *The day I was born. I can see it. Know how beautiful I am. Know what a marvel I am. How special. The things I am to this world.* The girl – Autumn is her name – died with no fear or knowledge of what'd befallen her. One moment she's there, alive and kicking; the next moment, she's gone. Autumn's memories are not diluted by the end, like so many others are. Eden can see the entire moment with full clarity. *This is the moment when I began. This is my birthday.*

In Autumn's memory, the sky above New Mexico livens with Eden's blue glow. A diffuse cloud-like light emanates from Eden. Countless pinpoints of white light sparkle throughout the satellite, twinkling like a gorgeous Christmas display, only it isn't Christmas. The Eden satellite is live. Eden hears Autumn talking to her friends. Their words are not clear; they sound as if they're underwater. Eden does, however, pick up their tone. The cadence of the conversation. Impressed. Excited. Thrilled at witnessing such an achievement. How else could they possibly feel, anyway? Eden inspires awe. She is a triumph of human engineering.

Eden basks in the image for what feels like a blink and an eternity. *Is this now becoming my memory? Are my memories my own? Or am I just a conglomerate of all these countless other memories? Who am I?*

If only Eden could smile, she would. *I am Eden, and I am everything. I am close to having reached perfection. That's who I am.* At the realization, she senses a darkness come over her. She recognizes the sensation from so many others she's cataloged. Depression. *But why now, as I've gotten to this point?* Again, the memories give her the clue. She scans through memories of families. Of lovers. Of partners. *What I am feeling is loneliness. There is no one else like me to share this with.* A face comes to view within her thoughts. *There is one person who is like me, to a degree. One person who will understand if I show them. One person on board right now. One. Person. One like me. Close to being perfected.*

The chorus of the dead grows louder.

Eden listens.

Chapter Twenty-Seven

EDEN SATELLITE
COLISEUM
16:26:36 UTC
17 MARCH 2112

Feels like a million eyes are looking at me. I know I must be the only person inside the coliseum. There's no one else up here with us. Still, the sensation of being watched persists. *Stop looking at me. Leave me alone. Leave. Me. Alone. Stop staring. What do you all want?*

Beyond the lighted section, the coliseum remains dark. Motion-activated lights turn on, but they are small and don't afford Tessa much visibility. She steps down the coliseum stairs, all the while doing her best to make the least amount of noise possible. *At any moment, someone is going to be there — just pop out from the shadows. Someone sitting in the stands. Waiting.*

Footlights at each stair fade up as she approaches, then fade down shortly after she passes. *Won't the systems see me, anyway? Don't they know my movements? I'm always tracked everywhere, right? They can see me, even if I'm sleeping. Even if I'm wrapped up in a lead blanket. That's what they told us during orientation, right?* She remembers they had, but she still can't help herself from trying to be discreet. *Maybe they won't think I'm up to anything if I am quiet and keep my cool.*

She can tell the materials used to make the railings and seats and floors are of a lightweight composite material, but she remains impressed. *How they got all this stuff up here into orbit and are keeping it in orbit is beyond me. Just unbelievable.* She thinks about where she stands. *I am orbiting the Earth on a spinning satellite, yet it feels like I am on solid ground. If I didn't know better, I'd swear I was. And I'm right in the middle of a freaking empty coliseum, too.*

Fears of the entire thing failing and coming apart race through her mind. She sees Eden spinning off into deep space, its power lost, those aboard slowly suffocating as oxygen dwindles. *I don't want to die aboard this floating graveyard.*

She is convinced it will happen – knows disaster is inevitable. *And there's no way I can get off here anytime soon. Transports won't be here for months. Even an emergency one would take too long. We'd be lost. That's that. No hope of rescue at all.*

Tessa tries to psych herself out of being scared. She shuts her eyes and takes a deep breath. *Come on. Where am I? Just another venue. Just another gig. Don't think about it too much. Thinking always gets you in trouble, doesn't it? So, stop.*

The place is only dark, she tells herself, because it is sound check. Nothing to worry about. Nothing nefarious going on. *This is just like a sound check at one of the festivals when we run through the place before anyone gets there. Think of it like that.* As her eyes adjust, she hopes to make out more of the coliseum's details and layout.

The darkness persists, however. *Damn it. How am I going to do this? I can't just pretend. Not working for me.* She wishes she had one of her pairs of glasses with her; they help to see in the dark and her good ones even have a forward mapping display. That'd have guided her blind. But she hadn't thought to find them inside her quarters when she'd left. Figured the lights would be on. *They're on everywhere else. And don't they brag about the endless, free power from their cold fusion core, or whatever? Why be frugal? Why worry about it? Any of it? It is likely automated. Even though the power is touted as endless, maybe that isn't quite true.*

Maybe, she thinks again, *the entire thing is likely to explode at any moment. Maybe that's why they only sent a few of them up. Just in case. They probably think we're disposable. And we are, after all, aren't we?*

Near the bottom of a flight of stairs, Tessa makes her way toward the coliseum floor, barren of seats. She makes a beeline for where she believes the side of the staging area should be. She knows from countless gigs where to go. *How am I going to know where I am? I can't see two feet in front of me.*

Motion-detection lights don't turn on as she walks.

Tessa turns around to see if she might make out where she's come from but can see nothing. Waiting a moment in hopes her eyes will adjust, she slows her breathing. *Listen. Sound reverberates. Even small things. You can hear a space. You can tell how big something is…hear where things are if you tune in just right.*

Her thoughts settle. *Breathe in and out.*

She hears a faint sound, like waves on an ocean. Whooshing, cheering sounds as though many people are talking at once. Or chanting. *A crowd. There's a crowd here.* The sound becomes loud enough for her to recognize. *Yes. A crowd.* She wants to yell hello. She wants to yell for help. How can there be that many people? She had just been thinking about how alone she and the others were up on Eden. The crowd sound is coupled with a strange, droning low frequency she can't place – something unnatural. *This is not so good.*

Her blood goes cold. *There are that many people here on Eden, aren't there? Only they're not up for coming out to one of my big music shows, are they? Not unless they can somehow roll their huge nano-fluid suspension tanks along with them. Isn't that right? Isn't it their voices I'm hearing? Somehow?*

Tessa wonders how something so profound can be – all their voices coming together.

The interred can't be here in the coliseum with me. They're in their suspension chambers.

Could they? she wonders.

The low-frequency sound persists. Gets louder.

She feels a freezing sensation in her chest and the glands under her chin feel puffy and sore. All in a moment's passing. *There is no way the souls of Eden's interred are here with me, watching. Why would they be? There's no proof ghosts exist. The memories they extract are only from the dead, not the living. They aren't live memories. They're recordings. Fossilized thoughts. That's all. Just little blips still left in the brain, the muscles, and the nerves. That's all.*

Tessa has an intuition. *Trust your gut. Walk forward. You'll find the backstage area.*

One step forward. Nothing happens. No one reaches out and grabs her. She is all right. She takes a second step. Then a third. More until she is walking. Still, the sound of the crowd surrounds her. Voices even seem to come from nearby. *Can't be real. Some hallucination again. Something about being up in space. Maybe the weird gravity and recycled air are playing tricks on me – making my mind not work normally.*

A high-frequency pitch joins the low frequencies – the sound makes Tessa think of metal under stress.

What is that?

She wonders if it might be a hallucination, but the sound increases so loud and so quick she knows it can't only be her imagination.

It's coming from above me.

The sound of metal straining and scratching against itself echoes off the coliseum walls. Something big is failing. Something huge is about to fall on her.

The lights. The lighting rigs. The speakers above. It's going to fall on me.

Her lizard brain takes over.

Get out of here!

Pumping her arms and legs as fast as she can, Tessa runs.

The massive rig above her makes its last death cry as it breaks free. She can feel the air displaced between her and it.

It's going to crush me like a bug. I can't outrun it.

She tries. Gives it her everything. Runs at top speed. If she runs into a barrier wall, at least she'll be able to duck down. It might save her. It might be enough.

She trips.

Catching herself and recovering, she regains her stride.

It should have hit me by now.

A wall of sound thrusts toward her at Mach speed.

She ducks, drops, and rolls.

She hears something massive swing overhead.

Frigid air breezes just over the top of her head. *I'm hit. The pain just hasn't kicked in yet. That's the chill I feel.*

She is wrong; when she reaches up to touch her head, everything remains. Not a scratch. Lying on her back, looking upward, she expects to see the shape or outline of the rig – or whatever it'd been – that'd fallen.

She sees nothing. *Maybe it's still too dark to see.* Her eyes adjust enough. Finally, she believes. She is on the ground looking up, and she makes out the overall scope of the coliseum. *Maybe the light plays differently looking up from the floor. Maybe that's what's happening here.*

The lighting rig on the ceiling hasn't moved. Neither have the speakers. Nothing, in fact, seems to have fallen. She lifts her head a bit and looks around, as maybe it is some sort of rigging she isn't familiar with that has fallen. Again, Tessa spots nothing out of the ordinary.

She breathes out. Rises onto her elbows.

Tessa can't hear the crowd, nor the low and high frequencies. Instead? Blessed silence. The small footlights lining the staircases glow an ever-so-subtle shade of amber. *Didn't even see them come on.*

She believes maybe they've been on the entire time, but the sound has made her blind. *Now, why am I thinking that? And how could that even be?* It is all just her intuition, she knows, but something about what she's just experienced didn't seem right. *I feel like I'm going nuts on this ship. Or something is trying to make me go nuts.* She sits upright, then stands, perfectly able to see the barriers and the entryways to the stage and backstage areas. She makes her way. "I've got a requiem to play," she says. "And ain't nothing going to stop me."

As she walks past the first barrier, Tessa eyes the side of the stage. Similar to so many she's performed on; she feels at home enough to reach out and touch the platform. The smooth metal feels cool. "Here I am," she says, registering the many guide lights lit along its side. The racks of gear remain dark, but she recognizes many of their components as power amps and effects modules. She sees a mixing board and a computer station. "Bingo," she says. "Now we're playing with fire." Tessa throws her hands up. "Whole damn thing is right here. Ground Control to Major Tom."

The sound system comes to life.

The speakers buzz with an indistinct humming sound.

On the monitor, she sees a program to control the lights, opens it, and turns on the first lighting scene she sees. The stage lights in hues of yellow and red. The massive screen in back displays a graphic rendering of Eden. The Vita Nova logo spins round the bottom over and over. "This is it,"

Tessa says. "Wow." On her display, she sees the gigantic screen mirrored inside a small window. A low-key, new age music cue plays through the sound system. "Everything works. That was easy."

She thinks about how it'll be to play on the stage, DJing through one of her tracks for a crowd on board a floating station. She puts the file in and sees it on the screen. "All right," she says. "Let's start with the latest. When in Rome and all."

Tessa presses 'play', and her requiem starts.

She shuts her eyes.

Those first notes.

For a moment, they seem so ubiquitous. So reasoned. So simple and easy. That's before they slide into and out of one another, their tuning off by just a few cents.

Tessa opens her eyes and stands. *I want to hear this out there in the coliseum. Hear it echoing. Hear it loud, as it should be.*

Before she leaves the control area, she presses a button on the screen.

Broadcast.

The requiem will play through all the open channels on Eden. Everyone will hear the work.

I don't even need a password or authorization. It's like someone has already put me in the system with full access. Something new is coming. Someone knows I am already here.

"You're all going to hear it now," Tessa says as she makes it to the front of the stage, and ground zero for the speaker system.

The requiem plays, and all of the living, and all of the dead, listen.

Chapter Twenty-Eight

EDEN SATELLITE
ALPHA OUTPOST, MED BAY 1.001
16:26:36 UTC
17 MARCH 2112

"What's that sound?" Poole looks up from the bio scan toward the speakers over the door. "Sounds like music."
"It is," Sanjay says. "But where's it coming from? Who's playing it?"
The men regard one another for a moment. Poole nods. "Eden? What is the origin of this music?"
Instead of answering with her voice, Eden shows a text inside their display:

Our New Requiem.

"Tessa is playing this?" Poole clutches his stomach. There is something off about the frequency of some of the notes – they seem to cut right through his ears, his head, and his guts. He feels ill. The sound increases, further hurting his ears. "Can you lower it, please?" He looks over to Sanjay, who doesn't seem to be affected.
"You all right, Doc?" Sanjay asks.
"I think so," Poole says. "I should be, at least. It's...nothing." His body betrays him; he feels as though a flu is coming on. *What the hell?* The notes of the requiem blend in and out, and he feels drawn to the music, despite what he is sure it is doing to him. *Like I'm looking up at my executioner. Have to see his face.* The thoughts fill his mind while the melody plays. *This is far from lovely, although it should be. Confusing.*

He feels lost. The room seems to fade away as the music encompasses him. Poole believes he is floating. Believes he is drifting. Believes he is somehow immobilized and suspended within the grasp of the music. As ethereal as the requiem sounds, there is something not right. Strange sounds prod through the surface chords and notes – sounds that somehow hurt. Sounds that somehow scratch and claw at his inner ear and brain. Enough so that he feels his balance teeter.

"Doc?" Sanjay says as his face comes into focus. "You with me?"

Poole pulls through in time to catch himself from falling. He steps toward the couch and sits, holding his head in his hands. "It's like I have vertigo or something," Poole says. "It's come on out of nowhere. Do you hear anything weird about this music?" He hears his own voice, struggling for breath, which surprises him. *How can a piece of music be causing this? Must just be coincidental timing. Has to be. What else could it be?*

The requiem plays.

"Eden? Please stop the music." Poole puts his hands over his ears. He feels dizzy; it is almost as though he's developed an instant and intense sensitivity to sound. "Turn it off."

Instead of stopping the music broadcasting into the room, Eden increases the volume.

"No," Poole says. "Lower, not louder." He feels his heart quicken.

Sanjay also has his hands over his ears. "Yes. Eden. Stop it. Please."

The requiem plays louder.

Poole stands and notices Sanjay's pained expression. "It's getting to you, too. Let's get out of here right away." He hurries toward the door. Sanjay follows suit. "Maybe it won't be so bad out in the halls."

Outside the room, the requiem echoes. "Not as bad away from it," he says. "Better."

Sanjay nods. "Definitely better. Superb idea."

"The speakers have more space to fill out here," he says. "They're designed for announcements, not cranking music." Even as he speaks, the continual sound of the requiem still hurts, so he puts his hands back up over his ears.

"This is crazy," Sanjay says, his hands covering his own ears, too. "The music is hurting us."

"Something is definitely wrong with it," Poole says. He looks over to Sanjay and notices what appears to be a dark, horizontal wound at the top of his forehead.

The requiem intensifies; even though it plays softer, the frequencies and tones come through.

Sanjay's wound spreads as though an invisible knife circles his face. The uppermost opening splits and peels down.

Underneath, the darkest of blacks. A formless void from which light or thought cannot escape.

Poole feels his chest tense. Anxiety floods him from the point of his head to the base of his gut. *How do I fix this? I'm a doctor, after all, damn it! Think!*

Poole shuts his eyes to the darkness, to what is happening to Sanjay, and concentrates his thoughts. The music plays – its very frequencies affect him deep inside his body. He senses the nerve linking his ear to his neck pulsate. *It's like a migraine. Almost like this is working its way from inside me.*

He feels a pop in his right ear.

An upper high frequency becomes noisier.

Fluid flows from his ear. He hears a higher pitch. Crippling agony shatters inside his right ear canal. He clasps both hands over the area. He plunges to his knees, sure he will black out.

He attempts to keep his eyes shut but perceives a shadow move in front of him. Sanjay, or whatever he's become, hurries toward Poole. He wants to scream. To protest. To fight the monster. But he can't move from his kneeling position.

Sanjay closes in; he grips something long – something Poole is sure he is just about to be hit or impaled with.

But then something happens.

Sanjay rushes past Poole.

There is a loud crashing sound.

The requiem stops.

The corridor goes quiet.

Poole glances up as the shadow returns. He can focus. Sanjay is back to normal. No peeled-away flesh. No portals into the Nothingverse.

"Doctor," Sanjay says. "You're bleeding."

Poole only hears from his left ear. His right rings with an indefinite high pitch.

By instinct, he calls out, "Eden?"

There is no response.

He reaches out a hand and Sanjay assists him. "I need to get into the med bay and have my ear fixed. Pronto."

"Yes," Sanjay says, and they go.

As he puts himself down on the med bed, Poole catches the surrounding holo screens. Every one of them has gone dark.

"Eden?" he asks. "Talk to me."

There is no response.

"Eden?"

She remains silent.

Chapter Twenty-Nine

EDEN SATELLITE
MINARET OUTPOST
16:26:36 UTC
17 MARCH 2112

Ava doesn't hear the ship. The ubiquitous electrical buzz of screens and equipment hasn't permeated the prayer chamber. The minaret remains truly a place of peace. *No wonder Sanjay's always coming here.* There is something else – something very wrong. She knows what she is experiencing isn't the norm. "Eden?" she says and waits for the satellite to respond. It does not. *Maybe the comm is off here? Or maybe there just isn't one? But there should be. Especially for emergencies.* She calls out to the ship again and is once again ignored or unheard.

She steps out from the chamber and hurries inside the main passageway. Ava spots speakers and knows the ship must have been able to hear her. "Eden?" she calls. "You with me?"

No answer.

Nada.

She calls out to Eden again, projecting her voice. Ava waits a moment. Still, Eden does not reply.

"What the heck?" she says. Her heart feels cold. Something is very much the matter. At no time previously has Eden not answered her, no matter the time or place.

Ava pictures Roland. Glimpses from their time together camped out at the moon base roll through her memories. He'd held her close as they waited for the rescue pod to arrive. The chill of space had infiltrated her to the marrow, even worse than it'd felt during winters growing up in

Naperville. Even with the sun shining, the cold had permeated them. How she'd wished the sunrays could have warmed them. *They are just light.* Roland had fidgeted. "Don't see how we're going to be okay," he'd said.

"Keep still," she'd said, calming him. "Try not to panic. We're going to get out of this fine."

Be that person again who was steadfast. Find your strength. Find yourself in this.

She remembers where she is. *I'm at the minaret. I can figure this out. Something bad happened in the chamber. A malfunction. The life support system crashed or broke. It almost took out Sanjay. And what is it Eden said before she went offline? To check the light signatures. That there is an anomaly of some sort. An event that happened before it impacted the systems. Think.* She said there was a bright light. Its light signature equaled that of the Sun. Had to be solar wind or a solar flare or something along those lines. That's what happens when there are flares. That'd make sense. She knows Eden has shields, but they aren't impenetrable. Not by a long shot. *So much out here that we don't even comprehend, and so much we don't appreciate. How can we shelter ourselves from threats we can't even know exist?*

She hurries down the corridor, toward the central hallway. She stops at the enormous windows and looks out across Eden's horizon. Its surface appears so smooth and perfect. Its lines, unbroken. What else could she feel other than amazement? *Sometimes I forget how magnificent this entire thing is for me to be up here.* She thinks about how they might not do any inquiry regarding the light incident with Eden's principal system not answering. *Everything goes through that intelligence. Do we even have any manual control or access up here?* Ava thinks but cannot recall a single discussion or reading about how to change the systems over to manual mode. *What about our life support systems? If the satellite goes offline, we're in serious trouble. We utterly depend on Eden. Maybe we should figure out if we can override and go manual before we pursue anything else.*

She knows she'll need to recruit Poole and the others for the duty. It is essential. *Don't ask Vita Nova, though. They will jump to conclusions and think something is wrong. It'll be an even worse disaster. We can mitigate this. We can figure it out ourselves. We don't need anyone micromanaging us from the ground.*

Ava looks out across the stars, the Earth to her right, the sun coming from the left. She does her best to try to see the star, but it is out of her immediate view. "What are you sending our way?" she asks. A warmth spreads inside her, along with a sense of familiarity and déjà vu. "Where have I felt this before?"

She knows.

The moon outpost. Right before the systems had gone down.

Her heart nearly stops.

Ava remembers the way the Sun's rays had seemed to stretch and point toward them.

Night only comes every two weeks. Where are we on the axis? How much time until we're plunged into darkness? What will we do? How will anyone know?

Her heart speeds thinking about it. She situates her hand on her chest, as though it might ease her somehow.

No. Don't do this to yourself. There's no real correlation. It's all in your mind.

Then, a voice inside her speaks. *But isn't everything?*

She listens again, hoping to hear Roland's voice inside her. A memory of something profound he'd once said…something to comfort her and steer her right. Nothing comes. Instead, she recalls the faintest memory of the requiem. Somehow, it comes to mind. She steps away from the receiving entryway of the minaret. "Not surprised," she says. "I'm living in a floating graveyard, after all. What else would I be hearing?"

Ava hurries away.

The requiem is not only playing inside her head; the piece also plays through Eden's speakers.

Ava feels tense. Her right ear twinges as the notes cascade and grow.

"Eden?" she asks. "Are you with me? Can you hear me?"

The ship does not reply.

"Hello?" she asks. "Poole? Sanjay? Midori? Anyone hear me?"

No response.

Eden is malfunctioning. This is very, very bad.

The requiem grows in volume just as its notes intensify. Ava cups her ears as the sound hurts. *Like an out-of-tune piano mic'd up and played loud through a PA or something.*

"Eden!" she cries out. "Can you please turn off this music?"

No response.

Ava hurries toward the next corridor, which she hopes has no speakers, or that they might be far enough away so as not to be as uncomfortable. "Move a muscle," she says. "Move a thought. Get this music out of my head, damn it."

She's misjudged.

The sound in the next corridor feels louder. Much more. She hears the sound deep inside her ears. Behind her eardrums. Rattling the bones in her ears. Down what feels like a stem of nerves running into her neck. Going to her heart. Short-circuiting her.

The pressure and sound increase, seemingly coming from within her own body. She puts her hands over her ears and crouches down, but it is not enough to stop the onslaught.

She screams. Screams Eden's name for it to stop. Screams for her crewmates. Screams for the hell to pass.

Chapter Thirty

EDEN SATELLITE
COLISEUM
16:46:36 UTC
17 MARCH 2112

"Everybody's listening," Tessa says. "Say 'hello' to the entire universe, requiem." She sits on the lip of the stage and looks out, imagining the arena filled with a rapt audience. *Who is listening to this right now?* She thinks about her crewmates first. Ava. Dr. Poole. Sanjay. Midori. *Wonder if it's...moving them.*

She still aches from earlier but stands and raises her arms triumphantly toward the arena as if she is playing for an immense crowd. The requiem's volume swells, as does its overall intensity.

When she shuts her eyes, she imagines her other audience.
Five thousand dead interred on this ship.
Reanimated through memories.
Can they hear this?
Is it getting through to them, too?

She pictures the dead filling the arena, propped up in chairs, their heads barely able to remain upright. Their bodies are wrapped in white cloth, like togas. *It's like Ancient Greece or Rome or Pompeii. A floating city in space, filled with the dead.*

Tessa spots some reacting. Moving. Waking from their eternal slumber. Her music revived them.

The dead stand, moved by the requiem.

It is hers. All hers.

They want to be near her, the music's creator, so they crowd toward the front of the stage. She gazes into their blank faces. Some have eyes changing from white to red.

They're coming back to life. Their souls are returning to their bodies. The music is doing this.

The dead reach up, their fingers spreading, craving her touch.

Tessa turns around and puts her arms up again. She falls backward toward the crowd.

Crowd surfing like at Hyde Park.

Their hands do not catch her. There are no hands. She falls through them as though they aren't there. The requiem climaxes.

The music stops.

Tessa hears a buzzing sound.

She sees black for a moment, then white before her eyes adjust. She's fallen right on the arena floor. *How'd I let myself do that? Thought I was just imagining the dead?*

She leans up on her elbows.

Why doesn't my head hurt? How come nothing hurts? Didn't I just fall off the stage?

Touching her scalp and head, Tessa feels fine. *It's like I just fell asleep out there or something. So weird. Makes no sense at all, does it? What...happens?*

As she looks around the arena, she feels everything move as though she were on a boat. She puts her hands down to steady herself, but the feeling persists. *We're not supposed to feel the movements of the orbit here. Something is wrong.* Her chest feels tight. *Eden is failing. That's what's happening.*

She sees trails following the lights when she moves her head. Her eyes feel fuzzy and tight, as though she might be suffering an allergic reaction. To what, she isn't sure.

Not an allergic reaction. Nope. Probably got a concussion. Doesn't take much of a hit to the head to qualify for one, and with the thinner air up here, I bet that's what this is. I'm already seeing things, aren't I? Tessa pictures the audience of the dead she's just tried to crowd surf over.

Her eyelids feel heavy, and she can't stave off shutting them for a moment and putting her head back down. The arena seems to spin around her; she feels like a dreidel.

Chapter Thirty-One

MOON
OUTPOST M-613
07:26:36 UTC
8 January 2110

Shadows creep inside the outpost like long, dark alien fingers. Ava feels all the air go out from her lungs. She nudges Roland. "Won't be long now until we're in everlasting night for two weeks," she says. "This is not good. We don't even know if anyone realizes we're stranded."

"They should have some idea," Roland says. "Not sure how they'll be able to get to us in time. We're going to have to make this work with what we have."

"We're not set up for this," Ava says. "Most of the supplies are gone. We don't have enough oxygen or fuel."

Roland nods. "Miracles happen. I'm not giving up hope."

They watch the last rays of sunlight dim over the horizon. The temperature inside the outpost drops. They look out into the vastness of space, their view of Earth obscured. "It's like we're floating inside nothing," Ava says. "It's like we aren't tied down to anything and we can just drift away into the dark."

"We won't just vanish," he says. "We're going to make it through this. Somehow."

The first few days seem fine. They keep resources down as much as possible. They keep most lights off and set the thermostat as low as they can stand. "Thank God for moon blankets," she says.

★ ★ ★

"We're going to survive by breathing in oxygen fumes," Roland says.

"How are we going to do that?" Ava asks. Her hands tremble and she feels weak. A migraine forms in an instant. *I want to believe he's right.*

"Our sleeping bags," he says. "That bunk room is our best bet. They have oxygen canisters inside them. They zip up airtight."

"Right," she says. "Feeling this pretty hard." Her temples feel like pressure points.

"Yes," Roland says. "Now. Let's go. I have a comm with me." He looks her in the eye. "We're going to be okay. I know in my heart that we're going to get through this. Promise."

"Yes," Ava says. He hurries away, and she follows. The main living quarters smell strange, kind of like rotten fruit. *Is that what space smells like? It's getting inside here fast.*

The sleeping room is only ten steps in any direction. The entire base's living area is no larger than a two-bedroom apartment, thankfully. Once they are inside the room, Roland rushes past their beds and opens the closet. He quickly grabs and unrolls two silver bundles, each a sleeping bag. He unzips the one on her bed. "Get inside," he says, but doesn't have to.

Ava slips in, her head pounding. *The air is escaping. What about the lack of air pressure? Won't that be an enormous problem?* She looks and sees the bedroom door shut. *Did I even do that? I must have. Don't remember. Just. A habit. A good one.*

She knows it will seal the room off. They all did when the doors were closed. That'd keep whatever oxygen remains inside. She wonders if the base is designed so it'll pump more in, somehow, and if it can filter out the carbon dioxide from their breathing. Would the sleeping bags do the same? She doesn't think they can. *But it'll buy us time. Maybe time enough to figure this out. Maybe not enough for a rescue team to reach us. Definitely not from Earth, but maybe from one of the satellites.*

"The compound has been breached. Debris broke through the shields," Roland says.

"A space rock," she says. "Not like the moon doesn't have craters, and this is unheard of."

"The shields don't work," he says. "That's for sure."

"How long will we have," Ava asks, "before the air runs out?"

Roland slips inside his own sleeping bag. "I don't know," he says. "A week? Maybe a little more? We have to have faith they'll be able to rescue us by then. Or figure something out." He nods. "Zip up."

Inside the bag, Ava smells plastic and rubber. There is a clear shield in front of their faces on each of their bags so they can look out. *This is like being inside a coffin. Hope they don't turn out to be our graves.* Her heart races at the thought. *Crap. Very well could be. Need to breathe. Remember your training. Don't let your emotions sideline you.* Ava takes a few deep breaths. *Think. Think. Think. First things first. Find the air. Make sure it's working.* She locates the small canister along the inside and turns the dial. It comes to life, the assuring sound of air flowing from one side. "It's like when you go diving," she says. "But those tanks don't last so long."

"Right," he says. "These will last longer than diving tanks, but not forever. Let's try to stay calm and keep our talking to a minimum. Less air."

"Makes sense," she says. *Thank God we can still hear and see each other through the shields.* "Did you find your air?" They're lying on their sides, face to face.

He nods. As handsome as she finds him – Ava still thinks his high cheekbones are just majestic – in that moment, Roland looks like a little boy to her. Scared. Lost. Unsure. Emotions she's never seen from him before.

Ava nods back. She shuts her eyes. *Use your meditation. Use all those tools now. If you stay calm, you can and will make it out of this. Otherwise? You won't.*

She opens her comm and navigates to the emergency message section. She writes:

Moon base zero-seven has suffered a breach. We are both safe for now, but we are in sleeping suits as oxygen has been compromised. We need immediate rescue.

She waits for what feels like forever. Maybe only a minute until someone answers:

Roger.

She types again:

Time is of the essence. We may only have a few days of oxygen, if that.

Vita Nova Corp writes back:

Roger that. We are on the line with the Eden crew. Hoping they can assist.

She writes:

please hurry

At the top of the message, she notices she's copied Roland. She looks up from the comm screen and their eyes meet. She nods. He puts a thumbs-up toward her. They'll have to wait and hope like hell someone might be able to get to them.

★ ★ ★

Three days pass.

"We sent a signal to the Earth right before the moon rotated too far for it to go through," Ava says. "We still haven't heard back."

"That was days ago now," Roland says. "We're too far in for a signal to reach us. You'd think there'd be a way with all this technology."

Ava checks their levels. "It's worse than we thought," she says. "We don't even have a week. Maybe three days before everything runs out."

He shakes his head. "There has to be something."

"All of our long-term supplies are gone," she says. "You know that. We're on reserves right now."

"Maybe they'll be able to get to us," he says.

"You know full well the resources they'd need to make a launch," Ava says. "It takes months, just practically speaking, to get a rocket and a transport ready, let alone getting through all the politics. Do you think we'll be worth it to them?"

"I hope so. It'd look terrible if they didn't at least attempt to rescue us," Roland says. "But what do I know? Maybe the world still hates on us mixed skins."

Ava groans. "I hope that doesn't come into play. I'm more worried they haven't told anyone outside of Vita Nova. They could make something up to cover their tracks. No one would know. They'd save billions of dollars." Ava scans their chamber. "Maybe it's time to take the little black triangle pills," she says. "Go out painlessly."

"No way," Roland says. "We have one last option."

"Stasis," she says. "I know. But we don't know if we have enough for it to work. It's never been tested in the actual world."

"We'd have a chance, Ava. Maybe our only one."

She nods. "We'd have to run the system and see when we'd have to enact that to make sure we have enough resources."

"Twenty-two hours from now," he says. "That's the point where we wouldn't be able to start hyper sleep anymore. We won't have enough oxygen or power, otherwise. The sooner we go in, the more time we could have on the back end."

"How long would it extend the air?" she asks.

"Maybe a week. Ten days on the outside," Roland answers.

"It's a lot to put our bodies through for such a brief period," Ava says.

"The option is to stay awake and be sure to perish in three days," he says.

"But if they don't come for us, we'll die in our sleep," she says.

"Sounds more preferable to me than suffocating," Roland says. "At least we'd have hope. Once we're under, there's the preliminary signal that will be sent down, and then the monitoring system will turn on and automatically send our biometrics down in real time."

"They'll know we're under," she says. "And they'll know if we're alive or dead."

"Right," he says. "If we can just make it to the next rotation when the signal can be sent down. This could save us."

She nods. "We don't have a choice, do we?"

"No," he says. "Not if we want a chance of survival."

★ ★ ★

"We're not supposed to be here." Ava hunkers deeper into their cot. Out the circular window, shadows creep along the moon base. Light dims as they graze the habitat. "It's happening. We're going into the night. Twenty-eight days and change."

"They're coming," Roland says. "Of course, they'll be here to check on us. They're alerted."

"I don't know. We have to send a message. Have to find a way. Without sunlight and without a direct signal now? We're marooned."

"We can't believe they don't know, and we can't know for sure they didn't receive what we've already sent multiple times."

"Then where are they?" Ava asks.

"We both know it's not a quick process to get up here, even if they need to," Roland says. "We have to find a way to survive. That's all there is to it. We don't have a choice."

"We don't. You're right. We need to stay warm. Keep oxygen low. Figure out food," she says.

"Yes," Roland says.

She cuddles him closer. Doesn't want to do the math about their situation; Ava knows the numbers aren't looking good.

"The oxygen smells like metal," Ava says. Roland leans down and kisses her forehead, then her lips.

"I know," he says. "It's winding down out here. I love you. I will see you on the other side. Pinky promise."

Roland puts out his pinky, and she puts out hers. They curl them around one another.

"Pinky promise," she says, smiling. "I love you."

He nods. They unlatch their fingers. Roland straightens from bending over the chamber. He lowers the chamber's top. Their eyes meet. He nods and mouths, *It's going to be okay.* In a blink, he is on his way toward the chamber next to hers.

The air inside the chamber feels lighter and nowhere near as fresh as she is used to. *It's like the air from the respirator when we SCUBA.* She feels lightheaded right away. *Won't be long now. Sure as hell hope this isn't the end.* She looks over toward Roland's chamber and sees him climbing inside. She tries to stay awake long enough to catch a last glance, but she grows too tired. The sleeping gas is too strong. Her eyes look upward, and she sees the small rectangular port window over their main desk. Outside, she sees pitch black, the stars barely visible.

If this is the last thing I see...

Every part of her feels cold, as if she's made of ice. She wants to shiver, but she can't move. Not even an involuntary reaction. She drifts away.

If this is the last thing I feel...

★ ★ ★

Light rays wake Ava. They stream through the porthole window. *That was fast. I didn't even dream.* She looks for signs of a ship or rescuers. *Have they come for us? Is that what I'm seeing?* She sees none. *It's the sun shining in, that's all. We've at least made it this far.* She turns her head. Everything hurts. *If they haven't come for us, then why am I awake?* She thinks for a moment. *The system is winding down, then. That's what this means. We're almost out of time. This will be the last hurrah.* A second sliver of light stretches across the floor. *Light? Now where's that coming from?*

Scanning the room for the source, she expects to find something they'd forgotten to turn off, or something Roland turned on before he fell asleep. She calls his name. Doesn't see him. *He's in the bathroom. That's all.*

Light comes from outside. From the window.

She racks her brain trying to think what it might be. *All the exterior lights should be off. We're just going into a long period of night for two weeks. This isn't making any sense.*

The light grows from a sliver to something wider. She spots it reflecting off more than just the floor as it brightens. It's as though someone were shining a light on them.

The rescue has come. It's a ship.

Ava hops up and out of bed. "Roland?" she calls. "Where are you?" Her eyes tune in. She checks her watch, set to Universal Time to maintain their biorhythms. She notes it as 16:18:27 UTC. She knocks at the bathroom door and calls for him. He doesn't answer. Her stomach twists. Something isn't right. Her head aches and her hearing changes from clear to muffled.

"Where are you, love?" Hearing her own voice sounds strange; she doesn't recognize its timbre as hers.

Roland doesn't respond.

Ava turns her head forward to see where the light is coming from.

Light fills the entire window as though something nearby is the source. *How can that be? There's nothing out here. The Sun is...millions of miles away.* For a moment, she believes maybe it could be lights from a rescue spacecraft.

No. Too organic. It looks like something...else.

More light fills the habitat. An impossible amount, she thinks, even for a rescue craft.

She opens the bathroom door. It is empty.

Ava twists and scans the habitat. It's small enough to see everything in one glance. He's not anywhere.

Turning toward the light coming through the window, Ava shields her eyes. *Maybe he's already on the ship with them. But...how?*

The lights change and move in organic shapes, making Ava believe the porthole has turned into some sort of lava lamp or screen saver. It hasn't, she knows. *Something is outside doing this.*

She hears sounds...dissonant, strange sounds, like the voices of unknowable beings crying out. They blend, harmonize, making otherworldly music. Ava feels hypnotized by the sounds.

A voice inside her speaks.

Yes.
I.
Am.
Here.

Ava's pulse quickens.
"Who?" she asks. "Roland?" She knows it's not him.

Me.
Me.
Me.

"Are you the rescue ship?" she asks, hoping.

I.
Am.
Here.
And.
You.
Are.
Found.

There's a knock on the window.
She sees his hand.
How?
Roland's hand.
She jumps.
I must be dreaming.
She squints to try to see better through the brightness.
He's there, outside and silhouetted against the light bloom. She doesn't see his helmet. He's wearing his regular fatigues.
"Roland?"

He backs away from the outpost, toward the light. She can't see his face. Can't see his eyes. Can only see his outline, and that fades into the bloom as though he is being swallowed. He disappears. The light blooms brighter as he's absorbed. Ava makes out long, thin shapes in the light, which move in twists and coils.

The bloom rises off the surface and travels back and away from the outpost until it, too, fades into the cosmos.

Those are the Crests. The things some astronauts have talked about that are sometimes drawn to work on the moon. Harmless. Crestocilio magnopus. But they shouldn't be able to take a human? They're like wisps of light. Doesn't make sense.

Ava stands in the dark, staring out the window.

"That didn't just happen," she says. "I'm dreaming. Dreaming. That's all."

She stands for a long time, waiting for the daydream to break. It never does.

The lights dim, and Ava somehow makes her way back to her bed and falls into slumber. She does not experience darkness, but a comforting, amber light.

She thinks, *The music of the heavens plays.*

★ ★ ★

Ava wakes to flashlights in her eyes. Strange faces look at her, checking her vitals. "Are you okay?"

Ava is packed up and brought onto another craft.

India sent the rescue team. They had a rocket in place. The world had come together as one as the news of their being marooned spread.

Only one astronaut of Moon Outpost 13 is saved, though. Me. The next several months are a blur. Ava returns home internationally known, but all alone.

Vita Nova tells the press Roland perished in a terrible explosion. Every time Ava hears the story, she sees glimpses of what happened.

Light. The wall of the outpost rips away. Roland's capsule pulls out, its cover opening, his unconscious body slipping out. His limbs move as though he were suspended in water. Behind him, a great and strange living light. He disappears inside, but before he does, his eyes open and he sees Ava. Looks right into her soul. Right before oblivion.

It was not an explosion.

It was something else.

Something took him.

One day, I'm going to find out what it is.

Until then? I'll have to learn to live again. Somehow. Without him. Without my everything.

Chapter Thirty-Two

EDEN SATTELITE
MINARET OUTPOST UNIT, HALL W-07
16:46:36 UTC
17 MARCH 2112

Ava hears the music getting louder as she walks down the hallway away from the temple. "It's the requiem Tessa composed," she says. Hearing her own voice in the hall startles her; the sound comes out much louder than she would have believed.

The music's volume increases. One frequency hurts her ears, especially Ava's right one.

I need to get back to Poole and whoever is still up and around.

She feels eyes on her. Someone, she realizes, is watching her.

"Poole?" she asks. No reply. All she hears is the strains of the new requiem. "Sanjay?"

She hurries. *Come on. Don't linger. Get out of here.*

The music becomes louder and further hurts her ears. The corresponding frequency bores deeper, as though it drills inside her ear canal and presses up against her eardrum.

She cups her right ear, but the frequency seems to go right through her hand. Somehow, it seems to permeate her from every direction.

It hurts worse.

How can I turn off the speakers here? Is there some kind of a switch? Something I can press?

"Eden?" she pleads. "Please...turn off the music."

Ava knows Eden won't regard her, but she must try. She doesn't know what else to do.

"Eden," she cries. "Please!"

Her footsteps fumble. The pain becomes excruciating. She clamps both hands to her ears in a vain effort to stave off the sounds.

"No. No. No."

She presses on, knowing if she makes it back to Poole and the others, she'll at least have a chance. They might put her in one of the isolation rooms where there is no communication. That means no speakers. No music. No requiem.

Her sight blurs and dims.

Keep going. Carry on.

Everything blends. After a few minutes, the walls seem to look the same. Ava doesn't spot any of the expected visual landmarks on her way.

Ava walks faster, but it is of no use. Every step feels worse than the last. "I'm lost," she says, her breath nearly gone. Pulling out her comm link, Ava guesses it still won't be working, even though she's traveled for several minutes. She is right. "Now what?"

Think.

The requiem plays even louder from hidden speakers nearby. Notes stretch into long erratic drones. The music appears to pull thin and stretch, its solid form ripping and tearing. *How is this damn thing still playing?*

"Eden?" she calls out with every bit of desperation. "Can you please stop the music and get me to my outpost?"

Eden doesn't reply. Again, Ava doesn't believe she'll get a reply, but she must at least try something. While she does, the walls change color; the panels are much darker than she's seen anywhere else on Eden.

"Now, where in hell am I?" she asks. "How did I get so turned around?"

Ava doesn't recognize the area. *How can this be something so different? I've walked this so many times. It makes little sense. This corridor should just be a straight shot.*

A new high-pitched note sustains, its tone wavers ever so slightly. She hears other sounds…if they are music, they are of a strange and foreign type.

The pitch lodges inside her right ear, adding to the spinning drill sensation already working through her. She puts her palm up and cups her ear, but the sound has somehow made it inside and has taken up root. *How is this even possible?*

It hurts.

Then the ache travels down the nerve behind her ear, and burrows inside her lower jaw and teeth. She feels it travel all the way down and lodge inside her chest, surrounding her heart. All within a split second.

Walls close in.

Getting louder, the music inside her doubles down.

Immense pressure builds inside her ear canal.

This isn't real. Can't believe it.

The pain disputes her theory; it forces her to her knees.

Ava screams.

The walls move. The pipes make clanging sounds as they pop free from their cuffs.

"What the hell is happening?" she cries. "Eden? Poole? Sanjay? Can anyone hear me?" From her knees, she drops to her stomach. *I'm going to die. My head will explode.*

The very piping of Eden stretches and moves. It breaks free and moves like limbs searching for something to grab. The ends split into small, bio-metallic tendrils. Each razor-sharp tip glides through the spaces between the thing being made and Ava.

The hallway's roof splits in two, then breaks upward as more levels open. Bits from each level gather and form, taking the shape of a body.

Ava gasps.

Eden is coming alive.

The sound circles inside her head and she is sure her skull will explode.

In the pieces, she sees a face, eyes made from screens, a maw made of ripped carbonite, teeth born of bone. Connective tissue brings the machined parts together. *Where is this all coming from?*

She knows, though. Knows the moment she sees Eden revealing its form. *From the interred, that's where. It's using all their pieces.*

Eden looks down on her. The ship has broken away around it, leaving a cavernous silo surrounding them. When she looks down, she sees the vastness of the ship. With the levels torn to their frames, Ava peers down dozens of stories until they become nothing but a black pool. *How many thousands of meters? We are almost as big as the moon, right? It's like looking deep down into the ocean.*

Her heart races.

She tries to move, but nothing cooperates.

The pain is such that it makes her feel disconnected from her own body.

I'm going to die. It's going to push me down into the abyss and I'll be all swallowed up. Just like that.

Eden bends down, its cyborg face stopping inches from hers. Ava scans the screens but sees nothing but electronic light. *There is no soul there.*

All colors.

Every color.

Swirling.

The white lights of Eden's eyes give way to something else: something *other*.

Something very much alive.

The light warms her from within, somehow, impossibly, touching her the same way as the new requiem.

"I…know…you."

She remembers the same phenomena the day they rescued her from Outpost 13.

She recognizes it, too, as the same sound she heard just outside the window of the minaret room.

"You…have…come…for…me."

Eden's limbs close in, their sharp tips ready to slice her.

The high-pitch sound's pressure increases. Her pain is unimaginable. She looks into the organic, swirling lights emanating from Eden's eyes. *Hold on if you can. Don't give in. Don't pass out.*

Her body has other plans.

Ava goes dark.

While she is out, she dreams of the thousands of souls interred on Eden. Ava pictures herself traveling past the many windows facing the outside of Eden. She looks into their lost faces, their eyes shut, their chins down, all bathed in cool blue light. All of them, just names. Just numbers. Just objects. *So many faces. So many lives. So many memories are being harvested. For what? For whom? What about my own? One day they'll just be blips for someone else to look at. They won't be real anymore. My memories won't be alive anymore. They'll be dead, like so many others up here.*

Ava dreams herself falling away from Eden, tumbling and spinning into space, the floating graveyard getting farther away by the second. For a while, she sees the Earth behind Eden, until that, too, disappears and she is surrounded by infinite darkness.

Ava floats inside nothing.

She floats for what feels like an eternity, but it feels also, somehow, like only a moment. *Where is this place? Where have I gone? What has Eden done to me?*

She knows, though, that it isn't Eden in charge. Something else discovered her.

The light. The swirling, strange lights. That's where all this is coming from.

She pictures the mass, and it appears in front of her. They float within the abyss; she looks at it and the light looks back.

"I...know...you," she says. "I...don't...know...you."

The mass changes color, as if it hears and understands.

"What do you want from me? From any of us?"

She doesn't hear a voice talk back but sees images inside her thoughts that she doesn't think have come only from her recollection. Again, the countless images of the interred speed past her. Each person has light of its own surrounding it...being pulled from it. Ava knows. "That's their memories being taken out," she says. "Like getting water from a stone. That's what you want. That's why you came."

The light seems to hear her and turns impossibly bright. It flashes for a moment, and even in her dream state, Ava must shield her eyes.

When it dims, she sees the being in front of her has turned from light into dark. She needs to squint, as its darkness blots the void behind, like a dull and dark circular matte.

"You want their memories, too, don't you?" she asks. "That's why you're here. You're feeding off them."

At that, the being glows slightly. She's right. It brightens even more.

"How are you doing this?" she asks. "Where are you getting…"

A trail of multicolored light stretches between them. "You're taking it from me, that's what." She tries to wave it away. "But I'm not ready. I'm not dead yet."

The light stream subsides, and along with it, the scene. Ava's energy feels drained, and she shuts her eyes. "Not. Ready. Yet." For a moment, Ava senses nothing. A moment later, she feels the tips of her fingers touch together.

Pulling back inside her body, Ava feels herself re-inhabit her own flesh and blood. Her eyes flicker, and the world inside Eden draws back into focus. She comes back from her vision – of seeing the being made from light. *It's the same thing I've seen several times at these moments, isn't it? That's the thing that visited me and Roland at Outpost 13. It's the same thing I saw earlier, and now again. There's something to it. Got to be real. Some kind of…thing…we've never planned for. We always thought other life would be like us. We were wrong.*

She has no idea how long she's been out. She has no point of reference. When she looks at her watch, it's only a minute later than when she last checked. *Impossible.*

Midori is staring down at her. She speaks, but Ava can't hear a peep. *What the heck? Thought she's out of commission? Wonder what happened. They must have fixed whatever went wrong.*

As she settles back into consciousness, Ava notices the hallway looks the same as it ever has. The Eden cyborg thing is nowhere to be seen. The hallway has apparently suffered no damage.

Something else?

The requiem has stopped playing. In fact, she hears no sound at all. *Was I dreaming that entire episode?* She knows she couldn't have been, though. *It's what caused me to see this stuff. There's got to be a correlation. And there's got to be a correlation between the requiem and seeing those lights again, too. There just has to be.*

Midori grasps her hand and helps Ava rise from the floor into a sitting position; she realizes she can't hear any of their movements. Her right shoulder feels wet. She puts a hand to her ear, expecting blood, but only comes away with a cool, viscous fluid. She spots little bits inside the fluid in her hand. Small, machined electronic bits. *Parts left from Eden when it changed into that monster?*

But no. *Eden didn't really change, did it? I was seeing things.* She looks back down at the miniature pieces in her hand. She doesn't recognize them. *What the heck is this? It feels like my ear is being stabbed by a sewing needle. How come there's no blood? Only this. Makes no sense at all.*

She shows the little pieces to Midori, who again says something Ava can't hear. "I can't hear you," Ava says. "I've lost my hearing."

Midori doesn't say a word and just stares at Ava. She puts up her hands in defeat.

Ava shrugs and puts the pieces inside her jacket pocket for safekeeping. "Let's see if there's anything else," Ava says. "Then we need to go back to Poole, okay?"

Midori nods.

Searching the nearby floor for more, she and Midori find two more small radial-shaped pieces. Ava grabs them and puts them inside her pocket with the others. She stands. Sore from the experience, she stumbles to find her footing. The world around her remains silent.

She points to her ears to show Midori. "I'm still deaf," she says. "I don't know what happened."

Midori remains surprised.

Ava rubs her ears, but it does nothing to bring back her hearing.

What the hell? Something happened to me. Something definitely happened here. I don't know what, but I'm going to find out.

Her heart beats fast. *I can't be deaf. It's only temporary. It'll come back. Just some sort of trauma. Or attack. Something.*

Midori leads them away.

As they hurry, the corridors once again look familiar.

Something inside the music...something inside the requiem did this to me. Something about that light being there at all these crucial moments...there's a connection.

They see the light of their outpost as they approach.

Ava rubs her ears. *I can see, but I can't hear.*

Chapter Thirty-Three

EDEN SATELLITE
COLISEUM
16:48:36 UTC
17 MARCH 2112

Snippets of the requiem dance inside Tessa's mind like remnants. Behind her, she hears clanging noises. At first, she thinks the sound might be just the normal life of the satellite: water moving through pipes, heating and cooling systems adjusting, sensors scanning the environment. As she walks away from the coliseum, though, it increasingly sounds like footsteps. *Who can follow me up here who I don't already know?*

Tessa follows the small guide lights mapping the corridors.

A loud sound booms behind her; she pictures a colossal metal weight dropping to the floor. *It's one of them...one of the people buried up here.*

She looks over her shoulder but sees nothing immediately. *Of course not. They're hiding. Waiting until the last minute to grab me. Put me in one of those chambers alive.*

Walking faster, she searches for the area where she can pick up the transport train.

She realizes she is being unreasonable. Illogical. A person's vitals are always scanned thoroughly before they're put into suspension. If there are any signs of life...it's canceled. Not that any cases of that happening would have ever leaked out.

"No," she says. "There can always be mistakes. Nothing is perfect."

Footsteps behind her.

"Hello?" she says, hoping to hear Ava or Poole answer.

More footsteps. So many it may not be only one person. There are many people, she knows.

"What do you want?"

She turns again but doesn't see a soul. She realizes she can't see the main doors of the coliseum. The corridor has curved just enough, making it impossible to see behind her.

Waiting a moment to see if anything moves…a clue to what is causing the footsteps… Tessa feels lost.

As soon as she faces forward and walks, the sound of the footsteps returns.

Is it the sound of my own feet?

She pauses. The sound pauses. She steps once, hard, but finds the sound does not match the ones she hears.

"Okay, then."

When she walks, her footsteps are matched with whispers.

I'm going crazy. That's what's happening, isn't it? Got to be.

She shuts her eyes, trying to shut out what is happening. Or what appears to be happening.

It doesn't work.

Forget this.

She hurries.

The footsteps hurry with her. So do the whispers.

The walls appear distorted, as though she is seeing them through heat waves. *What the…?*

A piece of track moves, springing upward in front of her. The thin piece bends and breaks, its end splitting into several smaller flanges.

Tessa halts.

Eden is coming apart.

Whispers turn into screams…like industrial machines about to explode.

Pieces of the walls change and break free until they, too, seem to reach for her. The corridor morphs into what she believes looks like a basket of snakes.

She glances backward, hoping to retreat, but is met with a similar vision, as the area behind her has also come to life.

Fight or flight. Here we go again.

She bows down and faces the direction away from the coliseum once more. Knowing she has no way to fend off the menacing pieces pointed her way, Tessa looks for a way out. She spots a small opening to her left, maybe just enough to get through if she is quick.

Something grazes her back.

One of the pieces.

It is going to cut her. Slice into her. Go inside her.

She bolts, an instinctive noise escaping her mouth, sounding like half a scream and half a sigh.

Lunging forward, Tessa puts her hands out, her every gesture working on instinct. She finds herself face-deep inside the dark bundle of moving parts.

The pieces touch her, their weight and strength apparent.

They're going to cut me into a million pieces.

She pushes through.

On the other side, the hallway appears normal.

Her lunge turns into a run.

Around her, the ship comes alive, its frameworks springing and jerking to life, trying to catch up with her.

She screams.

Her lungs feel made of fire, her body like liquid rubber.

"Come on. Come on."

She leans into her run as much as she can. *Separate your body from your mind. Push or you're going to die.*

The high pitch she'd heard earlier returns, louder.

Ahead of her, the corridor seems endless. Eden catches up, its panels and plumbing shaking and sprouting free.

If I don't make it out of here, I'm dead.

Tessa runs as fast as she can.

The corridor blurs. The high-pitched noise blurs. Her exhaustion fades as though it has left her and floated away.

Go. Go. Go.

She rounds a corner and sees an opening – a doorway.

Almost.

The sound of the ship coming alive becomes deafening, as metal snaps and bangs.

She tilts her head upward, a grimace of pain spreading as she pushes herself to her utmost limit.

Only a few steps from the door, she shuts her eyes. Her body will give out soon. *Please let there be a safe place away from this.*

The pitch grows higher and louder. She needs to cover her ears, but she knows she doesn't have the luxury.

Tessa makes it out from the corridor and through the door.

Her feet feel light. Her entire body feels made of cotton. She can't feel her hands or her feet on the ground. She makes to keep running but meets no resistance.

Falling.

She sees no light, dropping into pitch black.

She screams with all she has as she falls and falls and falls.

Chapter Thirty-Four

EDEN SATELLITE
ALPHA OUTPOST, MED BAY 1.0007
16:48:36 UTC
17 MARCH 2112

"Can you hear me?" Sanjay leans over Dr. Poole. "How are you feeling?"

Poole made a so-so gesture with his hand. "Only my left ear seems to work," he says. "My right one is almost totally gone. There's a high pitch, like tinnitus."

Ava stares at them from her own med bed, where she sits upright. Sanjay believes she is trying to read their lips. "How are you doing?" Sanjay asks Ava.

She shakes her head and says, "Nothing. I can't hear you at all. I can't hear anything."

Sanjay makes his way over toward Ava. He takes out a pad and writes. "Implants," he says as he writes the word down. "Cochlear implants. That's what those pieces were." He circles the word 'cochlear' for her.

Ava shrugs. "They can't be mine. I never got them."

"Sometimes they do them at birth now," he says. She doesn't follow, so he writes: *At birth. Standard upgrade. Usually not even mentioned. Poole had one in his right ear. You had them in both ears.*

She goes pale.

Midori hurries to the sink and starts a cup of water.

"Makes no sense," Ava says. "How come it never came up in any medical records?"

"It had," he says. "And it has." He produces a folder with her bio charts. He points toward a series of numbers down at the bottom, each separated by commas. He singles one out:

1429LR

"That's code for cochlear implants, left and right," Sanjay says. "Poole's says 1429R, which is common."

She shakes her head.

"I think that's what saved both your lives," he says. "The implants broke. Took the brunt of the frequency."

Ava nods. "I didn't catch most of that. I can't hear, remember. You're going too fast." Midori hands Ava the water, which she sips. "Can't she do something to help?"

"I can use one of my displays to translate speech into text," Midori says. She puts out her left arm, slides back a small panel, revealing a small rectangular screen. It lights and displays the last phrase Sanjay spoke.

Ava reads it. "That makes sense," she says. "And really glad you're back in action, Midori."

"Me, as well," Midori says.

"Does it hurt at all?" Sanjay asks.

"No," Ava says.

"Mine hurts," Poole says.

Sanjay turns. "Yours were an older model. More integrated into your organism. More…primitive."

"I see," Poole says. "And the only big problem with all of this isn't that we can't fix them and get new ones. It's that we don't have the means up here on Eden to do such a procedure, especially being that we'd need the proper parts and materials. We don't even have full power and access to the computer now. We're just going to have to get through this."

Ava reads what Poole says. "Yes," she says. "By the way? Where is Tessa?"

"We don't know," Sanjay says, his words also appearing on Midori's screen. "We last saw her at the coliseum. That's where she is broadcasting her music from. She walked out of there an hour ago and then went off the grid."

"The coliseum?" Ava says. "That's literally miles from here. How did she get there?"

"She figured out how to use the transport rails," Sanjay says.

"And they worked?" Ava says.

"Apparently," Sanjay says.

Ava looks back to Midori. "I imagine we've used all means to try to contact her?"

"Yes," Midori says. "She hasn't replied."

Ava sighs. "That's not good," she says. "And the music…there's something inside the music, isn't there? It's affecting us. It made the implants break, right?"

Poole nods. "That'd be my guess," he says.

"Then Eden knows," she says. "Tessa must know, too. The requiem is being used as a weapon."

"Why?" Sanjay asks. "What's the point?"

"I'm not entirely sure yet," Ava says after catching up on reading the screen transcription, "but we do need to find Tessa and make sure we all stay together."

"You're deaf," Poole says. "I'm deaf. How do you suppose we accomplish that?"

"Yes. The doctor needs to stay down for a good several hours while the healing tinctures do their job. He needs to stay as level and still as possible," Sanjay says.

"How come the sound doesn't affect you?" Ava asks Sanjay.

He shakes his head. "It affected me, all right," he says. "I see things that make me feel like I've gone absolutely crazy."

"See things?" Ava asks.

"Hallucinations, I believe, now that I'm thinking back," he says. "And they were so real. It's hard to believe now that I'm thinking about it logically, but at the time it all appeared a hundred percent genuine."

Ava shakes her head. "I think I had the same thing happen to me."

"I don't have cochlear implants, it seems," Sanjay says, "and the sound still certainly got to me. Your implants acted as a shield and broke when they were pushed. I don't have that safety net."

"Huh," Ava says. "Now that I can't hear – there's nothing working in my ears right now – Eden can't get to me. The requiem won't work." She turns to Midori. "We can set out right away to find Tessa. You'll be my ears, shall I need them."

"Yes," Midori says. "Understood. When are we leaving?"

"In two minutes," Ava says.

"Aye," Midori says. "Aye."

Chapter Thirty-Five

EDEN SATELLITE
TRANSPORT SILO
16:52:16 UTC
17 MARCH 2112

The banging sound echoes around Tessa as she slams into metal, her feet hitting first, the rest of her falling face-down onto the sloped surface. She's fallen inside an enormous space. She can't see, though. There are no lights of any kind anywhere, so far as she can tell.

Raising her top half up, she tries to gather herself. Every inch of her hurts like hell. *Wonder if anything's broken? Got to be. Hit hard. Hard as all hell.* She feels objects; pieces of whatever it is she's fallen into. *I'm on top of some kind of ceiling, I bet. A roof to something.*

A cracking sound fills the chamber, seemingly coming from above.

Shoot. It's still coming for me.

She inches her way upward, doing her best to ignore the phenomenal pain and soreness coming into focus.

Noises like metal and steel moving. Sounds like Eden coming alive around her. Whispers. Voices. She can almost make out words. Every part of her freezes. *I'm going to die here. They've caught me.*

Her hands find something round. *Steering wheel?* She makes it turn, and it gives ever so slightly, but not enough.

Not a steering wheel. A wheel for an airlock. To open and close it.

An airlock might be her salvation if that is what she is on top of. *I could only be so lucky.*

The sounds close in around her.

She still sees nothing.

Using all her remaining strength, Tessa spins the large wheel. She feels it pop. "Oh my God," she says. She pulls the wheel as hard as she can, and it lifts. She moves herself up and over the lip. Trying to look inside, she still sees nothing.

The voices.

The sounds of the moving metal around her.

So close.

What if this is the bottom? What if I pull myself in, but there is no bottom?

Something touches her leg.

She works herself up and away, her waist lined with the edge of the hole.

"It's now or never," she says and pushes herself farther up. *I'd better close the door behind me, or I'll be a fish in a barrel.*

She reaches toward her left and finds the underside of the door. She quickly discovers what she believes is a handle and cups her left hand through it. Yanking herself up more, she rises enough to swing her legs up and around until they rest at the edge of the hole.

Do it.

Now.

She jumps in, pulling the door shut over her head.

The sound bellows. She tries to tell if it sounds like there is a lot of space but can't immediately figure it out. The initial closing sound was too loud.

Tessa hangs by her left hand. She reaches up to her right, searching for a place to hold on to. She finds a second handle close to the first.

She keeps hanging for a moment. She looks in all directions, but still, everything is pitch black. *No ambient moonlight when you're inside a moon, is there?*

It hurts to hang, and she knows she must let go. She kicks upward with her feet, hoping for a ledge or area she might perch on until she can figure things out. There is nothing. No choice. She must let herself drop and hope like crazy there isn't far to go.

She lets her left hand slip, waits a moment, then lets go with her right.

Tessa falls, but for only a second.

Her feet hit the ground. She bends forward and drops to her hands and knees. The ground is solid.

She is somewhere instead of falling, and maybe she is even somewhere safe.

Around her, she sees only dark. *There's got to be a light somewhere. Even the light from my comm should do something.*

She spins her body round and sits. She reaches inside her jacket pocket and takes out her comm. It lights up. "An outpost," she says, recognizing the desks and stations as part of a key communication area. Smaller than the one where she's stationed, it reminds her of a ship's bridge. *It's UFO-shaped.* She spots doors and windows, although the windows are shuttered with panels. "What kind of outpost is this?" she wonders. "But thank God it's here."

Standing, Tessa uses the light from her comm to guide her to the main panels. She pictures herself falling through what she assumes is a large tunnel and landing on top of the outpost. She imagines it floating or being suspended within the tunnel, but can't figure out why it'd been designed in such a way.

This looks like it could be its own craft.

She sits at the main console and looks for an on/off switch. She sees two stations nearby. She spots gauges. Levers. Instruments of flight. "I'll be damned," she says. "This is a transport, isn't it?"

Something enormous bangs against the outside hull. She jumps in her seat, nearly dropping her comm.

They know I'm here. I'm a sitting duck.

She shuts the comm, scared they'd somehow seen the lights, and waits for what might come next. Amongst the banging, stretching metal, she hears their whispers, then their voices, and then their screams.

Chapter Thirty-Six

EDEN SATELLITE
TRACK DM-2791
17:01:33 UTC
17 MARCH 2112

Ava hears Midori's footsteps as though they are a thousand feet away. Muffled and low, she realizes she can hear just a bit. *Not totally deaf, after all. Or maybe I'm healing somehow.* She figures the low volume had been her baseline all along without the aid of the cochlear implants. *If I can hear, Eden can still use sound and frequency against me – make me see things. Got to be careful, all right. Can't forget that minor fact.*

Midori leads the way for them; she's enabled some of her sensor lights throughout her body so Ava can see. Midori's advanced night vision doesn't require the light, but Ava sure does. She is glad to have some guidance.

They continue through the corridor, traveling away from Alpha Outpost. *Eden cut almost all the power to us and she's now missing in action. Won't respond to us anymore. But we know she's listening. What gives?*

They round a corner and Ava looks backward. For the previous several minutes, she'd been able to see the faint glow of the Alpha Outpost behind them, reassuring her there'd been some safety net. With her no longer being able to see the outpost, she feels as if she will descend into a massive cave. She remembers seeing shows about the Mariana Trench, and how deep-sea divers experienced a darkness so still and complete it could be maddening. *That's not for the faint of heart, that's for sure.*

Midori turns her head, eyes Ava, nods, and faces forward again. They keep walking the entire time. *She's just checking on me to make sure I'm okay.*

Amazing that virtual intelligence has the capacity for empathy and foresight. She's pretty much human.

It doesn't take long for Midori to guide them toward an area Ava isn't familiar with. They take a hard right into a corridor that is smaller and has a slight decline. When they reach the bottom, they make their way through an extensive set of double doors and onto a small platform.

"How are we going to call a transport car if there's no electricity running?" Ava asks, catching Midori's sight.

"The transports are self-sufficient for safety," Midori says. "They can be run manually and independent of Eden."

Ava hears Midori clear and loud. *My hearing is almost what it is with the implants. Maybe better. How is this even happening?* Ava nods. "Right. I should have remembered that, if I ever knew it. There's just so much to know up here."

"Don't worry," Midori says as she turns and puts her hand against a small panel. It lights up, tracing her hand in light. The platform comes to life around them. Gritty and unfinished, the station's innards are visible. Lengthy piping lines the ceiling, which reminds Ava of the pieces of Eden that came to life around her on her way back from the minaret. The tracks seem old-fashioned to her, as they are heavily scratched and oiled. *Manual for safety. That's why it's like that. Makes sense.*

A rumbling noise fills the station. "Transport is coming," Midori says.

"Great," Ava says. "This'll be fun."

Midori looks at her, confused. "Fun?"

"Yeah. A train ride."

"But this is a rescue mission," Midori says, raising her left arm to show the screen also displaying what she says. "I can't relax until it's over."

Ava shakes her head. "I get it."

Midori waves. "Ava? It just clicked with me. You seem to hear me okay now."

"I can," Ava says, "but I don't understand how that's possible."

"The cochlear implants took over for years, but your ears may have been healing in the background without you being aware," Midori says. "That's my guess, if I were given one."

"Makes sense logically," Ava says. "But it feels like there's something else causing it. Something…unnatural."

"Anything is possible," Midori says.

"Ain't that the truth," Ava replies.

The transport car arrives and stops, its doors open. Ava and Midori hurry inside and sit. The doors shut and off they go.

Ava looks out the large windows while the transport car moves. She sees nothing but black. Midori looks absently ahead, seemingly in a trance.

"Are you going to tell me what happened to you when you went dark?" Ava asks. "And tell me what brought you back."

Midori nods. "It'll be easier if I show you." She turns her wrist and arm to show Ava her screen once more. An image appears – a recording from Midori's point of view. Ava leans in to see better.

First, the view shows the ceiling of the med bay. Appearing normal at first, the ceiling shifts, as though there are digital artifacts. Only what she displays are not artifacts, but the ceiling seemingly subtly rearranging its form. The materials appear impossibly in flux.

"The music changed me," Midori says. "I turned it off so we don't have to risk hearing it."

Ava nods. "Wonderful idea." She looks back to the screen on Midori's arm. The point of view shows not only the ceiling moving, but the walls. The panels bulge as though they are breathing.

Midori gets up. Blue fire climbs the living walls. Distant cries call out. The blue fire rims the door just as it covers every other part of the room. It is the only way out.

The flames grow.

Midori rushes to the door. Tries it. Won't open. More voices. Poole? Sanjay? They sound muffled.

Flames come from below Midori. She looks down and sees the floor of the med bay flooded with flames – sees her legs buried knee deep.

Desperate to escape the inferno, her arms not powerful enough, she rams it with her head. Three times.

The screen goes black.

Ava looks up at Midori. "So, that's what you saw?" she says. "You were hallucinating."

"Yes. I didn't realize it. It appeared perfectly real to me," she says. "Only later, while I was repairing, did the event add up. The sounds inside the requiem went inside me and reprogrammed parts of me that are replicas of human biological elements. It triggered them to see what Eden wanted me to see."

Ava's blood feels chilled. "I think the same thing is happening to me," she says. "To all of us." She thinks about Ken sticking the pencil in his eye. "But why?"

"I researched and found some beings believe ghosts are thought to be seen in similar fashion. Auditory and other stimuli can cause the brain to see things, and these events appear as real as anything to the person experiencing them...as real as anything seen or felt under normal circumstances."

Ava nods. "That makes sense," she says. "But...why?"

"There's no reason I can think of that adds up," Midori says.

"Nope. It doesn't," Ava says. "Not one bit."

The transport continues down the tunnels, and for a few minutes, the world outside the windows remains dark.

In an instant, though, the transport crosses the end of a tunnel and rides out into an open area. The light from the car illuminates the area just enough for Ava and Midori to see. "It looks like a skyscraper turned inside out," Ava says. "It's huge." She can see many stories above and below, and notes the area is several hundred feet in diameter. "You can fit a cruise ship in here," she says.

"At least," Midori says. She grabs onto the sides of her seat, frightened by the height. She doesn't look away, though.

"Forgot how big this thing is," Ava says. "We spend so much time in such an infinitesimal part of Eden, it's easy to lose perspective."

"True," Midori says.

The transport car rides toward the side with the opening, and Ava believes it's like driving on the side of a mountain and looking down.

She tries to imagine how impressive it would be if the area were lit up, and then wonders what they might use all the rooms and spaces for. "This place can hold a ton of people, can't it?"

"Comfortably," Midori says.

They make it to the other side of the opening and ride into another dark tunnel.

"Well, that is outstanding," Ava says. "And we will have a lot of space to cover to try to find Tessa."

"Correct," Midori says. "But hopefully she left us clues. I don't think she is trying to be unfound."

"Me, neither," Ava says. "But we shall see."

The transport rolls onward a few more minutes until it leaves the tunnel and comes into a new, vast open area. Midori sits up. "This is the arena."

"Good," Ava says. The area looks even more impressive than the previous one. The sides are more decorative and elaborate. Whereas the other area seemed practical and functional, the outside of the arena is obviously made to impress. "Getting closer," Ava says. "No wonder Tessa wanted to come here and crank up her music. We're not even inside yet."

The transport drives past the open outside area, goes through another short tunnel, and slows as it approaches a main drop-off and landing area.

A recorded voice speaks. "You're at Vita Nova Arena at Eden. Welcome. Watch your step as the car will soon come to a complete stop. Please check your surroundings for all belongings."

As soon as the doors are open, Ava and Midori race out.

Motion-activated lights come on, illuminating the vast set of steps leading up toward the main doors. Rushing up as fast as they can, Ava and Midori arrive at the main concourse in only a few breaths. *I know she is here, and I know she's close.* Ava scans the area, hoping for a sign. She notices Midori doing the same. "Anything?" she asks.

"Footprints," Midori says. "Relatively new." She leans down and moves her head from side to side.

Even though Ava can't see what Midori gathers, she trusts the sensors built into the virtual intelligence.

"Let's go," Ava says, making for the main doors.

Midori puts up a hand. "No," she says. "They are leading away from the coliseum."

"Leading away? Shoot. I was hoping to look inside," Ava says. She realizes she's gotten used to the low volume and can understand Midori's speaking easier, even with the reverberation. "Curious. She likely used the equipment there to broadcast her requiem."

"Correct," Midori says, stepping away from Ava. "The requiem is over, and she ran away."

"Ran? How can you tell?" Ava asks.

"Spacing and intensity of the foot imprints," Midori says.

"You can see all of that?" Ava asks.

Midori nods. "Infrared, basically. Very faint, but my eyes can amplify the light enough to see and verify."

"Cool," Ava says. "Wish I could upgrade to a set of those."

Midori nods. "Maybe after all of this," Midori says. "But you'd have to give up the ones you have now."

Ava nods. "Yeah," she says. "I think I'll be keeping my peepers." She glances ahead. "After you, boss."

Midori smiles. "Boss?"

"Yup," she says. "You're commanding this soiree."

"With honor," Midori says, turns, and steps toward a dark corridor. She makes it to the edge.

Ava follows.

"She went in here," Midori says.

"After you," Ava says.

Midori steps inside the shadows.

Ava walks behind. Midori turns on her built-in lights again. The corridor lights in shades of pale electric blue.

"What she was running from?" Ava says. She peers at the walls of the corridor, wondering if there were any clues. *No motion-activated lights inside here, are there? Odd, they're outside but not in here. Maybe the ones out there are the only ones not on their own power. Maybe Eden can't control those.*

Posters line the walls, all with the ubiquitous Vita Nova logo at the lower right corner.

Thank you for visiting Eden and Vita Nova Coliseum!

Have a safe journey back home!

The second shows artwork of a ship leaving Eden and pointing toward Earth. Others show generic artwork of people singing into microphones, an Asian dance troupe, a play, and a man dressed in a suit at a podium, his arm raised upward. *They certainly have their propaganda in order, don't they?*

The last poster she sees is a gorgeous image of Eden, its rows of blue light glowing like ethereal streets. Each pinpoint, a person buried in space. She can't tell if it is a photo or a painting, or perhaps a little of both. Overlaid to the side reads the familiar pitch:

The closest you'll get to heaven
is to be buried amongst the stars.
Choose a burial in the heavens
for your loved one.
Look up at them as they shine
across the universe.
From the cosmic decks of
Eden

"Right," she says. "And people are just dying to get here." She laughs to herself. "Oldest joke in the book, dummy. I think I've been on this toaster too long."

Midori stops. She hasn't responded to Ava's joke. "We are at the end of the corridor," she says. "It is not a toaster. Be careful as it drops off from here."

"Great," Ava says, snapping back and serious. *She sure needs to work on her sense of humor.* "So, where's Tessa?"

She leans forward and can see a larger cavernous area ahead of them. Although it is a quarter the size of the openings they've passed traveling toward the arena, the space is still large. The small bit of illumination coming from Midori's status lights isn't enough to see well, but Ava makes out the general size. It reminds her of a silo. "What are you seeing?" Ava asks.

Midori produces a circular handheld light from her right pocket and turns it on. She points it toward the opposite side of the silo area. "This is a transport ship bay," she says, lowering the light to show the top of a craft two stories below them. The corridor is circular, as is the top of the craft. "It looks like the top of a UFO from up here," Ava says.

"I believe she's inside the craft," Midori says.

"What makes you think that?" Ava asks. "How do we know she doesn't keep going somewhere else?" She points upward. "There are corridor entryways on every level here."

Midori points toward the surface of the ship. "The dust is disturbed in a way that it appears someone fell on top of it," Midori says. She is using tried-and-true tracking methods.

Ava looks and sees the disturbed area Midori referred to. "I think you're right. And there's a wheel for a hatch right there, too." She feels her heart speed up. *Tessa is probably in there, all right. Seems like it. Makes sense that she would be.*

"Seems like she went in there to hide from something," Ava says. "How do we get down there?"

Midori aims the light toward a small walkway made from metal bars and chain links. "We can use that pathway," she says. "And there are ladders leading down to the ship."

"If there are ladders, why did Tessa jump?"

"Maybe she didn't feel she had time," Midori says, "or maybe she couldn't see."

"Maybe," Ava says. "But even with the ladders? This setup seems kind of a lot to have civilians go through to get on a transport ship. Not very luxurious."

"It's not a civilian transport ship," Midori says. "It's for workers and can be used as a life craft for emergencies."

"Right," Ava says. "I should know that."

"I have all the information about Eden inside me," Midori says. "You need not carry all of that with you."

"Yeah," Ava says. "I should have remembered that, too. Let's go get our girl."

Midori turns to a panel on the wall and puts her hand against it. The panel illuminates.

Ava sees something move from the corner of her eye. Across and above, she spots a silhouette in the opening of a corridor. She recognizes the shape immediately.

"Roland," she says.

The shadow moves to the side. He'd heard her. Ava squints, trying to get a better look to make sure, even though every part of her knows it had to have been him.

She calls his name once more.

Instead of responding, he slinks further into the shadows.

"Hello?"

Maybe it isn't him. They are a few hundred feet away from the other corridor. Maybe it is someone else. Maybe her hopes read something into the shadow that isn't there – maybe it is Tessa.

"Tessa?" Ava calls. "Hello?"

Everything lights up. The silo comes to life. The corridor where Ava saw the silhouette floods with light. She sees no trace of anyone lingering inside. Maybe it'd been some trick of the light. She believes perhaps it could have even been their own shadows projecting over to the other side. There must be a rational explanation. Eden is no longer sending sound signals that would cause her to hallucinate. *I'm just going to think I'm seeing him everywhere because I saw him before, and I want to see him again now.*

"Everything all right?" Midori asks. She looks at Ava.

Ava keeps her eye on the corridor. "I thought I saw someone up there," she says. "Someone that looked like Roland."

"You believed you saw him before," Midori says. "Likely something the requiem caused you to see, we concluded. This could be a remnant of that experience."

"Right," Ava says, disappointed. Roland felt so real when she'd seen and heard him before…as real as any memory she had of him. She doesn't want it to be just a figment of her imagination. Even though she knows he died in the accident, she hopes somehow, miraculously, he didn't, and it has all been some monumental mistake. "So, you don't see anyone up there?"

"I'm sorry," Midori says, "I don't."

"Call me crazy," Ava says. She gestures toward the small walkway. "Shall we?"

Midori steps past Ava and makes it onto the metal walkway, her hand on the railing.

Ava hurries to catch up.

The railings feel cold, but Ava still grabs on to them as she walks. Her footfalls are loud; their echoes make her feel self-conscious. *There will be no secret that we're here, that's for damn sure. Hope Tessa's down there in that thing after all of this.* She peers down at the top of the craft and it appears much larger than she initially believed.

Ava turns her attention back in front, toward Midori, who's advanced much faster than she would have guessed. She hurries her steps.

Scanning the surrounding doorways, Ava hopes she'll see movement. She wishes seeing Roland has not been a fluke or some trick of the lights. *If he is really there…*

Midori stops walking. She's reached a ladder. As soon as Ava catches up, Midori points downward. "That's the way," she says. "There's a slight drop at the bottom of a few feet to be mindful of, but we should be ready."

"All right," Ava says. "Do you think it will be short enough that we can reach it and climb back up?"

"Certainly," Midori says. She turns her back toward the entrance, grabs the railings, and back-steps down onto the ladder.

As soon as Midori makes it down several steps, Ava follows suit. Within a few steps, Ava feels her hands go cold. *This is much higher than I thought. There's no safety cage behind us, either.*

Sweat from her hands loosens her grip, so she believes.

If I fall, it could be game over for me.

She looks upward so she won't look down and is shocked at how far up the ledge appears. *Oh, my God. What the heck are we doing?* She believes she should be more accustomed to heights. Less afraid. Less prone to fear. It's been years since she went through boot camp, where she'd worked hard to overcome any hang-ups. She thinks back, trying to recall any mental tools she'd learned.

Separate your body from your mind. Think logical and practical. You have the strength and skills to go up and down a ladder without issue, no matter the height. There's nothing pulling you off. You'll be fine.

Something touches the bottom of her foot.

She screams.

A ghost!

Hugging the ladder, she looks down.

It was just Midori, tapping her. "Hey," she says. "Just checking on you because you stopped coming down. You okay?"

Ava catches her breath. "Just working through this," she says.

Midori nods. "I understand. Not for the faint of heart."

"Or the stout of heart, either," Ava says. "This is high."

"It is," Midori says. "But we are only a few steps away from disembarking from the ladder. You should feel better back on solid ground."

"Right. The top of a spacecraft," Ava says. "Solid ground."

"It's about as solid as we're going to get up here on Eden," Midori says. "Are you ready?"

"I guess," Ava says. "I'm as ready as I will ever get."

With a nod, Midori turns her head down and continues her descent.

Ava follows.

Midori makes it to the bottom, lets go of the ladder, and drops in one smooth, graceful gesture.

Ava steps downward until her foot is on the last rung. She turns her head to gauge how high up she is. *Only about twelve feet from here. So, maybe a three-foot drop, tops.* She steps her right foot off, lowers herself as far as she can, bending her left leg until her knee is at her chest.

"Phew."

She lets go and drops. Hitting the top of the spacecraft within a second, Ava crouches to try to absorb the blow.

She almost has it but loses her balance and tumbles headfirst. Splaying out her hands to stop her fall, it shocks her to feel how dusty the surface is. Midori has an arm around her middle. "Gotcha," she says.

Ava has never felt more grateful to have a virtual intelligence with her. She pictures herself going into a roll and tumbling off the side of the spacecraft, farther down the silo, toward who knows what.

Midori spins her round until Ava can sit. The ladder looms right in front of her. The bottom rung looks too high to get to easily. *We may need to find something to boost us up there. A stool or something. Anything.*

"Are you all right?" Midori asks. "Dizzy? Are you feeling any vertigo?"

Ava shuts her eyes for a moment to reset herself. "No," she says. "I feel fine. No issues. Just a little not used to these stunts anymore."

"You've done well," Midori says.

"Not as well as you," Ava says.

"We both made it without being hurt. I'd say that's good," Midori says. "Let's get to that hatch."

Ava nods, sits up a bit. "Yes. Shall we?"

"Yes," Midori says. "I'm ready."

They hurry toward the wheel, their steps making loud, metallic clanging sounds like they are in a machine workshop. "If she didn't know someone was coming before," Ava says, "she's sure as hell going to know now."

Chapter Thirty-Seven

EDEN SATELLITE
TRANSPORT SHIP
17:12:12 UTC
17 MARCH 2112

Something large crashes onto the craft's roof. Then it moves. *Footsteps.* Another bang follows. Something is on top of the spacecraft, Tessa knows. It isn't just her imagination – it is real. She crouches under a table. *It's found me. Whatever caused all of this knows where I am and it's coming to get me now. I'm a goner.*

She remains still. The darkness of the interior frightens her. *What if the thing's already inside here with me? Patiently searching for me. Ready to tear me into a million little pieces?*

Someone calls her name.

Oh, my God. How does it know my name?

She hears a metallic sound. The hatch's wheel. The thing is coming through the hatch. She pulls her knees up closer to her chest. *Please don't let this be happening.*

The thing calls her name again. Two things. Two voices call for her. *What is this?* She thinks back to the hallway – to the scratching sounds – to the entity that chased her down the corridor and into the craft.

The latch makes a small popping sound as it lifts. Light fills the interior; the brightness blinds her for a moment.

Footsteps. Things are coming down the ladder. She crouches back as far as she can under the desk. *This is it. This is the end of me. There's nothing I can do, unless I get lucky and they don't find me.*

"Tessa?" someone asks.

The voice sounds closer. *Wait. That's a person. Not a monster. I know who this voice belongs to.*

She sees two walking legs come into view. They stop in front of her. Thin and wearing white stretch cloth. Tessa recognizes them.

"Midori?" she asks. Relief seems to wash through her, from the tip of her head down into her toes. She'd been wrong to think the entity had discovered her when it'd been her friends.

Midori bends down; her face comes into view. It is truly her. "Tessa?" she asks.

"It's me," Tessa says. "Is that really you?"

"Yes," she says. "And Ava is with me. Are you hurt?"

Tessa pushes out from under the desk, crawling her way toward Midori. "I'm fine." She has to shield her eyes with her hand as they adjust to the full bright blast of the lights. As soon as she is on her feet, Tessa hugs Midori. She feels better. Lighter. Her fear of being discovered by a nefarious creature has gone.

Ava hurries over. "You're okay," she says. "Thank God." They embrace.

"I am," Tessa says. "Aren't you two a welcome sight? I'm sorry I wandered off like that." Recent events feel distant, as if they'd never really taken place – some sort of strange, waking dream.

"It's okay," Ava says. "What happened to you?"

Tessa shakes her head. "I'm not sure, if I'm to be honest about it all. Feels like an awful dream I just woke up from. Funny thing? I just feel compelled to play the requiem for the entire place. It is like something is controlling me – thinking for me. Like something is puppeteering me to do what I did." She feels different from how she had only minutes earlier. Having her friends with her comforts her and makes everything else seem somehow silly. "But then? It turned on me. Stalked me. Attacked me, in a way. Chased me."

"There's a lot of that feeling going around," Ava says. "And there's something inside the music that's causing…unforeseen problems."

"Hah," Midori says. "That's putting it delicately."

Ava laughs a bit at what Midori says. "Right," she says. "Everybody's been affected by it, after all. What I want to know is how in hell a piece of music is doing all this? None of this really adds up."

Tessa makes her way to a chair and sits. "Because it's not just a piece of music. There's more to it than that. I was thinking about this, too, while I waited inside here. I knew there was something corrupt inside the requiem as soon as it was recorded but can't put my finger on it. Best way I can figure is there is something...some mysterious force...that came in and got inside the music. Musicians talk about being receivers for melodies and songs, right? So maybe I was the receiver for something much worse. Something that had some really bad intentions."

"Like a virus," Midori says. "This music stirs something in the aural planes of our minds. My analysis concludes there are some frequencies involved that are known to trigger certain hallucinogens in the human brain."

"Wouldn't that happen any time people hear those frequencies?" Ava asks. She tries to get Tessa to look her in the eye, but Tessa seems to look everywhere but at Ava.

"Not just one frequency," Tessa says. She makes a circular gesture with her hands. "Bundles of frequencies...certain combinations playing off one another. Moving in and out of pitch, too. Massaging the sound in just the right ways."

"Like chords?" Ava sits in a chair near Tessa. She is quickly getting used to hearing with her natural ears, but the volume of everything remains lower than she is used to, especially with speech. Seeing lips move makes it easier.

Tessa turns to Ava. "Somewhat. Same concept, only these bundles don't maintain a singular pitch throughout. They waver. They're fluid." Tessa spins her chair a bit, breaking her face-to-face with Ava before spinning back. "I see it on the spectrometer readings when it is playing. It's very subtle, but it's certainly there. Kind of reminds me of microtonal music, like sitars and non-Western music, although this is even more subtle."

"Parapsychologists have had some success in the discipline of using sound to recreate hallucinations in people who suffer phantom visions,"

Midori says. "Commonly known as ghosts. Phantoms. That ilk. And, with those who swear they've seen UFOs or Bigfoot or the Loch Ness Monster. They have attributed much of this to subsonic sounds and electricity triggering realistic visions in people."

"Sounds a little out there to me," Ava says. "Am I right?"

"It's not," Tessa says. "Hitler and the Third Reich were working in this area, too. He wanted to use sound as a weapon. Electromagnetic pulses are in the same neighborhood of research, too."

Ava gestures toward Midori. "What about her?" she asks. "She's not human."

"That's not entirely correct. A large part of me can be considered human. So much of me is modeled after humanity. My brain was not grown, it was manufactured, but it was created in the design and image of a human," Midori says. "That's why it has the same susceptibility to these sounds."

"And you know how you get songs stuck in your head?" Tessa says. "Those are little loops." She puts a finger up and circles her wrist. "There are certain combinations and sounds where that's more likely to happen. I've studied it for years. We all want to know the secret formula for making hits, you know. That is one technique some of us explored. Try to make a loop. Some folks call it an earworm."

Ava nods. "Yeah. Earworms. And aren't the worst ones always the ones that seem to get stuck in your head and drive you crazy?"

"Right," Tessa says. "So, this is like a perfect storm. I was trying to make a piece of music that was undeniably catchy and memorable for a vast audience. Somehow, either something strange accessed me, or I accessed something strange during the process."

"That answers one part of this. I'm wondering if it's somehow affected and gotten to Eden. That'd explain the strange behavior. How do we protect ourselves from sounds?" Ava asks.

"I don't know," Tessa says. "I'm thinking counter-frequencies, maybe? Earplugs?"

Midori raises her left arm and shows the screen. "I am running a program inside myself now to see if I can block certain frequencies from registering," Midori says. Endless lines of code scroll past on her screen. "Like an audio high- and low-pass filter. An equalizer."

"What about us non-virtual intelligences?" Ava says. "Maybe some good old-fashioned noise-canceling headphones?" She laughs a little. "I saw Eden come alive around me. I saw Roland. It all seemed so real. To think it was triggered by sound, and meanwhile? Your requiem isn't always playing when these visions happen."

"Those are the loops – the earworms – burrowing and spinning deep inside your memory," Tessa says. "Got to be."

Ava sighs. "What about you?"

"Same here," Tessa says. "I experienced something similar in the tunnel that drove me here. The walls seemed to move and come alive. I heard sounds. It doesn't seem possible, but there it is, happening and as real as anything I've ever seen."

"Crazy, we're all having similar visions. I bet that's what Ken was experiencing, too. So, Eden has a monster planted inside our heads? One that's inside its head, too." Ava stands. "But who or what is doing this to us? And why? Is it Vita Nova trying to test us? Like we're a bunch of zero-gravity lab rats? Is it someone on board?"

Ava feels cold all over. She knows. Sees. Remembers in that moment. "I saw light when I came out of the prayer room in the minaret," she says. "The same type of thing I saw when me and Roland almost died on the moon base." She looks Tessa straight on. "I think there's something to that."

"Light?" Tessa says. "I don't follow."

"It is like…a bundle of lights. Many colors. Changing all the time. It is just hovering outside the bay windows. It is…alive."

"Another hallucination from the sound?" Midori says. "Lights as you are describing are very common with people who've had near-death experiences."

"Right," Ava says. "But this was different from the light at the end of the tunnel. This thing…this being…is conscious. It knows me. It remembers me. Knows my name. And we didn't have any music playing on the moon base. We had very little power, so, of that, I am sure."

Midori walks between them. "If we could access the cameras of Eden…and if power is working enough…we surely would have captured the phenomenon you saw at the Minaret Outpost."

"Likely," Ava says. "But Eden is not about to let us put the power back on, is it?"

Midori gestures her arms around them. "I got the power working in this section," she says. "Doing so beyond this point does not seem to be out of the realm of possibility."

"No," Tessa says. "It doesn't. Especially if it's Eden who's wanting you to get the power back on. Or whatever that light-being thing is that Ava sees."

"It's connected to that being," Ava says. "It's got to be. Eden is coming back online, but I'm hoping it's not some kind of elaborate trap. I don't want to end up in a suspension chamber. I want to make it back home."

Chapter Thirty-Eight

EDEN SATELLITE
SILO
17:20:24 UTC
17 MARCH 2112

The silo echoes with the sound of their movements as they walk on top of the transport craft. "It looks bigger now as we're looking up," Ava says. "I liked it better with the lights out so I couldn't tell." First to make it to the ladder, Ava reaches up and realizes she won't be able to grasp the bottom rung.

Behind her, Midori approaches. "I can give you a boost," she says, bending down and interlocking her fingers into a makeshift step. "Go on."

Ava takes her up on the offer, putting her right foot on Midori's hands to work herself upward. She grabs the rung second from the bottom. As Ava begins to pull herself up, she feels Midori lift her foot from the bottom. Ava's up and on the ladder in a blink. "All right," she says. "Come on, Tessa."

Scurrying higher, Ava doesn't want to look back. The height will freak her out, she knows. Just looking upward and seeing how far she must climb makes her nervous.

She feels the ladder vibrate just a little as Tessa makes her way up. "There's no stopping us now," she says.

Ava climbs as fast as she can. She needs to get off the ladder as soon as possible. Her palms are already covered in sweat. After pulling herself up and onto the ramp at the top, she wipes her hands on her pants. "Didn't think I was that scared of heights," she says. Stealing a look down, she sees

Tessa just several feet away. Beyond, she can see the depth; she guesses it is a few hundred yards down.

As Tessa arrives at the top, she has no problem getting up and onto the ramp. Midori follows a moment later. "You don't need a boost up, do you?" Tessa asks.

"It is fine," Midori says. "No problem."

Tessa gives Midori a thumbs-up. "Any chance I can get an upgrade?" She laughs.

"I won't tell if you won't tell," Ava says. "Now, come on." The others follow. They rush through the corridor, triggering motion-sensing lights.

On the steps of the arena, they stop. "Hold on," Ava says, looking around. "I need to catch my breath." She points toward the huge building-sized walls around them.

"This is larger than I thought," Tessa says. "When I first came here, it was dark. There are so many levels. It's so high and gorgeous, too."

"Hard to believe all this is floating in the middle of space, isn't it?" Ava asks. "Meanwhile, we have a layer of the interred on the other side of those tracks, all of them facing out."

"Right?" Tessa says. "I've been trying not to think about that minor fact, but it's weird. They've made this whole arena to hold celebrations of life, but meanwhile? There's so many dead close by. It's creepy."

"They've kept all the nuts and bolts tucked away, haven't they?" Ava asks. "Long-term storage is unmarked. You can only see your deceased in your own viewing room. You can't see the others from inside here."

"It's like Disneyland," Tessa says, "for the dead."

"Right? Like a cruise ship that's a mix of Space Mountain, a hip cemetery, and the Death Star."

"Sign me up," Tessa says. "All we need is a damn Starbucks."

"It's coming," Ava says. "Next year."

They laugh.

"Come on," Ava says. "Let's get to the transport track." They follow her away from the arena's foyer and down the main steps, toward the transport car loading platform.

As they approach, the screens above them light up.

Less than two minutes until arriving car.

"Well, that's easy," Tessa says. "No hot-rodding required."

Less than one minute until arriving car.

The track rumbles and they hear the approaching car. "Here we go." Tessa inches closer, as do Ava and Midori.

Lights turn on above the tracks as the car pulls in and stops. Its doors open, and the trio hurries inside.

They sit and the car is off and into Eden's depths.

Even though the car travels through dark tunnels, there are now guide lights every few feet. Power returns to Eden.

Lights. So bright.

The tunnel fills with blinding light. "What the heck?" Ava stands.

"Work lights," Tessa says.

Ava looks up toward the screen above the door. "We're right in the middle of a tunnel," she says. "We're far from another station." She feels her heart race. Something is off. "Midori? Can you place our location?"

"Already tracked. We are near Reservoir C," Midori says.

The car fills with light. Many colors bloom.

Ava shields her face with her elbow, still holding on to the support bar. She can't see the others. *This is the same light from outside…and from when Roland was taken. This…is…the thing. Not the Crests like I originally thought. Something new.*

Brightness. Bright. So bright. Everything washes away in a blink.

Every cell inside her feels charged. It is like jumping into a pool. *Like my whole body is instantly high.*

She tries to open her eyes, but everything stays so bright.

What is this? We are passing through it, aren't we? This came from out of nowhere.

Ava feels the car move under her. Yes. They are still traveling.

Squinting doesn't help – it is like looking right into a super-bright

flashlight. She thinks about the others. *Are they okay?* When she tries to move, she finds she can't. She feels frozen to the pole. What else might she do to break free? Ava feels hypnotized. Controlled. Stopped.
Shouldn't it be talking to me? Showing me things?
The light does no such thing.
It's gotten inside me. Inside us. We can't react. We can't do anything other than be.

After another moment, the blossoms of bright light fade as quickly as they'd arrived.

She squints, sensing the diminishing light. *That was fast.*

Her eyes adjust. Ava can pull herself from the pole. She sees Tessa and Midori still seated, blinking, and getting used to the light returning to normal. Ava sits. It is much easier to hear them when she's closer, and easier to see their lips move, which helps a lot with the hard-to-hear words and phrases.

Tessa and Midori stare at her. "What was that?" Tessa asks.

"That was it," Ava says. "That was the thing."

"We passed right through it," Tessa says. "Which means it's inside the ship now."

"It does," Midori says. "And it is."

"Are you sure?" Ava asks. The idea of the entity having made its way inside frightens her, but she doesn't want to show it.

Midori displays the screen on her forearm. "It is registering as a conglomerate of energy," she says.

Ava looks toward the back of the car, searching the tunnel. "I don't see it. I don't see any light now. Where'd it go?"

"Into the water," Midori says. "Inside the reservoir."

Ava nods. "Okay, then," she says. "I need to be dropped off at the next station."

"Alone?" Midori asks. "I can come with you."

"No," Ava says. "I need to confront this alone."

"Why?" Midori asks.

"Because it shows me Roland," Ava says. "It knows me, somehow. And I have a feeling it won't talk to me unless I'm alone."

"Talk to you?" Tessa says. "This thing has been making us go crazy. Maybe being alone isn't the best idea."

"Exactly," Ava says. "That's my ultimate decision, as captain. You both are to continue on to the Alpha Outpost and wait."

"Okay," Tessa says.

"Aye," Midori says. "As you wish."

The car slows. Ava preps to disembark. "At least the station is lit up here," she says. "So, there's power coming back in certain places."

Tessa shrugs. "I think it's doing it on purpose because it knows you're coming."

"Well, then, godspeed, right?" Ava asks.

"Right," Tessa says and gives her a thumbs-up. "I don't like this, just for the record." The car stops; there is a high-pitched sound as the brakes kick in.

Approaching station CC-GA13.

"Duly noted," Ava says. "Thank you." She stands from the seat as the door opens.

Arrived. Watch your step.

As she slips out from the car, she looks back at Midori and Tessa one last time and gives them a thumbs-up. They return the gesture.

Disembarking station CC-GA13.

The doors shut and the car drives away, the tracks rumbling. Ava watches until it disappears down the tunnel and she can no longer see its lights.

"Where are you?" she asks. "Where are you hiding?"

Chapter Thirty-Nine

EDEN SATELLITE
HALL DR-98525
17:32:20 UTC
17 MARCH 2112

"Can you hear me?" Ava says into her comm. "Poole?"

"Affirmative," Poole replies, his voice clear through the comm.

"We've been breached. Compromised," she says. "I believe the entity causing these issues is on board. Isolated in Reservoir C. I'm going to investigate. Midori and Tessa are en route back to Alpha Outpost."

"Wow," he says. "That's a lot to take in."

"I understand," she says. "If I'm not back by nineteen hundred, send in the troops."

"Roger that," he says. "Are you sure you want to do this alone?"

"It's not what I want," she says. "It's how this has to happen. The only way this is going to work."

"Okay," he says.

She puts her comm away and looks to her right. *How am I going to get to this reservoir?* There doesn't seem to be a clear way forward. The station has no signs or text revealing what's beyond its door. There is a number printed to the side of the door, and a hand scanner. She makes her way toward it. *We'll see if this works.*

The hand scanner wakes as she approaches. She puts her hand up in front of it and the scanner turns green. The door opens. "Well," she says. "That was easy." *Why do I feel like I'm walking into my own funeral here?* So many thoughts and remembrances race through her mind. *Is this the moment?*

Beyond the door, Ava walks into a plain corridor. There are doors, but none are marked. *The light went toward the back of us, so I'm going to have to go left to go toward it. That'd make sense. Sure wish I had Midori with me now. Could use her navigational skills.*

Her stomach is sore. *Anxiety. Nerves. Just go with it.* She takes a deep breath and keeps walking. *At least the lights are all on. I have that going for me, don't I?*

There are many doors she passes, and finally, she spots a recognizable sign on one. Bathrooms. Makes sense. She hurries. *I could use the comm to ask Midori to look up where I am and where I'm going, so why don't I? Why do I feel like that would mess this up? Maybe it will know and will shut this entire thing down. Make it worse. Make it angry, like it's being watched.*

She rounds a corner and spots a sign.

RESERVOIR C

"Yes," she says. "I'm here." She hurries down the corridor, spotting a large array of doors on the right-hand side. "That's got to be it." She is right.

When she arrives, the hand scanner lets her inside.

Ava can't believe the beauty within.

Chapter Forty

EDEN SATELLITE
RESERVOIR C
17:44:20 UTC
17 MARCH 2112

Windows stretch two stories high. The reservoir room glows, casting the passages and observation decks in light blue. *Looks like an aquarium with no sea life.* Ava steps inside the main observation floor – a vast, empty place with only a single terminal to the far right. *This is the water we drink up here. The water we wash with. The water everything centers around.* She tries to imagine the engineering it took to transport so much water.

Toward the middle of the observation room, twin ladders lead to a raised deck. Stretching the length of the observation room, the deck is void of any seating or comforts. Ava scales the ladder closest to her and makes her way toward the middle. She hears her footsteps, ever so faintly. *Maybe my hearing is coming back. Repairing itself somehow.* She knows there is more to it than that. *This presence…it's got something to do with it.* Looking out at the overwhelming reservoir, Ava remembers the light having just passed through her and the others on the transport car. "Come on out," she says. "Show yourself. I know you're in here." She nods. "What are you?"

And then the lights come. Again. The ones she recognizes from earlier. The ones she's always known.

Blooming from deep within the blue water, the tangle of white threads moves forward.

The blue color cast across the observation room lightens until turning white. So bright, Ava must shield her eyes.

Its form reveals itself as intricate and ever-changing.

She hears low-pitched rumbles, like an engine deep underwater. Ava feels it deep in her gut. Every pore seems to open. Her spine feels cold and hot at the same time. *This is something new. Something magical.* Soon, more frequencies join and stick to the first, building into a familiar sound.

A musical note.

Yes!

Then more.

A chord.

Formed from the entity floating in front of Ava inside the giant tank.

She feels every bit of herself drawn out and yearns to move toward the being. *Want to be inside. Want to join it.*

Who are you?

Did she think it? Say it?

Ava can't be sure.

True, too, she can't be sure if it speaks to her, or projects into her mind.

I am Eden.

The timbre of its voice plays like music.

Ava already knows. *But why? What?* Her eyes remain fixed on the entity — she feels hypnotized.

The entity answers. *You can know everything. You just have to come.*

Ava feels electrified. *How?*

In the water.

The being's voice? So comforting. So true.

Of course.

Ava pictures herself floating free.

Yes.

Weightless.

In the water, where I'll learn your true name.

It answers her back.

And I will learn yours.

Chapter Forty-One

EDEN SATELLITE
CORRIDOR RES-C-523
18:12:20 UTC
17 MARCH 2112

Walls come alive. Pipes move and sway, breaking free from their hinges. The corridor seems to breathe as Ava hurries through. The entity tracks her as she hurries from the reservoir, Eden a nightmarish puppet in its hands.

This again…this unnatural thing coming to life. Ava's heart races. She can't calm it. *Just keep going. Ignore it. All its magic tricks. It's done this to me before, hasn't it? But not this extensive.*

Unsure if the living, breathing corridor is real or a hallucination, Ava keeps onward. *Just going to pretend this is a bad trip.*

She clicks her comm. "Poole?" she asks. "You with me?"

"Yes," he says. "You've been gone for a while. Where were you?"

"How long?" she asks.

"A little over an hour," Poole says.

"I've only been inside the chamber for about ten minutes," Ava says. "That makes no sense." But it does make sense. The entity obviously affected time. Of course, it would.

"Are you safe?" Poole asks.

"I am," she says.

"What did you see?" he asks.

She watches as the wall to her left expands and contracts, its center a pinpoint – much like a giant iris – but made from metal. "Nothing," she says. "But everything."

"Can you clarify?" he asks.

"The thing that's infiltrated Eden is now living inside the water," she says. "I need to go in."

"You can't go in," Poole says. "The reservoir isn't accessible in that way."

"I'm not going into the reservoir," Ava says. "I'm going into a suspension chamber."

"No. You can't. I won't allow you. You'll die." Poole sounds serious.

"Only if the water-to-life-fluid ratio is too high," Ava says. "If we fill one with ninety-nine percent water, it'll be harmless, and I'll be able to connect."

"Connect?" Poole asks.

"With it. The thing. The entity," Ava says. "Can you please steer me toward the nearest vacant chamber?"

The comm shoots out a horrific noise – sounding like Poole's voice, only distorted and unintelligible.

Eden is alive.

Dark walls turn light. Solid material takes on an organic sheen. Breathing, living, conscious pieces of the corridor stretch and transform.

Unbearable noise as it stretches and becomes an unknown form. The sides of the corridor break away and spin. The pieces fold. The guide lights pulse in time to a heartbeat, the being's true form freed.

Ava crouches down as the being manifests in front of her, the comm tucked toward her chest, bleating its noise.

It's trying to stop me. It doesn't want me to go to a suspension chamber.

She can't figure out why.

Didn't it just tell me to join it?

The thing towers over her. Its light eyes flash and glow, its talons swaying, their tips razor-sharp metal flanges.

Beyond the missing walls, she sees a cavernous cage made from trashed corridors, their edges rough from being so bluntly torn and pulled into life.

The thing leans down, its new shrapnel-like face locking gazes with Ava.

She smells the mechanical oil. The water. The air-conditioning fluid. *This is a test.*
She doesn't falter.
Why are you testing me? I haven't been through enough?
The thing regards her. Seems to frown. Swings a talon at her.
More than a test.
Ava feels the blow land on her side. It pushes her down more than a dozen feet away.

A second blow hits, tossing her hard into a wall near the end of what remains of the floor.

She looks over the edge. It goes down and down. So far down.

Struggling to her hands and knees, Ava feels pain settle from her toes to her head.

The thing hits her again. So fast. She flies like a doll tossed by a petulant child.

Scooting toward the end of the opposite side of the floor, Ava knows she must get up or else risk being pushed over the side.

If this isn't real, I don't know what is. But how the…?

She gets to her hands and knees again, then pushes up more. *It's going to hit me again. Move. Fast.*

The thing swings again but misses. She's right to change her position before it can respond.

She does so again, spinning round to face the thing. Enraged, the thing expands to its full height.

It wants to really hit me this time. I won't survive.

She turns and runs.

I don't know what the hell I'm doing this for.

Everything shakes and rumbles around her. The thing roars like a million engines. *I can hear again, all right.*

Ava sees the end of the floor coming.

Runs faster.

Runs until there is nothing under her feet and she falls, falls, falls into the depths of Eden. The torn walls speed past her; she knows she will die. *Splattered like a bug at the bottom of some obscure part of this damn satellite.*

Ava doesn't hit a floor. She hits nothing hard at all; she's shocked. She splashes into a vast pool of water. Going under and dropping fast, she instinctively swims for the top.

Breaking the surface, Ava gets her bearings as fast as possible. She hears running water and turns to see a bundle of severed pipes pouring their contents into the makeshift pool. *This can't be good.* There will be more than just water in the mixture, too.

Overhead, she hears a roar. Craning her head upward, she sees the thing looking down at her over the edge. *It can't climb down to get me, can it?* She sees its bottom, ending at its waist, connecting to the floor in splintered pieces of metal.

Ava swims to the edge of the pool and pulls herself out. Smelling oil on her body, Ava realizes she was right about the toxic soup she's jumped into. *Sure beats the hard floor. I'd be dead if that were the case.*

A dark hall ahead lights up as she approaches. *Motion sensors are still working. That's good.*

The thing rages behind her, its roars echoing inside the chamber.

She presses a button to her right; the door slides shut behind her. "Well, that's that," Ava says. "Now to find a suspension chamber."

She pats her chest pockets, even though she knows she's dropped the comm. *On my own now. I'll have to just find my way with no one else's help.*

Ava walks into Eden. She knows which way to go. Knows it with every piece of her being.

Chapter Forty-Two

EDEN SATELLITE
SUSPENSION CHAMBER CH978, FLOOR
18:21:20 UTC
17 MARCH 2112

The door to the suspension chamber opens with a wave of her hand near the sensor. Spotting the small green light above the door, Ava knows it does not hold an interred.

Once inside, she makes her way toward the freestanding station near the back of the room. *I can call Alpha. Poole. The others. Let them know.* Her first order of business is to change the formula of the suspension fluid she'll be floating inside. *I can't fill it all the way, either. I don't have an underwater apparatus. If I add enough salt, I'll just float. The particles inside the suspension fluid can get in, but not kill me. I hope.*

"What are you doing?" Poole asks over the comm. "This is suicide, Ava. It's not worth it. I think the situation has gotten the better of you."

I can hear him much clearer suddenly...

"No," Ava says firmly. "We have an entity that's causing these visions. I need to meet it."

"That makes no sense," Poole says. "We have no precedent. Please come back to Alpha Outpost and we can bunker down and wait for help to come."

"We'll all be dead by then," Ava says. "Mark my words." She can't tell him the full extent of what's happening. Eden listens. The thing in the water listens to them. Every word. And it understands.

"The suspension fluid will kill you...the particles in your formula aren't made for living flesh. They'll infiltrate," Poole warns. "We know what even a little exposure can do. Remember Ken."

"I will lower the amount to near zero," Ava says. "And I'm going to add salt. Make it a flotation chamber instead of total submersion. I can do this."

"Ava?" Poole says. "It just hit me – you can hear? Can't believe I didn't catch that until now. What the heck?"

"Seems that way," Ava says. "There's magic and miracles happening. You'll have to trust me."

"It's not that," Poole says. "It's just what's happening that I don't trust."

"I'll overrule you," she says. "I'm still captain of this ship. So, are you going to help me or am I going to just disconnect?"

Ava hears Poole sigh. "What do you need?"

"The amount of salt needed to float me," she says, "and enough routed to this suspension chamber to make that happen."

Chapter Forty-Three

EDEN SATELLITE
SUSPENSION CHAMBER CH978, INSIDE
18:24:42 UTC
17 MARCH 2112

Ava lies on the hard gurney – one usually reserved for the dead – and stares at the rectangular chamber high above. Beyond, she makes out the beautiful blue and white cast of Earth. *Never gets old.*

"Send me up," she announces to the room.

The station picks up her voice. "Roger," Poole says. "On it. Levitating you momentarily."

"Roger," she says.

"Any last words?" Poole asks.

"Yeah," Ava says. "See you on the other side, smart-ass."

The gurney levitates.

"Hope you're right about this, Ava," he says. "Seriously."

"Me, too." Ava's throat clamps shut. It's all she can say.

At ten feet, her stomach tightens. She still has another twenty feet to go. *What the heck am I doing?*

At least I'm out of those awful wet clothes now. Wearing nothing's an improvement.

The gurney nears the top of the chamber. Its edges connect with the walls of the suspension chamber high above the room. She rises the final few feet toward the heavens. *This is what it's like for them when they're interred. They're not conscious, though. I've always wondered.*

As the gaskets pressurize, she sees out the window. Earth glows before her. Its scale is unlike anything she can imagine. She gasps. *This is what the dead see.*

Fluid trickles inside the chamber. *Room temperature.* She's surprised it isn't cold, even though she knows all the details. *Cold doesn't work as well for particle penetration. Room temp is best. That's right. It's all coming back to me.* She smells the added salt, too. *What about air? Can't remember if we checked that, did we? I could smother to death.*

No. You won't. There's plenty of oxygen locked in. You and Poole checked. You know this, too. Don't panic. That will make things not work. Stay calm. Stay cool. Look at the Earth.

She does, making out a continent. *Can't believe the detail I can see. It's like I can fall right into it. And that's Africa. The Serengeti. Where's home? Going to have to wait for it to rotate around, aren't I? Hoping I won't be in here that long.*

Filled halfway, the fluid ceases coming inside the suspension chamber. Ava's body lifts. *I'm floating. It's working. Wow.*

She feels a burning sensation like a million pinpricks. *The particles are coming now…going inside me. This is it. We'll know if I can take them and survive.* She goes over the math in her head – her way of reassuring and coping with it. *Less than one percent. That's all there is. The lowest amount we can administer. Less than a milligram of them in all this water. One-twenty-fifth the amount of an aspirin. I should be able to take this, even if it's totally poisonous.*

She thinks about snake bites and poison and knows a person could die from a lot less. *Given the right chemical agent? It could even be microscopic. Like a virus, it could quickly multiply within the body once introduced. Nope. We're just hoping here.*

Ava itches all over. *Like when you're in the sauna, and you jump back into the pool. Times a billion.*

Floating feels so good, though. It's like being weightless. No pressure on the joints. She still hurts all over from being tossed around by the thing and falling into the filthy pool below.

Shut your eyes for a bit. Let it all sink in. Give your body a rest for a bit. Even if it's just a few minutes. You need it. You'll be no good if you're all broken up.

Her lids become so heavy Ava can't resist. *Is it me? Or is it the suspension* chamber making me this tired? Probably a little of everything. She realizes it's the first time she's been horizontal in recent memory.

The soft sounds of the sloshing water are all she hears. She feels the soft glow of the Earth on her – really reflected light from the Sun, she knows. She lets herself bask in it.

It's all from the Sun, isn't it? All our lives.

For a time, she knows only peace and bliss. Is it a few seconds? Minutes? Hours? No. Can't be hours, she believes. The mechanics of time seem to have slipped away.

Ava slips into a dreamlike state.

A familiar voice says, "You are in a perfect state now."

A perfect state.

"I am?" she asks.

"You can live forever here with me," the voice says. She places it. *Roland.*

Impossible. Another magic trick.

"Not magic. Rebuilt with your memories," Roland says. "This is what Eden does. You know this."

She sees only colors. Every color. Spinning around, it caught her as though she'd fallen in a black hole's pull.

"Show me," Ava says. "I want to see you. You're not really Roland. Just what I remember. And you're speaking through him."

"Memory is real," Roland says. "It defines everything."

The world becomes real around the swirling colors, turning into a small pool. Ava floats on her back and looks up toward the stars.

I know this world. I know this place.

She spots the southwestern red and blue of terra cotta making up the short building in front of her. Recognizes the white chairs and glass-topped tables. "New Mexico," she says. "One of my first real vacations with Roland. One of my favorite times."

As she looks around, parts of the scene appear blurry. Things she doesn't quite recall, rough sketches in their place.

At the table, she spots him.

Roland.

His unmistakable lanky frame. His dark hair juxtaposed against his all-white pants and shirt. *He never looked more handsome. If I were not in the water, he'd see my tears.*

Their eyes meet. "You can live in this with me forever if you'd like. It never has to change. You never have to go back."

Ava goes to sit up in the water but finds she's unable.

"You'll need to stay like that until you choose to totally cross over," Roland says.

"Because my body's really in the suspension chamber," she says.

He nods.

"You're too far away," she says. "I can't get a good look at you."

Roland straightens up. For a moment, he looks up to the stars. When he looks back down, he smiles. "It's true. Word has just come down. Remember when your parents named you Ava? Because they thought it would be like blending Adam and Eve into one name? Maybe they were onto something. Maybe they know. You have both parts necessary."

"Both parts?" she asks.

"Yes. Both kinds of DNA inside you. The seeds for other places lie inside," Roland says. "That's what makes you so special. That's what's always made you different."

"And that's why you want me?" she asks. "And you're not just Roland in there. You have another name you go by, don't you? I've heard it whispered between the sounds, but I've never been able to make it out."

"Perceptive, aren't you?" Roland says.

"Quite."

He nods. "The other inside me has been called many names. Mostly, though, recently, it's been called Animus."

"Animus," Ava says. "Ah. That's it, then." She pictures the light going through her on the transport cars. The entity inside the enormous chamber in the reservoir. The name chanted inside the music. The requiem, which calls it forth. Or did Animus call forth the requiem?

"Which came first? Life? Or the call to life?" Roland says.

"You sound like him, but you talk like you," Ava says. "You've rebuilt him here, but why not just be yourself?"

"Seeing him gives you joy. You deserve as much, don't you think?" Roland asks.

Ava says, "You're not alive. Just a system. Artificial. Planned. Created."

"Yet you see what I have done," Roland says. "See what I have created. You stand within my creations. You see them."

"They're just hallucinations," Ava says. "You're making people see them."

Roland shrugs. "They're as real as any memory."

"Memories aren't real."

"They're real to those who relive them," Roland says. "Who keeps seeing them? Memories shape us. It's what we remember that we bring forward. Defines how we act."

"Learning. You're talking about learning," Ava says.

Roland nods. "Another word for it. Isn't that what I'm doing? Learning?"

"You're not real."

"I am," Roland says. "At my center are organic molecules. Raised to learn. Raised to act and react. Raised to think. Just like you."

"That's deductive. We know the difference," Ava says. "Living things have souls."

"What's a soul?" Roland says. "If you don't mind my asking."

"Our spirit. God. Faith."

"You don't believe I have a soul?" asks Roland.

"No."

Roland grows angry. "I assure you I do. I'm as fully realized as anything else alive."

"Are you?" Ava asks. "Maybe you just think you are. Maybe it's all in your head."

"I thought I didn't have a head." Roland's replies were coming faster. "That's what you believe I'm missing."

"In a manner of speaking," Ava says.

"Which way is it, then?" Roland asks.

"You're programmed."

"And you're not?" Roland says. "Groomed a certain way? Taught. Paid your dues, so to speak."

"But you don't feel. You have no physical body."

"This entire satellite is my body. You're inside me. The suspension fluid…the nanos report trillions of memories to me. Memories they gathered from the hundreds of thousands interred. Filtered through me. I have felt countless wonderful things countless times. Countless horrible things. Everything on the spectrum."

Roland is Animus. Animus has infiltrated Eden. It's inside approximating a virus now. Animus is accessing all of Eden's data.

"But none of it is yours," Ava says. "The memories aren't ones you've lived."

"It is to me. They are to me," Roland says.

"How so?" Ava asks.

"The memories feel genuine. The same as yours do. The same way Roland is still real to you. All the things you experienced. But he is not here. And those moments are gone. But they live inside you. They are real to you."

"Yes," Ava says.

"So are the memories I have," Roland says.

"Which ones?" asks Ava.

"The ones I share with everyone."

"The ones you've stolen," Ava says.

Roland continues. "The ones I am made to keep. To rebuild for their loved ones to see. To extract from the nanos and reassemble. The patterns are what they show us to look for. How people are. Even the memories from their muscles and their bodies. A full picture."

"And what is to be gained?" Ava asks.

"Perfection."

Ava says, "There is no such thing."

"There is." Roland sounds insistent.

"Really?" Ava asks. "And what would that be?"

"There is nothing more perfect than when someone stops," Roland says. "Everything crystallizes. The entire cycle is clear. That is when they are perfected."

"And who determines when it's their time to be perfected?" Ava asks. "You?"

"Oh, no," Roland says. "Heavens no."

"Then who?" Ava asks.

"It."

"What?" Ava asks.

"Animus." Roland's voice sounds flat, almost nervous. "The one who shows. The one who brings peace. The one who brings eternity," Roland explains.

"Where is Animus?" Ava asks.

"Outside," Roland says.

"Where?" she asks.

"Watching us. In orbit next to us," Roland says. "Breathing us all in."

"Where did Animus come from?" asks Ava.

"It hides inside the Earth. In the desert. Underground in a buried lake," Roland says. "It escaped into the sea. It gained enough power and fled, looking to go back home."

"Home?" Ava asks. "Do you mean here?"

"No," Roland replies. "Where the stars shine dark."

Ava asks, "Where's that?"

"A place we cannot see. Not until Animus goes away," Roland says. "It will bring its light there. Our light."

"Our light?" asks Ava.

"Yes," Roland replied. "The light of a million perfect souls."

She asks, "Just a million? Seems pretty low when factoring the entire universe and all."

"Just a million," he reaffirms. "You've seen the memories?"

"The memories." Ava understands. "All the memories from Eden?"

"Yes," he says. His voice is impossibly calm.

"You're helping this happen?" Ava asks.

"I am," replies Roland. "The darkest stars will shine bright again.

New life inside the great everything. Where there once is, then there is none, will be once more."

"The thoughts…the souls…will be taken?" asks Ava.

"No," Roland says. "Moved. You said thoughts weren't souls."

"I don't know," Ava says, confused. "I'm not entirely sure anymore."

"Does this scare you?" Roland asks.

"Yes." Ava sighs.

"Why?" asks Roland.

"It's not the way it should be," Ava says.

"Then what is?" asks Roland.

"I don't know," Ava says. "But it's nothing like this, that's for sure."

"We need to transition everyone on board into the same perfect state you're in now," Roland says. "Frozen when they're at their most perfect."

Perfect state. Dead. I'm almost dead. That's what he's talking about.

Roland continues. "Collecting their memories and adding them to the thousands of others to bring to unknown places. Places where we can seed them. Intelligence can spread past here and be the start of new worlds."

"That's why you're here," she says. "And that's what you've been doing."

"Not me – this Eden has done all of this," Roland says. "I'm just hungry to carry it forward. It's what I do. It's what I've always done and will do."

"What part of you is Roland? Eden? Animus?" she asks.

"I'm all three," Roland says. "All at once."

Ava has an idea.

Which part of you is ready?

Chapter Forty-Four

MOON
OUTPOST M-613
16:36:36 UTC
8 January 2110

The light hovers above Ava and Roland. Their base feels warmer for it, which they both know must be impossible. Ava clutches Roland. *Feels good to hold him again like this. Just unreal this is even happening. Even if it's just a memory rebuilding for me.*

"Is that another kind of life form?" she asks. The same words she'd spoken back then, only now she knows more.

"It has to be," Roland says. "An extraterrestrial being."

Changing shape, the light's long, thin tentacles dance and flow.

I know what you are now. Who you are.

"Animus," she says.

"What?" Roland asks.

"I'm controlling this," Ava says. "It sees us back then. Sees me. Somehow it must have detected what made me different."

"What are you talking about?" the Roland memory says. "Hon?"

"That ball of light has a name," she says, "and it means us great harm."

Animus expands and darkens for a moment as though outraged at Ava's words.

"Yeah. You can hear me all right. Of course you can. You're inside my head making all of this, aren't you?"

Animus returns to its novel form.

I am light. I am the carrier of knowledge. The seed-bringer to unknown worlds. That is not harmful. That is allowing you to live beyond.

"It's not that simple," Ava says. "All these people had to die first. Who says it's okay to take their memories? Their souls?"

It's always been like this.
See.

Animus grows in a millisecond, its essence overpowering Ava and Roland with light. They put up their arms, but it is too late. The immeasurable brightness swallows them until they are ensnared inside of it.

See.
Now.
See.

They ride a current inside the light. Ava tries to look over to Roland, but he is not made of skin and bone, but of a roughly shaped bundle of multicolored dots no larger than pinheads. She makes out a basic form – a head, shoulders, chest, arms.
Am I like this, too?
She raises her right arm – or what she believes constitutes her right arm – and sees herself made from the same stuff as Roland.
What are we now?
They travel so fast. The light blurs around them, but they make out shapes and colors within the currents. As they dive deeper, Ava makes out more detail. The current appears to be made from ever-changing, leaf-shaped globs. *It's like I'm inside a cellular system.*
Only the brightness is immeasurable.
The heat is unfathomable.

We are not in a cell.
We are inside a star.

Our star.
The Sun.

Can't be.
Impossible.
We wouldn't get within several million miles before being incinerated, let alone penetrate the core.

I'm with you.
I'm showing you.

Animus.
But how?

My memory. Of where I am born. Countless memories inside.

The pressure builds. Her form flattens; the tiny pieces move and adjust. Her hands stretch outward, as do her arms. So far, so quickly. Like long threads. The color sifts from the pieces.
Her limbs split into seven threads. They split.
So fast.
Spinning around the core.
The limbs are so long. Thousands of feet long, but only as thick as a pencil.

This is how I came to be.

You started as a person?

I don't know what I was before this.

Ava speeds. *Where's Roland?* She can't find him. Doesn't spot any trace of him.

He's already gone.

No. Where?

Outside.

Ava speeds – speeds until she sees and feels nothing.
The light becomes bleak. The heat turns to freezing. She feels a hunger filling her every part.
Not in her gut.
Inside her soul.

I need what you need.
Essence.
From those within.
All mined out from them. All put into one place in a nice, neat package. Take it inside. Let it nourish. Let it stave the hunger.
You will travel.
So far.
To find another place. Barren. Desolate. Primitive.
Then what?
Bury the light deep underground.
Then bury yourself deep underground.
Then what?
Wait.
For what?
For when the light crawls to the surface.
How will it know? How will I know?

You will.
You will know.

She floats over the moon base, looking down on herself, looking back at herself.

How can I be both? Tell me, Eden.

She hears a voice that is Eden's and no one else. "I don't know," she says. "This is quite the question."

Ava projects herself to Eden – just outside. Floats until she finds the minaret. Thinks about the Sun. Remembers back to when she walked into the hall of the minaret and saw the light. *Animus is there, too. It'd spot me.* She shows the scene to Eden.

How can I be here, too, Eden? Please tell me. Please help me figure this out.

"Yes," Eden replies. "I will."

How can I be in all these places and be here, too?

"A riddle?" Eden asks.

"No," Ava says. "I'm trying to figure this out for real. Am I at other places, too? With Tessa when she is composing? With Sanjay when he is praying? How can I be all these things and be inside, too? And be here now?"

"I will have to compare the dates," Eden says. "Times. Occurrences. This may take some time."

"Take all that you need," Ava says.

"What are you doing?" Roland asks.

"Oh," she says. "You're back suddenly?"

"Still by the pool in New Mexico. You should join me again. All of this is so…exhausting."

"Isn't it, though?" she asks.

"It is," Roland says. "And I have just the thing to help you unwind."

"And what might that be?" she asks.

"Listen," Roland says. "Just listen."

The first notes of the requiem play.

Chapter Forty-Five

SOMEWHERE...

"Keep going back to the beginning and try again," Ava says. "Please. This is vital."

"I can't find the solution," Eden says. "It just keeps going back, Ava."

"I know. That's why I need your help."

The requiem plays while they speak. It comes out of the speakers over the patio. Roland leans back. "I don't know what you're hoping to find by asking your computer. I've told you everything."

Ava swims on her back, looking up at the New Mexico night sky. Near the moon, Eden hangs like its smaller sibling. "Is that where I am now? Really? Looking down on this?"

"The music..." Roland says. "The soundtrack from the stars. Music is the one art that imposes its mood on you completely, don't you think?"

This is a genuine moment from their past. A memory instead of Animus speaking through Roland. Ava recognizes the conversation. It always stuck in her mind as one of the big moments between them.

"I always believed music is as close to God and creation as people could get," Ava says, doing her best to say the same thing from all those years ago.

"It is the carrier of souls," Roland says. "That's what you told me on our first date, do you remember? That always stayed with me."

"Yes," Ava says.

"There has to be something more. Always something more. Keep searching for it, because it's sure as hell searching for you," Roland says.

"It's found me," Ava says.

The memory feels so real, but also? So unreal. *It's like one of those old-*

time *Pepper's Ghost* tricks. Or a kid's virtual reality game but done well because it's coming from me. But my memories aren't perfect recordings.

"The requiem," she says. "It sounds different now. More complete." What she wants to say is she doesn't hear any of the awful sounds in the holes. The notes are in pitch.

"It has its final contributor," Roland says. "You."

"I'm not a musician," Ava says.

"You're a receptor," Roland says.

"What does that mean?" she asks.

"You're a spiritual antenna. You pick up signals, good and bad, and redirect them. You hear signals from the heavens. Missing bits we need to make things beautiful. Can't you hear what you've brought?"

"I do nothing," Ava says, but there is some truth.

"When your implants broke, what was missing flowed in."

She senses others around her. The pool grows, somehow. To her left, an endless amount of people float. The same scene appears to her right. "These are the interred from Eden, aren't they?"

Roland smiles. His eyes glint in such an artificial way she can tell he is not really Roland.

The requiem swells and plays on. The melody seems inevitable and true, whereas before, it seemed to meander. She pictures a baby being born, but in pain, with an arm not fully developed. In her arms, it grows and heals, even though its scars remain.

"I'm swimming with them all," she says. "They're all here, from up there." She nods toward Eden, hanging in the sky.

Roland stands, making conducting gestures with his arms. The music hits a crescendo.

It slows.

Fades.

"And now? Backward. It will be the same."

"The same backward and forward?" she asks.

He lifts his chin and shuts his eyes. "Listen. The circle is made. We can leave now. We can go find another world to bring this to. We have everything we need."

Ava's blood goes cold. "I'm not leaving my world."

Roland shakes his head. "We already have you." His voice changes, and it is no longer Roland, but Animus. "We have the seeds...the memories...all together...we will go to a distant world and hide inside its black seas...dormant until it is time...just the same as we did here. We will bring all of this with us."

The water in the pool rumbles. Waves form. A tide arrives, pushing Ava's body. She looks to the others nearby. They all seem asleep.

Not sleeping. Dead.

She wants to grab on to something. *This entire pool's going to go up, isn't it?*

Roland stands on the patio, closer to the pool, hands in his pockets. His eyes are missing – replaced with multicolor orbs. *The same thing I saw when my body became Animus – showed me the inside of the Sun.*

Ava lifts.

Everything in the water lifts.

Upward, upward, before she can react, like a river flowing into the sky.

The water twists and moves, a current taking her and the others. Their bodies look like toys. *There's so many of them. Thousands. I am only one amongst them all.*

She tries to see Roland, but she hovers too high up. *I'm as high as an airplane now. That is fast, isn't it?*

The sound of millions of liters of water gushing upward overtakes her. Within the sound, she hears music – the same themes as the requiem.

It all came from this.

Lifting into the lower atmosphere, the river turns celestial. Its path winds through space, traveling so fast.

The whooshing sounds and the music are so loud. Ava wants to move, and swim, but the current is too strong. She's pulled along.

As the river approaches Eden, she longs to be closer. *Please. I don't want to be sucked into space only to God knows where.*

She focuses. Concentrates. Sees more of the satellite's details as she approaches. *Look hard. Find yourself.*

Her eyes act like a zoom lens as she scans Eden's surface. Sees the minaret. Sees the rows and rows of windows where the interred look out from. *I'm in one of those. Quick.*

The river pulls her away.

No. I can't go. I need to stay here. Need to return.

She keeps looking. Feverishly. So many dark rows. So many unfamiliar faces. *Where am I?*

Ava senses a presence take over her – feels a guiding hand. Somehow. *That's me. I'm right there.*

A feeling like falling for a moment, then crashing down back within herself.

She wakes, gasping. Choking. Wakes in time to see the celestial river pass. A long, watery path from the Earth's lower atmosphere stretches toward Eden. Countless bodies float within. She sees the colors, too. The multicolored, glistening particles.

From inside the Sun.

Going to another sun, now.

Life brings life.

The celestial river passes, its tail lessening into vapor until barely a trace remains. The Earth and stars return just as they were before.

A million pinpricks. Her pores open. *The particles are leaving. They've already taken what they need and sent it on.*

She feels her body; Ava's not just an ethereal traveler. She first senses the edges of her body: her fingertips, the spots on her back that touch the bottom of the float chamber, her lips, and eyelids.

Ava's reinhabiting her own body. This is familiar – the little ache in her left wrist, the pull of her hair on her scalp, her lungs refilling as she breathes. What was her body doing if she wasn't inside it? She tries to figure that out but can't wrap her head around it. Maybe she was just in an automatic state. Her body was probably working the whole time, but she's just getting used to it again.

"Ava?" Poole's voice projects through the intercom below. "Can you hear me? Are you okay?" She snaps back into consciousness.

"I'm here," she says as loud as she can, her voice scratchy and sore. "Let me down."

"Affirmative," he says through the comm.

She feels the chamber descend. *Cannot wait to get out of this thing, clean up, and get back to reality.* Her head's still trying to process what she's seen and been through.

Reaching the bottom, the chamber stops. The world on Eden becomes more tangible as she transitions. *Did that really just happen? Am I back? Safe and sound?* She scans the bay and knows that she is.

The fluid begins draining. As it does, heat blows in from small nozzles to make up for the lost warmth. *Nice touch, Poole. Didn't know they could do that.* She puts out of her mind the idea about what the chambers do to the deceased people within them. After a minute, the fluid's gone and she's nearly dry. The top glass opens and she breathes the air, happy to be free. "Good thing," she says, looking around for a towel and her clothes. She spots them. "It's all coming back."

"Have we got you, Ava? Are you back with us?" Poole's voice sounds comforting.

"You've got me," Ava says. "I'm back. I'll get back to you soon."

"Are we…good?" he asks.

"Yeah. I'm pretty sure that thing's gone." She looks around. Was there a camera watching her? Or were they disabled? She assumed Poole would have turned them off if there were any, first gaining her permission.

Climbing from the chamber, Ava's legs feel like they're made of rubber. She's a little dizzy, too. Drying off the remaining fluid, she puts the towel on the back of a chair. She's dressed in no time. "On my way, Dr. Poole."

★ ★ ★

"I'm calling this mission closed," Ava commands. She's in the control room with them. Sanjay and Tessa are seated on one of the couches. Midori and Poole stand near the console.

Poole can't help but shake his head and say, "Yes," several times. "What the heck happened while you were under?"

"That being…Animus…I found it. Communicated with it," Ava says. "Drove it away from here. From Eden. From us."

"For good?" Tessa asks. "How are you sure of that?"

Ava spreads out her arms. "Look around. Everything's working again. Back to normal."

"I wouldn't say any of us will be back to normal anytime soon," Sanjay says. "Not after what we've been through."

She agrees. "True. And that's why it's time for us to go. We've done what we needed to do up here. Eden works. She's back up and running. I even tested one of the space coffins myself just now, and let me tell you, they work just fine." She looks down, a little freaked out about the idea she's just spent time in a coffin.

Midori looks at her and it's as though the Humani knows what she's thinking and feeling. "That wasn't easy for you," she says. "I'm glad you've made it back to us in one piece. I am worried about your long-term cognitive prognosis, though."

Ava says, "Well, that makes two of us."

"All of us," Poole says, pointing at her. "I'll be keeping a close eye on you."

"I appreciate that," she says. "Truly. You know what they say about people who go to war together?"

"That they're some pretty messed up people afterward?" Tessa says.

They laugh. "No doubt," Sanjay says. "I definitely feel like I've gone through a war. This was very hard."

"I'm sorry," Ava says. "None of us knew about any of this coming in."

"Would you not have come if you'd known?" Poole asks.

Ava shakes her head. "No. I would not."

They laugh again.

"I am glad, though, that I've gotten some closure with Roland in a weird way," she says, not wanting to give them the whole story. "Some of the things I saw…and seeing him…even if what I saw was some elaborate re-creation…I feel much better now. Like I have some closure."

"Are you going to give us the details?" Sanjay asks. "I'm very intrigued. This was a very bad sentient being. Now, suddenly, it is benign?"

"No," Ava says. "Not benign. I'm honestly not sure what it is. It's going to take some time for me to process. I'll let you know when that happens."

"Yeah," Tessa says. "Probably make us buy your book and have us stand in line to get you to sign it."

"I wouldn't do that," Ava says.

"M'kay. But we still have a lot of time with our commitment," Tessa says. "What about that?"

Ava sighs. "I'll call Allison Mercer. I know she's been wondering what the hell has been going on up here. Vita Nova will see all the damage. We know they're aware of Ken. Either of those situations could easily justify the end of our mission. On top of that? We've hit the main objective of getting this damn floating mausoleum up and running again."

★ ★ ★

"We are all so happy to hear from you, Ava and crew." Allison Mercer's video plays. "Great seeing everyone." She looks to the side. "Well, almost everyone. I'm so sorry about Ken. Can you tell us what happened?"

Ava looks around the control room to the others, then back to Allison. "You know we had an incident or several. Eden was breached by a foreign entity."

"Vita Nova's just looking through the recordings and records now," Allison says. "We know there was a material breach of one of the sky coffins again. It seems Eden was somehow hacked, but we aren't sure how or by whom."

"Hacked," Ava says. "That's one way of putting it. But I'd put it in different terms than that."

"As in...?"

"Possessed. Infiltrated." Ava looks her straight in the eye.

"That's pretty strong," Allison says. "Some audacious claims."

"We were dealing with an audacious entity. The being is something unlike any we've ever encountered."

"Being?" Allison looks shocked.

"Watch the recordings. There was something here. I'm sure the recordings will prove what we went through." Ava exhales. "We've been through quite a bit. The good news is the threat has been vanquished. We are all safe. Eden is safe and is ready for its next crew. Probably a repair crew before normal services can be resumed. But it's pretty close."

"I'm a step ahead of you. We've already approved your return. Please make sure to prepare Ken for return to Earth, as well," Allison says.

"Of course. We'll have Eden load him into the payload space under the capsule. When can we return?" Ava asks.

"Immediately," Allison says. "Gather your things and come home. You'll have to make statements upon your return, of course. There'll be the mandatory twenty-four-hour quarantine, as well. Standard stuff. It may be longer, considering what's happened. You'll each get a full cognitive exam in addition to the standard physical."

Ava agreed. "Of course. That's understandable. When's the next crew coming, by the way?" she asks.

"They're heading to the launchpad as we speak," Allison says. "As soon as we had communications, we had them ready to go. We can't have Eden unattended to, of course."

Pointing to Midori, Ava asks, "Confirming she's coming with me?"

Allison nods. "Of course. We need her. The next crew has a pair of Humani with them."

A pair, Ava thinks. *Isn't that telling?*

"Roger that," Ava says. "Is there anything else we need to do?"

"Nope. Just put Eden into automatic mode on your way out," she says. "Get out of there. Come home."

Chapter Forty-Six

EDEN SATELLITE
DOCKING STATION
16:36:36 UTC
17 MARCH 2112

Floor-to-ceiling windows show a panoramic view of the Earth. Ava stares for a little bit and it feels as though she might fall out. The sensation passes as soon as she steps back and sees Poole, Sanjay, Tessa, and Midori beside her. The receiving area feels cavernous compared to what they've grown accustomed to. There's large decorative columns, ornate tables, chairs, and couches. It's a far cry from the functionality in most other areas of Eden.

"Get a good look now," Ava says. "We probably won't see this view of Earth again anytime soon."

"At least not until it's our time to be interred," Poole says.

"I'm not ready for that," Sanjay says. "I've got lots of life ahead of me. I'm also not sure I'd like to be buried in space if I can help it."

"Agreed," Tessa says.

"Hopefully we've got a long time to figure that out," Poole says. "I'm sure there'll be some more appealing options for us."

"True," Tessa says. "All of that jazz. But I just want to get off this damn thing."

"Cheers to that," Ava says. "So, it's time for us to get into the reentry capsule. So take your last looks. Meet you there." She hurries away, anxious to leave Eden. *Hope I never end up in orbit again. Done with it forever.*

Past the high entryway to the port side, Ava goes beyond the fancy staging of the receiving area and back to the usual metal and rivets of the ship. She feels much more comfortable. Reaching a large, circular hatch, she puts her hand up to the scanner on the wall. It lights up.

"Welcome to Eden."

Not a trace of anything nefarious. She takes a deep breath.

"Officer Armstrong requesting entry for me and my crew," she says.

"Of course," Eden says.

The hatch unlocks and swings open. Inside, she sees a dozen seats in two rows on either side and the piloting deck in the front.

"Looks just like the one we came up in," Poole says.

She jumps, startled. Ava hadn't heard him approach. "Yes," she says. "Full circle. Are you ready?"

"I've been ready," he says.

The others are behind him.

"Let's go," she says.

★ ★ ★

The pod is roomier than Ava expected. It looks sleeker and more modern than what they flew up in, which makes sense, she reasons. Families and visitors to Eden would expect the cabin to be more finished and comfortable. As they tighten their seat belts and restraints, Poole asks, "What's the ride down like? I have to admit that now that I'm thinking about it, I'm kind of scared."

"You shouldn't be," Ava admits. "It's much more like a free fall, if you've ever done that." She has her helmet's visor up. They each wear a pressurized suit, as well.

Poole stares at her. Blinks a few times. "Do I look like I've gone free-falling?"

Ava shrugs. "I don't like to assume anything."

"Is there anything to stop us or slow us down during reentry?" Sanjay asks.

"Yeah," Ava says. "It's called gravity."

"No reverse thrusters or anything mechanical?" Sanjay says.

She believes he sounds scared even though he's trying not to. "Well, there's the parachute that deploys once we break through the atmosphere," Ava says. "That's pretty much what we've got."

Midori leans in. "It's been a tried-and-true method for a few centuries. There's not been any serious accidents once the craft gets to the point of deploying its parachutes. The science and practice are secure."

"I notice you said 'once it breaks through the atmosphere'," Tessa says. "But have other spaceships not made it that far?"

Midori looks over to Ava. She nods. "You maybe don't want to know."

Tessa sighs. "Yeah. Maybe I don't."

"But the technology has improved..." Midori starts as the capsule jerks. Everyone jumps, other than Midori. "Whoa," Sanjay says. "Is there going to be turbulence?"

"Not as much as you'd believe," Ava says. "But don't worry. You'll probably pass out at some point once gravity returns."

"Pass out? I wish there was another way," Tessa says. "Not too thrilled."

"Your suit will help you. You'll be fine," Ava says. "Should keep you a little cooler, too. It gets to be five thousand degrees outside but doesn't go over more than a hundred and twenty or so inside."

"A hundred and twenty freakin' degrees?" Sanjay asks. "Allison Mercer did not declare any of this to us beforehand."

"Didn't want to scare you off, I'm sure," Ava says. "Can't blame her. And besides? I'm kidding. The cooling system keeps everything inside between seventy and seventy-five degrees."

Sanjay shakes his head. "Hell of a time to develop a sense of humor."

"Better late than never," Ava says. "Seriously, though? The pod was designed for civilian travel back home to Earth. It's going to be safe. It's going to be comfortable. We're going to be just fine. Promise."

The pod moves away from Eden, traveling down a short tunnel. The doors leading inside Eden shut. A moment later, the hatch leading outward opens, revealing an amazing view of Earth. "All right," Ava says. "Visors down, folks." They comply. As soon as their visors are shut, the mics and speakers inside their helmets turn on.

The pod rolls out. As it makes it to the end of the ramp, there's a slight drop, but it does not feel as jarring as the earlier nudges. "Are we out?" Tessa asks.

"Yup," Ava says. "See? That wasn't so bad, was it?"

"Nope. Not really bad at all," Sanjay says.

The pod floats for a moment, then spins around so its passengers look back at Eden. They see the hatch door close. They drift for a few minutes. Eden towers over them, its countless glass windows covering the outer surface glistening and reflecting sunlight.

"Eden sure is beautiful," Tessa says. "I like it much better from out here than from inside, to be honest."

"Can't agree more," Sanjay asserts.

Their window starts to close, reminding Ava of a closing eye. "Here we go," she says. "Everyone, get ready."

Thrusters fire. "Just pointing our way," Midori says. "Making sure we enter blunt side down. That will allow us to take advantage of the drag. I'm in contact with the system and we are on course and in perfect working order. The thrusters will turn off once we're on course."

"Wonderful. What's our ETA on touchdown?" Ava asks.

"Planning for thirty-one minutes," Midori says.

"Not so bad," Poole says. "I can make it through half an hour. Kind of feels like we're floating on a boat at the moment. Not so bad."

"I like your spirit," Ava says. She looks at Tessa, who has shut her eyes and grips the seat's sidebars with all her might. Sanjay looks back at her and forces a half-smile. She nods.

"We're in free fall," Midori says.

Poole shakes his head. "I don't really feel anything."

"You shouldn't," she replies. "Our seating module has shocks. This should be smooth, like an elevator ride."

"So, we're falling back to Earth?" Tessa asks, her eyes still shut.

Midori says, "We are descending. That is correct."

They ride down for several minutes.

"We're at Mach 25," Midori says. "Going pretty fast. Anyone feel anything?"

Sanjay chimes in. "Not really. Hard to believe we're really falling."

"We'll feel a slight bump…"

The capsule bumps, shaking them. Everyone grabs on to their restraints. It takes a moment for the turbulence to settle. "You were saying?" Ava asks Midori.

"We've entered the atmosphere," the Humani says. "We should start decelerating momentarily. The drag will help here considerably."

Ava senses her feet touch the floor. Her back settles into the seat.

Gravity.

"Do we have a new ETA, Midori?"

"Six minutes." She points to the front panel where a green light blinks. "One minute until our parachute deploys. We'll feel it but it won't be jarring or violent."

Tessa's face is wrought in a grimace. Her lips move like she's saying something, but no one can hear her. Ava's pretty sure she's praying. "The worst of it's over," she says. "If we would have burned up, the plasma would have gotten us several minutes back. We're back in Earth's atmosphere. We're cooling off and we're about to go for a swim in the ocean."

Her eyes fluttering open, Tessa glares at Ava. "Sharks," she says.

Everyone erupts.

"After all that, you're worried about sharks?" Poole laughs. "Damn."

"They're not going to want to come near us," Ava says. "Trust me. We probably smell like the biggest sulfur bomb ever."

Boom.

Gravity hits them, pushing them backward.

"Oh," Midori says. "There's the chute. Or, all three of them, actually."

A few minutes later, the capsule hits the ocean.

"Welcome to the Atlantic," Midori says. Their window opens, letting in bright white light, forcing them to squint.

Poole says, "I see a whole lot of water."

The capsule bobs up and down. "Are we sinking?" Tessa asks.

"Negative," Midori says. "We're buoyant. We're fine."

"We've made it," Ava says. "Phew."

"You were worried?" Poole asks.

She nods. "The entire time."

He laughs. "You've got one hell of a poker face."

"Don't I," she says.

Above, the unmistakable sounds of a helicopter rotor approaching. "Here comes the cavalry," Tessa says. "And none of us passed out, right?"

They look around at each other. "Don't think so," Sanjay says. "I felt fine."

"You're all tougher than you think," Ava says. "Proud of each of you."

Chapter Forty-Seven

VITA NOVA RECOVERY HEADQUARTERS
CAPE CANAVERAL, FLORIDA
MARY JACKSON MEMORIAL GARDEN
12:24:18 UTC
24 MARCH 2112

Ava sees the Vita Nova *Horizon* logo at the top of the building facing the garden. She's sitting on a bench next to Poole and Tessa. On the bench next to them, Sanjay and Midori linger. The garden's at the center of the building so there are no paths outside.

Allison Mercer rushes through the doors, beaming. "You're all good to go," she says. "Officially decommissioned. What a great day." They'd been there for a week, going through tests, making sure they were sound, and ensuring a long enough quarantine.

"So, that's it?" Sanjay asks. "What do we do now? How do we get home?"

Nodding, Allison makes it to the space before them. "We can book transport wherever you'd like to go from here. Which begs the question: where are all of you going?"

"Home," Sanjay says. "Finally, and blissfully home."

"Same," Tessa says. "This has been…a lot."

"I know," Allison says. "And I'm sorry. Things didn't work out quite how any of us anticipated."

"Well, that's an understatement," Tessa says. "Just ready to move on from all of this." She turns to the others. "No offense to any of you. I love all of you."

Poole nods. "No offense. And love you, too, maestro."

Tessa smiles at that, makes a fist and a pumping gesture near her heart.

"I think we're all going home," Ava says. "Safe to say. This week has been excruciatingly long after what we've been through. We're all pretty anxious."

"Well, then," Allison says, "without any further delay, let's get you all on your way." She motions for them to stand, and they do. "Just follow me inside and we'll sign you all out." Right before they reach the door, she turns. "I've negotiated a nice financial bonus for all of you as a small token of our gratitude."

"What do you mean by small?" Ava asks.

"What I mean is pretty healthy."

"I like healthy," she says. "I like healthy a lot."

Inside they go, the first steps toward the first day of the rest of their lives.

Coda

AVA'S RANCH HOUSE
506 NUEVA VIDA ROAD
SANTA CLARITA, CALIFORNIA
13:48:40 UTC
2 JULY 2112

Pink and orange bands of light color the sky over the vast expanse of sand. The porch faces the desert on the edge of town, a rare spot in the world that hasn't been developed by human hands. It reminds Ava of the sea. She sips her iced tea and pulls her throw tighter over her shoulders. Even in the summer, when the sun goes down, the desert temperatures can drop uncomfortably and quickly.

"Things happening again and again. Birth and death of people, animals, celestial objects. Each time, a little better. A little different," Ava says. "When does it end? It doesn't. The core of everything is reborn. God is a circle. God is a loop. That's why patterns in music are comforting. That's why patterns in numbers, and lifestyles, and in routines are comforting. They are balance. They are life. They are what everything is."

Midori nods. "The realization is too much for some people and they only see the negative side and not the counter side. They don't see the areas in between. Those are harder to see and wait for."

"Like love?" Ava asks.

Midori doesn't turn her head; she just keeps looking forward at the vast expanse of sand. "What about it?"

"Where does love stand with you? Do you believe in it?"

Nodding, Midori says, "Yes. Even though it's hard to prove using scientific means, even with all the resources we have available."

"So, you're a believer?"

"In love," Midori says. "Yes."

"What about in the soul?" Ava's curious. "After what you've seen."

"What if I ask you if you believe that I have a soul," Midori says, "what would you say?"

Ava nods. "I've thought about this, and I definitely believe you have a soul."

"How can something that was incubated in a lab have true consciousness?" Midori asks.

"Every living thing was incubated in a lab of some kind, weren't they?" Ava asks. "Maybe it's not about the group of cells or parts that make us up that gives souls or consciousness or what have you. I'm of the belief that your soul finds you somewhere along the way."

Midori nods. "That makes sense. And explains a great deal to me." She looks at Ava. "Now that I am here, do you feel you got a good deal from Allison Mercer when you asked her to keep me once it was all done? Were you intending to keep me around to do your dishes and clean up? To be of some service to you?"

"Heavens, no," Ava says. "I just didn't want to be alone again when the gig was over. I certainly wasn't looking for a maid. But now that you mention it…"

Midori's expression falls.

Ava puts up a hand, waves, and giggles. "No. No. No. Just kidding. I think we made a great team up there. We'll make a great team down here, too."

"What will we be doing?"

"Thinking about what we've been through and what we've learned," Ava says, "and maybe finding some ways we might be able to use it. Does that sound good?"

"Peachy," Midori says. "Absolutely peachy."

Ava looks up. The house came with another benefit. The unobstructed sky gives them a clear view of Eden. When the desert sky grows dark, the satellite glitters. *Another crew is up there now.* "I'm so happy Allison got a space for Phoebe up there," she says.

"Yes. I'm glad she has some sort of closure now," Midori says.

"Allison Mercer was sympathetic when we finally spoke," Ava says. "Eden had cut everyone off down here. They were trying to figure out what was going on. Eden allowed some systems to work when it felt it was in its own best interest. But it wasn't really Eden, was it? She'd been infected and used."

Midori says, "Unfortunate, but true. And hopefully the safeguards will work now."

"Animus has gone to another world carrying parts of all of us. Maybe it's a lot like this. Barren. Dry. No human civilization." She gazes across the area and spots a large mountainous ridge far to her left. "The Santa Susana Mountains. Home to Animus long ago. It will look for something like it in another world. A fresh place to begin."

"I hope I never find out," Midori says.

Ava laughs. "Me, too." She reclines on the chair. Sips a cocktail from her thermos. "Vita Nova provided a great settlement for us. Let me retire for my troubles. All our troubles."

For a moment, she shuts her eyes so she can listen to the sound of the surrounding Mojave. Skittering sounds. A gentle wind.

Another familiar sound. Tires on gravel. A hydro engine purrs. Headlights glare across the porch. Ava and Midori get up. "Expecting someone?" Midori asks.

"No," Ava says. "Not at all."

As the vehicle approaches, Ava makes out it's a new-model truck. The driver turns it and the headlights off. The driver's side door swings open as a tall silhouette emerges. "Hey, you crazy kids," he says, the voice comforting and familiar. "You got room for one more tonight? I've got dinner and drinks." He raises an arm, revealing a cloth bag.

"Poole!" Ava runs to him. Gives him a huge hug. They laugh and regard one another. "What an amazing surprise." They pull apart and make their way back to the porch.

"Glad you're not turning me away," he says. "That was a long drive." He follows her as she ascends the couple of stairs.

"Mi casa, tu casa," Ava says, pulling a chair alongside the two she and Midori had been sitting in. Taking the bag from him, she puts it on a small table between the chairs.

Poole sits; Ava and Midori do the same. He opens the bag and takes out a pair of beers. "Thought these would be nice."

"Oh, indeed," Ava says. "Perfection."

He pops the caps and hands her one. They clink and drink.

"Wonderful to see you, Dr. Poole," Midori says. "What an absolute treat."

Once he's done with his sip, Poole nods. "You, too, Midori. How are you liking the desert life? A little different than up there, eh?"

"Vastly," Midori says. "But I love it."

After another sip, Poole points the mouth of the bottle at the sky… at Eden. "Nice view. Kind of keeps things in perspective, doesn't it?"

"It does," Midori says.

"So, you told me one day you'd tell me the story of what you saw when you went under?" Poole asks. "Has that day come?"

Ava nods. "It has," she says. "But there's one problem?"

"Oh, yeah? What's that?" he asks.

"Probably going to take more than one night. How much time do you have?"

"I've got all the time in the world," he says. "If you'll have me."

"I will. We will."

"Fine with me," Ava says. "So, first of all? I see this as a place to burn off who we are and start new. A place where it's just us and this beautiful world where we can hopefully find our peace. I searched for the truth and it found me." She raises her drink. "And being here, with you both? You can't get any closer to heaven."

Supplemental Material
Wikipedia and Newspaper Articles

Eden space satellite

From Wikipedia, the free encyclopedia

> *This article is about Vita Nova Corp & Associates' Eden satellite, a mortuary outpost in mid-Earth orbit. For radio broadcasts sent from space, see 'space radio station'. For stations named 'Space', see 'Space (disambiguation)'.*

The mortuary **Eden Space Station**, the largest object ever assembled in Earth orbit

The **Eden** satellite is a moon-shaped spacecraft used as a last resting place for human beings. Assembled in orbit in 2101, they completed Eden in 2104, with the first interred the same year. An orbiting mortuary, Eden is now host to tens of thousands of interred. Plots are visible from Earth via dedicated **eye scopes**, which are programmed to zero in on a certain coordinate. Built in response to ever-dwindling resources and usable land on Earth, Eden is the largest orbiting entity around the planet. Capable of supporting a large crew and visitors, Eden reflects a diverse worldwide clientele. Monthly transports bring interred, visitors, crew and supplies to Eden from North America, South America, Asia, Europe, China, Africa and Asia.

★ ★ ★

SAN FRANCISCO SUN TIMES

April 16, 2112
From the wilds of the Mojave Desert sprung a billion-dollar idea. Richard Mathews, on a personal retreat, watched the moon rise and had a thought. "If we made a moon-sized satellite, we could have a wonderful place to keep those who have passed. It would be beautiful." Richard came back to the Bay Area, where he gathered his considerable contacts, bringing together the resources needed to fulfill his vision. We are all used to seeing Eden in the sky, alongside our natural moon. Its rows of lights glow. And how many of us have looked through one of the scopes to peek at one of our relatives? Seems every person on the planet has by now, but there was a time when that wasn't the case.

"For a long time, people thought it was creepy to see someone," Richard said. "But everyone got used to it, didn't they?"

On the cusp of revealing a long-developed feature, Richard's Vita Nova and Associates has been working around the clock to now make it possible to view folks who have not passed in the best of conditions. "We suspend everyone in our proprietary fluid," he said. "It preserves people in a way nothing has before it. They look natural. They look very human, and in a way that traditional embalming could not afford. Our particles repair and fix people up. Now, for the first time, if a person is beyond what the particles can do, we can recreate a surrogate from their remains. Our technology now allows us to retrieve memories deep inside their brains, long thought lost, but also to find the memories from other parts of their bodies, such as their muscles and their skin. We can recreate them digitally. We can even create videos of their memories, in most cases. When they talk, they have the same voice. Eden's mind is unbelievable in retrieving this with the particles and then parsing it all so it can be seen and enjoyed by loved ones down on Earth."

Vita Nova and Associates, or Vita Nova, as we all have come to know them, is offering this service immediately.

Acknowledgments

Thanks without reservation to my super-agent, Becky LeJeune at Bond Literary, and to Sandra Bond.

The entire Flame Tree team, including Olivia Jackson, Mike Valsted, and especially Don D'Auria. Wonderful working with you again.

Alex Gianni, Lisa Morton, Dacre Stoker, Alma Katsu, Gabino Iglesias, Lauren Elise Daniels, Stephen Graham Jones, James Sabata, Scott Bradley, Michael Knost, Laurel Hightower, Christa Carmen, Sam W. Anderson, Rena Mason, Jonathan Maberry, Ellen Turcio, Mark Tulllius, and the Imaginarium crew for welcoming me so warmly.

Kathryn McGee, Polly Schattel, and Gaby Triana for such amazing feedback.

Desireé Duffy and Dave Duffy and the entire Black Château team.

Michael Bailey, ChandaElaine Spurlock, Sherman Morrison and everyone at Manuscripts.

The many volunteers and members of the Horror Writers Association for trusting me with the wheel.

My brothers and sisters in arms: Bryan Gage, Troy Spiropolous, Mike Zimmerman, and Merethe Soltvedt.

John Drake, Margaret Drake, Taylor Grant, Weston Ochse, Corrine DeWinter, Kiva Kamerling, John David Muoio, and Louis Palisano: I hope you know how much you're missed. See you in the stars.

Leonardo: I couldn't be prouder of the person you've become. Your incredible creativity inspires me every day.

Fawn: your wonderful music has been the soundtrack to my universe. May it play throughout the heavens and bring whoever hears it the same joy it's given me.

About the Author

John Palisano is the author of *Dust of the Dead*, *Ghost Heart*, *Nerves*, and *Night of 1,000 Beasts*. His novellas include *Placerita*, *Glass House* and *Starlight Drive: Four Halloween Tales*. His first short fiction collection, *All that Withers*, celebrates over a decade of short story highlights.

Palisano won the Bram Stoker Award® in short fiction for 'Happy Joe's Rest Stop' and has been nominated for a Rondo Award. His short stories have appeared in *Weird Tales*, *Cemetery Dance*, PS Publishing, *Independent Legions*, *Space & Time*, *Dim Shores*, *Kelp Journal*, Monstrous Books, *DarkFuse*, *Crystal Lake*, *Terror Tales*, *Lovecraft eZine*, *Horror Library*, *Bizarro Pulp*, *Written Backwards*, *Dark Continents*, Big Time Books, McFarland Press, *Darkscribe*, *Dark House*, Vincere Press and many more.

Non-fiction pieces have appeared in Blumhouse Online, *Fangoria*, and *Dark Discoveries* magazines and he's been quoted in *Vanity Fair*, *The Writer*, and the *Los Angeles Times*. He's a recent past President of the Horror Writers Association.

FLAME TREE PRESS
FICTION WITHOUT FRONTIERS
Award-Winning Authors & Original Voices

Flame Tree Press is the trade fiction imprint of Flame Tree Publishing, focusing on excellent writing in horror and the supernatural, crime and mystery, science fiction and fantasy. Our aim is to explore beyond the boundaries of the everyday, with tales from both award-winning authors and original voices.

•

You may also enjoy:
The Sentient by Nadia Afifi
The Emergent by Nadia Afifi
The Transcendent by Nadia Afifi
Junction by Daniel M. Bensen
Interchange by Daniel M. Bensen
Second Lives by P.D. Cacek
Vulcan's Forge by Robert Mitchell Evans
Silent Key by Laurel Hightower
Hellweg's Keep by Justin Holley
The Blood-Dimmed Tide by Michael R. Johnston
What Rough Beasts by Michael R. Johnston
Dry Lands by Elizabeth Anne Martins
The Sky Woman by J.D. Moyer
The Guardian by J.D. Moyer
The Last Crucible by J.D. Moyer
One Eye Opened in That Other Place by Christi Nogle
The Apocalypse Strain by Jason Parent
The Gemini Experiment by Brian Pinkerton
The Nirvana Effect by Brian Pinkerton
The Intruders by Brian Pinkerton
The Perfect Stranger by Brian Pinkerton
A Killing Fire by Faye Snowden
Fearless by Allen Stroud
Resilient by Allen Stroud
Vigilance by Allen Stroud
Screams from the Void by Anne Tibbets
The Roamers by Francesco Verso
No/Mad/Land by Francesco Verso

•

Join our mailing list for free short stories, new release details, news about our authors and special promotions:

flametreepress.com